Fire Danger

Fire Danger

Claire Davon

Copyright © 2016 by Claire Davon
Print ISBN: 978-1-946621-03-0
Digital ISBN: 978-1-946621-02-3

Cover Design: Kanaxa
Editor: Jennifer Miller
Formatting: Jacob Hammer

Publishing History
First Digital Publication: June, 2016
Second Digital Publication: May, 2017
First Print Publication: June, 2016
Second Print Publication: May, 2017

Dedication

Many thanks to John and Stacey for your encouragement and subtle nudges. Also to the contest readers and betas who believed in Phoenix and Rachel. Thanks to you all!

Chapter One

"Stay back!"

The whoosh of his wings manifesting startled Phoenix, knocking him off-balance. They gathered behind him, sticking up from his body. Phoenix immediately crouched, his hands in front of him, trying to identify the cause of the danger.

His wings had so consumed his attention that it took him a minute to realize there was a voice in his mind that rang through like a bell. He jerked to a standing position.

"Get away from me!"

The mental voice was shrill and panicked. His wings unfurled fully, looming like large orange-and-red shadows above him.

"Dogs. Scary dogs. Too close. Snarling. Stay away from me."

Not his danger.

His workout DVD was no longer an option. Phoenix pressed Stop on the player, simultaneously reaching out with his mind to find the source of the signal.

"Big dogs. Too big. Run. No, don't run. They'll chase you."

The voice inside his head echoed. Phoenix opened the large plate-glass door that led to the patio of his hillside house and sought a direction.

The voice was female.

She was in trouble.

She was mortal.

No, he revised immediately. Not mortal. The strength in her mental cry meant something else ran through her veins, something that gave her the ability to call to an Elemental, even inadvertently.

"Nice dog. Handsome dog. Pack. A pack. Run! Run!"

He plucked the impression of very large dogs from her brain. He paused, revising his thoughts. Wolves. Werewolves.

Did this call for his intervention? It was not his concern.

The wings on his back did not appear idly. It was a lie that he wasn't involved.

Perhaps other paranormals would help her? He cast out mentally, searching for any sign that someone besides himself had heard her cry for help and was acting.

There were plenty of additional minds, but none seemed to be interested in her plight.

Typical. Most paranormals had a disregard for humans that bordered on disdain. Except she wasn't human. He recognized that she thought she was; perhaps that was why nobody appeared to be going to her aid. Whatever the reason, no help was imminent.

His task, then. Even if his wings hadn't appeared, he couldn't ignore the cry. Why, though? Why this mortal—or whatever she was—and why now?

Answers would have to wait. With a hop through the open door and a glide onto the wind, Phoenix was in the air. He soared upward, his red-and-orange wings unfurling fully when he found a good current. Focusing, he determined the source of the altercation was several miles from his current location. Oakland, east of San Francisco. Industrial. Dark. Perfect for an ambush.

The tableau started to coalesce as he got closer. Faint yips met his ears, an aural indicator he was heading in the right direction.

"No, don't come closer. Fuck, dead end."

Her distress propelled him to speed up, engaging his wings to make the most of the current.

The lights got dimmer as he approached the destination fixed in his mind. There was little traffic in this dilapidated part of Oakland. Many of the streetlamps were out, so there were long stretches of darkness, broken only by ineffective pools of weak light.

A woman stood her ground in the corner of an alley sandwiched between two large warehouses. She was trapped between the high fence guarding the property behind and the beasts in front of her. Werewolves, Phoenix confirmed as he got closer. Untrained, young, stupid werewolves. Their black-tipped fur told him this was Fenley's clan. Running in a pack, the wolves clearly thought they were invulnerable to anything but other predators of the night. Just stupid wolves out for some fun, terrorizing the local population, toying with a human.

Silently landing behind the wolves, Phoenix folded his wings, and they slipped behind his back until they looked like another grouping of large muscles on his already massive frame.

The woman who had inadvertently sent out the distress call looked over. Only the widening and slight shift sideways of her eyes told him that she had seen him.

She *saw* him. She appeared odd, though, as if she was caught in a dream of some sort. There was something off about her mental signature, but he couldn't pinpoint it.

It made sense if she was other than human. In his Phoenix form he was shielded from their eyes, looking like an ordinary man. His wings could not be seen by humans, only paranormals.

She coughed and shot him a look under the cover of her thick wave of honey-blonde hair, a motion unseen by the wolves. His warrior side approved. Whatever was going on, she seemed alert enough.

"Nice doggies."

It was a beautiful voice, with a low register and silky, rounded tones.

The wolves were growling, their teeth bared, slowly pacing in front of her, closing possible avenues of escape with their constant movement. Foam escaped from the teeth of the largest wolf, giving it a rabid look. Their heavy leg muscles bunched as they circled, a readiness to spring at any moment evident.

Phoenix's wing feathers brushed against the crumbling concrete wall he leaned against. The air smelled of grease and used tires. Old cigarette cartons, fast-food bags and other human garbage littered the ground. The wolves had a den in a park not too far from here, and this would be a logical area for them to rove in. But their lack of discipline in targeting a human surprised him. Stupid, to draw attention to themselves.

Glancing over, he registered that the woman was pretty, tall and solid, with an athletic build. Phoenix mentally calculated her bulk, considering how much her weight would affect his center of gravity.

The passionate side of him admired the blonde facing down three young wolves. She looked from one to the next, clearly trying not to show her fear. The shaking of her body and quivering lips told him that the effort failed, valiant though it was.

She continued to look at him, and her eyes were wide, as if appealing to him for help. She still had that odd overlay, almost as if she was sleepwalking while awake. When the woman shifted again, he acted.

"Children, children," he chastised them, getting closer to the wolves while still keeping enough distance for a quick getaway. Caught as they were between two buildings, it would be difficult to grab her and take off, the retreat a sharp trajectory up and out.

A fireball might help. With a flick of mental energy, it was there. Flame danced lightly over his skin and collected at his fingertips.

All three wolves whirled, haunches quivering as they assessed Phoenix's unexpected presence. Their eyes flicked to the fireball and then, strangely, to the woman.

The largest of the three moved toward him, making a low series of yips.

The yips translated as a demand for him to back off. Now.

Phoenix shook his head. They obviously knew who Phoenix was, as they should. All the paranormals were aware of the Elementals. When he arrived seven years ago, he had introduced himself to the locals, so the packs knew that he was currently in San Francisco. They also had learned he didn't concern himself with other paranormal business. He left them alone to conduct their affairs and asked that they do the same.

The one who looked the fastest also yipped, and he translated the feral voice in his mind easily, as if the wolf were speaking the English language.

"Whatcha want, Elemental? Can't you see we're dealing with business? Clear out. Leave us alone. This doesn't concern you."

Phoenix turned his attention to the wolf mind-speaking to him.

"The better to rend you with, my dear," the wolf said, his mental tone mocking.

Did humans know a werewolf had been the inspiration for the Big Bad Wolf?

"Mortals are off-limits," Phoenix replied in the yip of wolf language. His hands had tensed into fists, his wings silently spreading over his back under the cloak of darkness, but not yet ready for flight. *"Go play with something that can defend itself."*

The bigger one stepped forward with a swagger. Phoenix could see the ripple under his skin. It wouldn't take much for the wolf to attack. They were angry and they were...scared? The quivering of their haunches told him they weren't as fearless as they appeared. One of them had marks across his back, as if he had been singed. Phoenix sniffed the air, but the overlay of scents made it impossible to pick up anything else.

He focused on the woman again. There was something else there, something flickering beneath her surface. It called to him, spoke to him in a way he hadn't felt for centuries. Fire. He shook his head, and he tasted the air again. There was fear and...something else. Compulsion, perhaps, as if their minds weren't quite under their own control.

It stank of Haures. His Demonos counterpart had a hand in this.

The largest wolf gestured to the blonde, but Phoenix didn't follow his hand. The distraction technique was too obvious. The third one moved into a classic flanking pattern until they had him triangulated.

The woman shifted now, opening her mouth as she observed the last wolf fall into place. She had blanched when the wolves surrounded them but managed to keep her cool. Amazingly, she still had her handbag, which she had slung crosswise on her body.

"Sir, you, the d-d-dogs..." she started and ground to a stop.

Time for fire. He gathered the flames at his fingertips and, with what appeared to be a casual flick, sent them toward the wolves. Fire stroked their ruffs, singeing the black tips. They yelped but didn't stand down. The aroma of burned fur slid across his nostrils and was quickly gone.

The wolves were shaking, he confirmed, by turns frightened and hostile, their foaming jaws and quivering haunches indicating a desire to rend, destroy, ruin. They hadn't yet moved on him, just positioned themselves to attack. They were scared. Of fire. Of him. Of her.

Her. But why? Even though she was some sort of half-breed, she seemed harmless. Still, there was something about her that frightened the wolves. Delving into her mind revealed that it was clouded, but there was a ring of fire. Interesting.

"What's your name?"

"Rachel."

She glanced at the triangulated wolves again.

She did not appear to be hurt; he didn't see blood or torn skin or anything other than mussed clothes from being snapped at.

The wolves would live to see another day.

"Good."

Phoenix pushed on her mentally, and her unconscious body slumped to the ground.

With a swift movement, Phoenix unfurled his wings and simultaneously rushed past the middle wolf to grab the woman and haul her into his arms. Her weight unbalanced him, making him lower to the ground. He concentrated for a second, recalibrating his center of gravity. Then, with strong flaps of his wings, he soared upward and flew out of reach of the snarling, snapping wolves in two strokes. They jumped, leaping with strong movements of their hind legs, trying fruitlessly to catch him. The yips of frustration and fury faded as they continued into the sky.

He was Phoenix. He could destroy three werewolf cubs with one heated burst of flame, but that would antagonize the locals. Better this way.

It was clear the woman's predicament had been the reason his wings had appeared. There was no other possibility he could sense, on the air or in his mind.

It could only have been the shapeshifters and the scared woman.

The curses of the cubs faded in the distance as he flew, hampered by the woman in his arms. They thought they had been clever, but their efforts had been useless against a being that could fly. Recognizing him, they should have known that.

Then there was the problem of the woman. Her skin was soft and warm under his touch, and felt pliable. She couldn't be more than twenty-five. He looped her arms around his neck to keep her body stable, and the press of her left breast against his chest made his pulse increase and his body react. The muscles of her thighs over his forearms were taut and strong. She was big, but not overweight, a tall and well-built woman with solid warmth.

Phoenix continued his flight, soaring above unlighted or ill-lighted streets to get them close to the address he had plucked out of her mind. While he couldn't be seen, he wasn't sure about his passenger. There was a drumbeat of danger somewhere, and he wanted to get her home quickly.

The danger tugged at him. Challenge was coming, of that he was certain. Was this woman somehow intertwined with it? That would be new.

They reached the apartment building. Phoenix landed in the deserted street. He found the keys in her purse and sorted through them in his mind until the right one became clear. Just one lock, he noticed. Not secure at all.

It was a small one-bedroom, sparsely furnished and uninteresting. The only interesting thing was the intriguing woman who still lay unconscious in his arms.

Phoenix kicked the door shut behind them and strode to the open door of the bedroom. As in the living room, the furnishings were simple, clean but not expensive, and slightly used.

It was, at best, a middle-class lifestyle, he observed before settling her on the solid dark-blue comforter and laying her head on the matching blue-covered pillow.

There was a hiss and he turned to see a brown tabby cat growling at him, its ears flat.

His track record of cats disliking him stayed perfect, judging from the ears and the hissing. Tipping a wing at her small champion, Phoenix removed her shoes. Then he worked the comforter out from under her prone body and smoothed it over Rachel's form until it was up around her shoulders.

"Watch over her, kitty," he said, resisting an urge to press a kiss to her forehead. Something inside her called to him, something as integral to him as the fire he utilized. The cat continued to glare at him, its green eyes glinting in the semidarkness as he checked and locked the front door.

Either the door or a window would have to stay unlocked if he left without waking her. Choosing a bedroom window that faced a brick building next door, he gave the cat, and then Rachel, a final look. With a strange reluctance to leave the woman echoing through his body, Phoenix exited.

The green of the cat's disdainful eyes was the last thing he saw as he closed the window. The cat jumped on the bed as he watched. Phoenix hovered for another second, watching Rachel stir before he turned and soared upwards.

It would have been better to ignore her distress call. It was not his business. Even with Challenge upon him, he should have let it be. But he could not. If Haures had been involved, the reason was unclear. The woman's origin was also opaque, his sense that she had fire still dancing in his mind. It was a mystery, and he did not like those. Especially when it was time for Challenge.

He took to the air. His intention was to go above the clouds and float there, unseen, observing the Earth. It never failed to soothe him.

Except, perhaps, for tonight.

* * * * *

Rachel woke with a jerk, sweat beading her forehead and covering her body. Her hands clutched the covers. For a moment she thought someone was in the room with her, and she cried out before stopping herself.

Oh no. It happened again.

She glanced around wildly, letting the atmosphere seep into her mind. She heard little other than the ambient noise of late evening or early morning—she wasn't sure which. She focused. Birds, large birds, soaring and flying, darting in and out of her path until they became a tangle of wings and feathers. They appeared almost human as they dove, knotting her hair with their huge orange-and-red feathers. Wolves howled, their canines bared, trotting menacingly back and forth, morphing into humans and then back to wolves again. Rachel shook her head. The dreams, so real, whirred in her mind until she finally allowed herself to relax, seeing only the familiar lines of her apartment.

She found the nightstand light and turned it on. The halogen lit the small bedroom, flooding her with welcome illumination. It had happened again. Damn it, it had happened again.

Were there any fires? Any scorch marks?

Her cat, JT, was at the foot of the bed, his posture watchful, intent. When she focused on him, he started licking the fur on his ruff as if that was what he had been doing the entire time.

The last thing she remembered was… She concentrated, the details slow to focus in her mind. She recalled nothing after getting on the subway, and had no idea of where she had gone. She didn't remember coming home or going to bed. She didn't remember anything after she'd gotten on BART. Rachel peered at the clock, the LED numbers telling her it was twelve fifty-three. Damn it. She had lost several hours. Again. Luckily, she was home, and unhurt.

Rachel eased herself from the bed. Had those been the clothes she'd gone to work in? She thought for a moment and decided that they were. No shoes, though. She flexed her limbs one at a time, checking for soreness. She sniffed the air, tense with anticipation. Smelling nothing but night and a faint stench of her own sweat, Rachel let out a breath.

The dreams struck her again, and she staggered. Large birds, more human than bird; vivid dreams of a half man, half bird swooping down to rescue her from dogs? In the dream they felt like wolves. Wolves in Oakland? That made as much sense as bird/human hybrids did, she thought ruefully. That was how dreams worked. Fire was another component of her dreams, and not always confined to her subconscious.

Odd dreams had been part of her psyche since she was ten years old. If she'd had these types of dreams before then, she didn't remember then. Like most other things from her first ten years, they were a blur, the memories impossible to reach except in snippets.

Winged men. Wolves shifting. The dreams circled her vision, playing over and over again in her mind. Rachel cursed, and JT gave her a look of feline disdain.

No question her fugue states were getting worse. She focused, trying to remember something, anything, from her time on BART. All she could remember was wolves and men and the feeling that she had been saved by something she didn't understand.

She prayed that nothing had happened at work, but she couldn't be sure. One more blackout at the office, one more unexplained and unexplainable fire, and she was done for. Rachel wondered if that would be for the best.

JT jumped off the bed to stand in front of the window in the far corner of her bedroom. He meowed, then again, and a third time. It was a persistent, shrill meow, unlike his usual laconic sound. He continued until she finally rose and went to the window.

It was unlocked. She shook her head. Even in a second-floor apartment, Rachel made sure to keep all access points locked. It had been a habit of hers since before she could remember most things. She didn't recall why.

A ripple went through her body, goose bumps rising on her skin, making all the hairs stand on end. With a flick of her wrist, she locked the window again, testing the pane to ensure that it was truly sealed.

Satisfied, JT began licking his paw and then rolled over in front of her feet, presenting his back to her. Rachel reached down and scratched the brown-striped fur until he purred.

She'd been poked and prodded, and nobody had found anything wrong, but the fugue states continued. She'd seen a therapist who seemed more interested in her family life than the blackouts. When they happened, she would be unaware of her surroundings for anywhere from under a minute to several hours, like last night. She didn't normally associate the blackouts with flying man/birds, however. That was new. They were usually accompanied by something burning. Last night had been new in a variety of ways.

Her mail lay strewn across the large, round oak table by the door. It had been neglected the past few days. Maybe the task of sorting mail would soothe her. Unfortunately, the piles of paper did nothing to ease the images in her head. *Birds. Wolves. Fire. Fire. Fire.*

JT meowed again, and this time she picked him up, his soft fur tickling her cheek. She scratched the cat behind the ears, luxuriating in his loud purr.

"What do you think, JT?" She wasn't too fond of slobbery dogs, and cats were easier for apartment life.

Dogs. *Dogs.* Wolves. A sliver of the dream or her fugue state came back to her. When the first dog-wolf came trotting up, it had turned and snarled at her. Then the second one joined it and the third, all growling.

Rachel knew you were supposed to stand your ground in front of dogs and not show fear. She had a vague recollection, or perhaps it was a dream, that when they surrounded her, she had reacted by flinging her hands, and something had discharged from them. She thought she had smelled smoke. Then they had charged, their teeth bared, and she had run. They had loped after her, keeping three paces behind but not letting her out of their sight. Yelling for help had yielded nothing but the sound of her voice bouncing off the buildings in the deserted industrial area.

An image of the flying man came to her, in that foggy quality that dreams had. With her life in danger, she shouldn't have noticed him, but she had. Even with wolves barking around her, she'd seen that he was handsome in a craggy way, with short brown hair and a heavily muscled but sleek body, tall and fit. He called to the deeply feminine part of her that had been too often neglected.

Rachel shuddered. The door was locked and chained, but the window had been open. A flying man could have gone out that way. The drop to the ground would have been no obstruction to someone with wings. She almost felt the sensation of the wind on her face, and for a moment it seemed as if she had, at one point in her life, flown without a craft.

She shook herself, sending mail scattering across the table. Flying people didn't exist and neither did werewolves. It was a weird, bizarre, unexplainable *dream*. Either that or she was going crazy.

Sensing a tingle, she checked her palms. Had she been clenching her hands too tightly? Her palms were red in that blistered way of sunburns. There was an odd smell in the air, as if someone had struck matches and let them burn all the way down. She rubbed suddenly itchy hands together and stared at the mail.

Rachel wiped at a char mark on the table. It hadn't been there a week ago, but she had woken up from one of her fugue states to find it etched into the table and a piece of junk mail smoldering on the floor. She had put it out, the acrid smell of the coated paper as well as her fear searing her. It was similar to events she'd had in the office and, once, in her car.

What in the hell was happening?

* * * * *

The first ripple of the earthquake was so slight that Rachel would have slept through it under normal circumstances. Quakes were a fact of life in San Francisco, and small ones happened all the time. If you panicked over each one, you wouldn't last long.

JT flicked his ears at the slight ground movement but seemed as unconcerned as his owner. Rachel continued to sort through bills, noting that her shades swayed a little. She picked up the junk mail to toss into the recycling, and began to move to the kitchen area.

A loud rumble alerted her that she only had seconds to act. Dropping the junk mail to the floor, Rachel leaped for JT and scooped him into her arms before he could run.

A big earthquake was coming. A bad one too, if the rumble was any indication. Her building was relatively new and up to code, but there was never a way to tell for sure if a building would survive the big one.

She dumped the now-squirming cat into the soft-sided top-loading carrier that always stood open in the corner and zipped it up. If claws and teeth were any indication, escape was the only thing on JT's mind.

The quake struck, and she tossed JT onto the queen-size bed, joining him there. She'd taken some earthquake safety courses when she moved out to San Francisco, and one of the things they said was that the bed was one of the safest places to be. It was better than a slamming door in a doorway or under flimsy furniture. It was better than outside, with falling glass and exposed, live electrical wires.

The headboard slammed into the wall, and the shades and ceiling lights swayed. The room moved—*bam bam bam*—a hard jolt shaking the walls. Rachel clung to the carrier, JT yowling loudly, while holding on to the side of the bed with her free hand. Her body warmed, just as her hands had earlier. It wasn't the first time over the past few weeks that heat had flushed through her body. If she hadn't been twenty-five, she might have thought she was going into menopause. It felt as if bees were just under her skin, buzzing to get out.

Rachel visually measured the distance between the bed and the door in case the walls started to buckle. The lights flickered but didn't go out. Her skin felt loose and heavy, as if it were sloughing off her body. A quick glance outside showed that the outside lights were fine and...

Strangely, the streetlights weren't swaying or flickering. Beyond the frantic beat of her heart, there were no sounds. Car alarms should be going *woop woop* by now in shrieking disharmony, triggered by the motion of the rolling earth.

The hissing of her feline drew Rachel's attention back to the room, and she clicked her tongue in reassurance to JT, but her gaze lingered on the outside tableau. The room was still rolling and jerking. Rachel thought she saw...

Eyes.

There were eyes outside.

Red, glowing, very unfriendly eyes. Floating outside her window.

Rachel shrieked internally but showed no outward fear. Her skin burned, and she wanted to… What did she want to do? She wasn't sure.

* * * * *

Even if Phoenix had been sleeping, the shrill mental scream would have pierced his consciousness. He caught a glimpse of rolling furniture and red eyes, and cursed. Not his image, not his mind. The woman. The—whatever she was. Rachel.

First the wolves and now the shadow people? The paranormal had a hard-on for this woman.

No time for a shirt. His shirts were well crafted, but even the best stitching got in the way in desperate times. Sweats and feathers would have to do.

A peek into the woman's mind confirmed his suspicion. It could have been vampires, they had those red eyes—a trick of the light and the fluids that kept their biology going. But he was betting on the shadow people. He sent a quick mental blast to her, praying it would be enough until he got there.

"Hold on," he said into her mind, hoping she was strong enough to accept his mental signal. *"I am coming."*

What he got back was a sense of fear but also of heat, like she was ready to go up in flames. He hurried to the door.

* * * * *

"I am coming."

As the room rolled, Rachel glanced outside several times and confirmed that nothing else was behaving the same way. This event was confined to her apartment.

The dream last night.

Red eyes and then dark mist, shadowy forms and a hiss.

"Open the door."

"They" wanted her outside.

The dream last night. It hadn't been a dream.

With that acceptance, for the first time since her fugue states started, the memory flooded back. The strange dogs/wolves, the winged man, the flight home. Although she had been unconscious, part of her mind had been linked to his, and she wasn't sure if she was remembering or seeing through his eyes. There was the feeling of flight, the sensation of feathers on the wing and air currents passing them like strong wind in a storm, vivid in her mind.

Birds? Wolves? Red eyes outside? *This is crazy.*

"Open the door. Open the window. Let us in."

The room still rolled, and even JT had started to settle down, as the rumble showed no signs of abating.

"I am coming. Don't go outside." It was the man's voice, urgent, rushed and closer.

Was this earthquake real? Or was it in her mind? JT was feeling it, so it was somehow physically manifesting, but how? Her skin continued to heat and her forearms developed red streaks. Something deep within her stirred, an animal clawing to get out.

"Don't open the door. Don't open the window. Don't go outside. I am almost there." In the madness, the familiarity of the man's voice reassured her.

"Open the door. Open the window. Let us in." Rachel struggled between the two, trying to focus on the former and ignore the latter.

Rachel hung JT's carrier around her shoulder and then clutched her hands to her ears, as if that could keep the voices out. She wanted to run, wanted to yank open the door and go outside, obeying the commands of the red eyes. It would be so much easier that way.

Vampires needed to be invited in, didn't they?

Vampires? Really?

She heard a whoosh and a rustle as if wings were settling. The birdman... she groped for the name, found it...Phoenix. She had no idea how she knew his name, but it was Phoenix.

"Shadow people. Not vampires. I am here."

The voice inside her mind was different from the shadow people's voices. Rachel's body flooded with relief.

As if on cue, the room stopped shaking. The heat in her body began to subside. She still felt its lingering presence and saw the air around her shimmer as if a fire had burned in front of her.

"Get some things. You can't stay here."

Keeping JT slung over her shoulder, she grabbed her purse and a toiletry bag she always kept packed, tossed them into a handy tote, and went for the door. JT yowled, moving from side to side in the carrier.

Flinging the door open, Rachel gaped at the naked torso of the well-built man standing on her exterior landing. He seemed agitated, harried, his wing feathers askew. She squeaked but made no other sound when red eyes appeared behind him, several feet away but out of reach of his wingspan.

He followed her gaze and growled. The beings pulled back but still remained visible.

"Good thing you didn't let them in."

There was a hiss behind him. *"Let us have the human."*

"Not a chance." There was steel in Phoenix's tone, something she wouldn't have thought was possible when speaking telepathically.

"Come on, Rachel. We have to go. It's not safe."

The world was turning upside down in a big hurry, but staying there meant death. The shadow people, or vampires or whatever they were would find a way in sooner or later. The wolves would get her. Something. Something would get her.

Why?

"JT comes."

His brows lowered, brown slashes against his forehead. "He's your responsibility. We have to fly. Now. Are you ready?"

Rachel gestured to the tote. "I always have a bag packed."

"Just walk away." One of the red-eyed beings poked a finger at Phoenix, but

its eyes were on Rachel.

He motioned to her as if there hadn't been a mental voice. Rachel decided that it hadn't been meant for her to hear.

"Let's go," Phoenix said, his voice urgent.

She put her arms around him. Phoenix frowned at the touch of her body.

"You're hot," he said, his voice a growl.

"I know," she said and that was all there was time for. With a swift motion, they were up and in the air. Behind them slight, wispy figures lingered by the apartment, their eyes glowing in the night.

Phoenix and Rachel were flying near the clouds before he spoke again.

"Why do they want you so badly?"

Chapter Two

"Why do they want you so badly?"

Phoenix's words echoed in her mind as they flew. She had no answer to the question. The moon was in its crescent phase, its light dim. After a moment she identified their destination as the expensive San Francisco neighborhood known as Noe Valley, in the central part of the city. His trajectory took them closer to the ground, and one house started to resolve itself. Although much of it could not be made out, she got an image of a contemporary structure with a generous property line.

Only a plaintive meow could be heard from the carrier. JT had to be too terrified to do any more than cling to the inside of his kitty mover and pray whatever prayers cats made. Normally, Rachel would have reassured the animal wedged between their bodies, but all she could do was keep her arms around Phoenix. The world seemed far away and a long way down. Rachel shivered.

What time was it anyway? Three? Four? She had no idea how long the "earthquake" had gone on. Or why the red-eyed vampires wanted her.

"Shadow people."

The mind speak was going to get old really fast.

There was a light on outside the house. They continued toward it, and she caught glimpses of soft rugs she imagined were to assist landing.

Phoenix executed a turn, rotating until they were perpendicular to the deck, his orange-and-red wings slowing their flight until they hovered. Then they landed, their feet barely making a thump on the surface. Phoenix pushed the alarm code on a lighted pad and led her into the house.

He waved his hand, and the room lit up. It was a clean, neat, light-wood contemporary living room, sparsely furnished. A black leather sofa stood in the middle of the room, with a large TV mounted on the wall.

"Do you have a small room or spare bathroom? I want to put him somewhere safe." JT lurched from side to side inside the carrier, making it rock.

Phoenix indicated a door. "Through there," he said. "I'll get him a bed and some food. Then we need to talk."

After finding the bathroom tucked away off a back room, Rachel closed the door and let JT out. He cowered in the carrier, his nose twitching for a moment, then jumped out and ran behind the toilet. Once there he glared at her, his mouth opening in a soundless hiss.

"I know, honey."

After a cursory knock, Phoenix came in with two bowls and a large towel. He moved past her and arranged the items next to the shivering cat. Phoenix's torso was still naked. When folded, his wings lay smoothly along his back, blending in with the strong musculature. Only the colors gave away what they were.

Winged men do not exist, she reminded herself. She wondered if she was still in a fugue state. Maybe she only thought she'd woken up from a dream but was, in fact, still dreaming. That would explain the non-earthquake, her oddly heated body and the red, glowing eyes. A fugue state was the most likely reason.

She spread her fingers until they strained against the bone. It felt as if she was awake. Maybe the other fugue states had been like this as well. Wanting to blank the voices in her head, Rachel began humming an old nursery rhyme. It filled her brain until all she could think was "The Itsy Bitsy Spider".

His head rose. "That will do for a start," he said aloud. "You will need to learn to cover your thoughts better than that, but you have innate ability."

Phoenix met her eyes. He was as gorgeous as she had envisioned in her dream, if she wasn't still dreaming. With a face like an angel created by a macho god, he had great features and a body that would be at home on a fitness magazine cover. She was five foot ten, and he was six inches taller than her. And broad. His wingspan was wide, about twice the length of a person, in perfect proportion to his chiseled torso. Sweats covered his legs, but the loose fabric let her know that they were as well sculpted as the rest of him.

"Chestnuts roasting on an open fire, Jack Frost nipping at your nose," she thought.

He smiled, his lips curling back like a feral dog. Like a wolf. *Wolves.*

"Come. Your cat will be safe here. You look like you could use a drink, and we need to have that talk."

He made no comment that he'd heard her impetuous thoughts. Not that it mattered. After the last weeks, she understood now that her life would never be the same. A little admiration of a sexy male body was the least of her worries.

His wings vanished, disappearing into his shoulders. One minute they were there, and then there was a noise, like a sucking sound, and they were gone. The fact that he didn't move or otherwise register the disappearance told her this was something that had happened before.

Just like the rest of everything that had happened in the last twelve hours, it made no sense. Yet there it was.

He reached for a T-shirt resting on the back of the sofa and slipped it on. The selfish part of her missed the sight of all that beautiful naked flesh, but the logical part of her decided it was for the best.

"Drink?"

The skyscape out the large-paned windows showed the hill and the city beyond. With her salary, she could never have hoped to afford this upscale central San Francisco neighborhood. "This must have cost a fortune." Her hand gesture took in the house and the landscaping beyond. Even if the place had been a family inheritance, this area hadn't been affordable for decades.

Phoenix poured one neat shot of brandy and handed it to her.

"None for you?"

He shook his head. "Alcohol has no effect on me."

"Oh." *Too bad.*

He grinned and Rachel flushed, realizing her mistake. "It really sucks that you can hear me," she said, trying to sound casual. *"It makes me feel vulnerable."*

His gaze met hers. His eyes were a clear sort of brown that could be called amber in certain light.

"You are vulnerable," he said brusquely, moving toward her. "Sit."

She took the alcohol and drained the glass with one tip of her head.

Phoenix arched an eyebrow at the act. "Another?"

It would be nice to get drunk, to forget the craziness for a few hours, but all that would do was leave her with a hangover, a muzzy head and the same lingering questions tomorrow. Today. Whatever day it was, getting plastered wasn't going to help the crazy turn her life had taken.

If this was a dream, it was a hell of a ride.

"No, that's enough." There was that sensation again, like someone had placed a flame under her skin. Rachel rubbed at her forearm, trying to shake the feeling. "I don't get it, though. Why would the wolves, or you, care about me?" She waited, but he made no response. Was she really having this conversation, as casually as if they were discussing the weather?

"I don't know the answer to that question," he admitted. "I will need to find out."

"*We* will need to find out," she corrected.

He inclined his head, but his mind was shuttered.

"How do you do that?" she asked, tapping her head with her forefinger. "That whole not-let-others-know-what-you-are-thinking thing?"

"There are ways," he said, the amber-colored bottle still in his hands. "You will need to learn them, if there is time."

"*If there is time?*"

She didn't realize she'd echoed the words in her mind until he answered there.

"*If the world doesn't end first.*"

"Repeat that last bit to me?"

He turned to her, and his eyes were distant, as if focused on something far away. "Are you sure you're ready for the answers? You're a…damned if I know what you are. You're different. This shouldn't concern you, but it does."

This. Vampires. Shadow people. Wolves. This. It made no sense.

"There are many things mortal beings have no concept of." His voice was gravelly and suddenly sounded very old. He gestured to the sofa, and without waiting for her, sat on one side. The throw there told her this was the side he preferred. She took a seat as far away from him as she could, sitting primly on the opposite side of the sofa.

His brows knitted together, and his eyes focused in on her like a laser beam. "Who are you, and how is it you can call to an Elemental?"

Rachel wished she could have controlled her involuntary start. The sensation under her skin intensified. She was pretty sure she wasn't in a fugue state or dreaming, but now she wished she could wake up.

"Do you have gods or demigods in your family? Something from the pantheons would explain your powers a little better. If not gods, perhaps Cherufe? You smell of fire."

His words should have been strange, but they touched something inside her, a distant memory. She reached for it but it slid away, vanishing into the corner of her mind again. "Um. Do you read a lot? Or watch a lot of TV? Movies? Comic books?"

"I watch and read my share, but that is not why I am asking." His gaze was steady on her. "Who are you? What are you?" Phoenix asked the questions softly, but she could hear his words.

A woman could get lost in those eyes, with their promise of sensual pleasure and something else—a strength that could slay dragons.

Fire. Dragons. Heat surged through her and just as quickly was gone. She felt something in his mind at the word *dragon* and then it too was gone.

Phoenix's eyes narrowed, and there was an answering surge of fire, like incipient flames dancing on his skin. Then there was the touch of his mind in hers.

Screaming. Glass shattering. The call to "Run, Rachel, run!" from everywhere and nowhere at the same time. It was the first thing she had any clear memory of. The car accident. The day her life was shattered forever. Rachel tried mentally to retreat but had no power against his assault. A screech. A bang. Someone hovering. Hovering? Memories of fleeing from the car and then watching it burn, her parents trapped within. Then running, compelled by a voice coupled with fear that dug its claws into her and wouldn't let go.

"Maybe I'm a witch?" she forced herself to say, and felt the probe retreat.

Phoenix's forehead creased. "Witches have to have some innate ability, but for the most part they are taught their powers. You will need to find out. It's important."

Agitated, Rachel rose from the couch and went to the window, seeing but not seeing the twinkle of early-morning city below them.

"You are not going to your workplace," he informed her. "It's too dangerous."

She doubted work would want to see her tomorrow, or ever again. Rachel thought she had escaped before the fugue took her, but she was sure of nothing these days.

"Bogeyman going to get me?"

He shook his head. "They only come out at night, in a new moon. Aver, their leader, prefers it that way. You will see him if he is summoned, but not during the day."

Ask a silly question...

"This is crazy. I'm nobody. I have a nowhere job, a small apartment and a boring-as-heck life."

"Not anymore." Phoenix's voice was solemn.

She turned to face him. "You are going to have to give me a little time to take this all in. I've flown with you. You're real, I think. Understand that I've been having fugues for the last few months, so this could all be in my head. I don't get this. Why is this happening?"

"I don't know. Not yet."

Phoenix moved, his reflection in the glass giving him away until he stood behind her and put his hands on her shoulders. The tanned hands against her body were dusted with fine hairs the same color as the hair on his head, and appeared strong and unlined.

"Look, Mr. Phoenix."

"Phoenix. Just Phoenix."

Of course he would only have one name. "Is that what's on your driver's license?"

Phoenix gestured over his shoulder to the garage that she imagined was behind the house.

"I have a driver's license and a car but I rarely use them. I have no need for a driver's license most of the time. Between BART and my abilities, it's irrelevant."

She pointedly moved her gaze to his back.

His grip firmed and he turned her toward him. "As you can see, they come and go. When I have them, they cannot be seen. Humans are very easily led."

"You say that pretty arrogantly," she said. "They don't see what you tell them not to see?"

He shrugged. "Humans do not see the paranormal. They see paranormals as regular people. Those of us who function in the world as they know it, anyway. Those who function solely as paranormals they only see, or feel, in nightmares. As the Phoenix, an Elemental, I am invisible to them."

A play of emotions crossed his face, his brow creasing. The air wavered in front of her, as if a heat source were in the room. Him?

"You look like you're trying to decide what to tell me," Rachel said.

"Not what I can tell you. What I *should* tell you. The wolf cubs, the shadow people—they felt or smelled something in you. Either that or they were compelled to attack by my Demonos foe. You are involved in this. This is unprecedented."

The room dipped and swam, but Rachel managed a snort. So many questions danced through her mind, and she didn't even know where to start. Vampires? Werewolves? Demonos? A man as the mythical Phoenix? Maybe she had taken a wrong turn and landed smack-dab in Rod Serling's brain.

"Char and burn. If I thought it would do any good, I would make you forget last night and return you to your apartment none the wiser for your ordeal," Phoenix said.

Rachel pressed the back of her hand to her forehead. "Okay, stop. The fact that you can read my mind is weird enough as it is. Now you're telling me you could erase my memory?"

Phoenix focused on a spot past her, his expression discomfited. "Not erase but make it appear as if it had been a dream. A bad dream brought about by too much vodka and a late-night viewing of *The Howling*."

"Or *An American Werewolf in London*."

"Yes. But not *Teen Wolf*."

She was going to say more, but the heat under her skin intensified and she took a step back. Phoenix frowned again, checking her arms where she was rubbing them.

"Rachel?" he asked.

He had an accent, something old-world Europe. She studied him again but couldn't place his nationality.

"How old are you?" she asked suddenly. "I'm trying to figure out where you came from and I can't."

"I'm from what you would now call Germany," he said simply.

She made a small sound. "Don't think I didn't notice you only answered half my question." The feeling of heat faded, to her relief. Now it was as if something had tilted her world on its axis.

Phoenix smiled, sending a shiver down her spine. The danger she'd sensed in him earlier came flooding back, and she wondered just how formidable an opponent he would be when roused.

He moved then, coming to sit beside her. He met her eyes as he came closer until she could see the gold and black flecks in his amber-brown eyes and the sun-bleached highlights woven through his chocolate hair. Up close his face spoke of age without having a line or a wrinkle to mark him. She decided it was his eyes. They appeared to have seen far too much. Rachel tried to remember what she could about the legend of the Phoenix. They were associated with the sun and died in fire and were resurrected. Did they have control over fire? Did he have control over it? How much of it was true and how much fiction?

"You're projecting like a mewling werepanther. Try to shield."

His phone rang, interrupting them, the bell echoing in the living room. She started, the unexpected noise piercing through the tension in the room.

The sense of heat began to fade, and Rachel took a breath. It retreated like a banked fire, controlled but not gone.

"Call from Griffin," the talking caller ID announced. "Call from Griffin," it repeated.

That wasn't a last name. "Landline?"

"It's easier. Safer." Phoenix turned his attention to the phone. "Griff, they have clocks in Iceland," he said, after pushing speaker on the telephone. "What is it?"

The voice was tinny but clear, a lilting tenor. "Aleric, what is going on over there? Who is projecting so loudly half the paranormal universe can hear her?"

Phoenix's gaze was speculative.

"That is an interesting question, my friend."

* * * * *

The man blinked at the sun fading into the horizon as night approached. Tilting his head, he focused again. Whatever he had felt, it wasn't in the bazaar shop he was in. He set the object he'd been holding down and made his excuses to the shopkeeper he'd been dickering with. Running more than walking, he reached a secluded area of the city, ducking into a shop where the tourists had left for the day. With a nod to the proprietor, he took his winged form and made his escape, flying the short distance to his family compound. He quickly went into one of the small, empty rooms, trying to quell his excitement.

The first series of mental shouts had woken him out of sleep. He couldn't calibrate them through the chatter: even in the early hours of his day, there were too many minds around and he was too unfocused. Now it was later in the day and he was ready.

Possible or not, it was real. He knew that mental signature. Or rather, he had known the signature of the parent. It was familiar to him in that way that spoke not of the parent—impossible since she was dead—but of the child. Which was impossible and yet here it was. When he heard it again, an annoying rhyme he was unfamiliar with, he winced.

His dreams had been dark, full of death and mayhem. Some had been memories.

Flexing his leathery wings, he listened for the shrill shriek again, so familiar and yet unfamiliar as well.

The booming voice came into his head. *"I have need of you."*

"Who's that?" He hoped he didn't sound too eager.

A mocking laugh was his answer. *"You know the answer to that. I have need of your assistance."*

The voice wasn't of his clan. It was possibly a god or a demigod. A supernatural being, without a doubt. Someone who lived on the darker side of life. A Demonos? He gloried at the idea. The moment he thought it, he knew that he was right. A Demonos. It could only be one Demonos. Fire. The fire Demonos had contacted him.

"I would have her," he said out loud.

He didn't know how this child had escaped his wrath all those years ago, but it could not stand. He would fly now, fly to where this creature was and dispose of her.

His wings flexed and the horns on his forehead burned with fire. He would destroy this abomination. He would not tell his clan. It would be his little surprise. He would be able to fix the mistake, and once he had, everyone would see he had been correct.

"Yes. You shall have her. Come to me. Come now."

How she had eluded him and hidden all these years was a puzzle, and he would solve it. He focused on the picture the voice had given him. America. He was unfamiliar with most of their cities, but even halfway across the world, he recognized the Golden Gate Bridge. That must be where the atrocity was. She could not be permitted to live.

Time to fly.

Chapter Three

So many selections, the human assassin-for-hire thought, standing in front of the glass case of the gun store. *So many ways to kill.*

Wonderful.

"Need help?"

He shook his head, staring down the much bigger, burly man covered in tattoos. The other man didn't blink, crossing his powerful arms and flexing his forearms.

"Still deciding," he said. "I will let you know when I am ready."

The tattooed clerk moved down the line, giving another customer his attention.

The man called Ron resisted the urge to pat his pockets. His false IDs were safely tucked away, well crafted and perfect. They had already passed the highest tests, as was evident by the California driver's license and US passport, as well as a social security card and gas bill. More importantly, he had a clean record. Ron Davies was a good boy. He had never been arrested nor gotten as much as a moving violation. He had probably been a Boy Scout, or would have been if he had lived past the age of two.

The man's slight frame and mild, uninteresting looks were an advantage in his line of work. It was an effort to remember him, even if someone had met him more than once. The prison guards had only remembered him when the other inmates tried to fuck with him. Then, everyone remembered him. For a time. But violence was unremarkable in the prison system, and once again he was quickly forgotten.

This ordinary part of his persona made him perfect for the job.

The clerk was hovering again, giving him a narrow, stony-faced look. Ron had been lingering too long in front of the case. Would it be wise to go elsewhere?

He pointed to the gun case. "That one."

The rifle would do nicely. It was the perfect size—big enough to get the job done, but not enough to raise eyebrows. The weapon would be suitable after he had modified it and added a scope. He would need ammo, grenades, bomb supplies and other instruments of death as well. There were ways to get those things.

It would be perfect for the assassination. Killing someone could change the world. As he checked the sights, he tried to remember the name of the man whose death had caused World War I. He had been some dull piece of European royalty or petty tyrant, a nobody who meant nothing—until he died. Then his death pulled the major countries into a war that swept over the world and took decades to overcome.

Ron nodded his approval at the weapon and followed the clerk to begin the registration process. Registration wouldn't be an issue for Ron Davies.

That was the nature of things. You needed to know the right string to pull, with so many interlocked. The wrong one and your assassination would hit a dead end. The right one and the world would explode.

If what he had been shown was true, it would explode in fire.

He liked fire, but he liked killing more. The events he was going to set in motion might end in flames and destruction, and that would be fun to see. But it was the killing he would enjoy the most. He hoped his client would let him kill more when his task was done.

Once his mission was completed, Ron exited the store and headed for BART. A little sightseeing was in order. Fisherman's Wharf to start, and then Coit Tower and the Transamerica Pyramid. He was new in town, and San Francisco was a pretty city. He would explore it now, before he turned it into a battleground. Before he became that guy. The one who started World War III.

* * * * *

Rachel was still sleeping in his bed when Phoenix rose from the sofa. He glanced toward the bedroom with its shut door, missing the expanse of his king-size bed. Then he shook his head. It had been centuries, but there had been many times in his short human life when he'd been grateful for anything other than hard ground to sleep on.

The enigma of the woman in his bed tugged at him. It was crucial they quickly find out what supernatural blood flowed through her veins. Something in her spoke to the fire in his blood, but he couldn't put his finger on it.

Fire calls to fire, he thought and shook his head. That had been disproven a long time ago. He had almost died because of his belief in that silly prophecy. If she was fire, he should run hard and fast.

Griff's call last night reminded him of what they were facing. Challenge. Iceland's volcanoes were rumbling and his enemy had put in an appearance. Phoenix had yet to see Haures, his fire Demonos foe, but it wouldn't be long. He would need to call Sphynx and Ondine later, check in on their status.

Walking over to the computer, he jostled the mouse so the screen came up, cursor flashing on the password box. Time had been when all their answers had to come from educated guesswork and signs put in their paths. The modern age made it so much easier.

There was a plaintive meow from the bathroom.

Despite the animal's apparent dislike for him, Phoenix turned to the kitchen. No being went hungry in his house. After preparing some leftover steak and chicken he found in the refrigerator, Phoenix opened the bathroom door. The cat snuffled the air. Unlike before, he was quiet.

"Here you go, cat. Your mistress will be awake soon."

Phoenix put the plate down, and after a sniff, JT deigned to eat a bite, and then another. Satisfied that his task was done, Phoenix closed the door and returned to his computer.

He had learned over the centuries that there was rarely such a thing as coincidence in his world. He'd been idling around, making nowhere in particular his home until San Francisco. An Elemental house, one of many owned by their company, had been where he'd ended up. In this day and age, even supernatural beings had an LLC.

He had not expected his Challenge to include an unawakened woman who had no idea of who she really was. Whether she was intended to help or hinder his Challenge remained unknown.

The local news talked of many routine things. Earthquake preparedness. The San Francisco 49ers. Tourist traffic. The mayor of Chicago was visiting the San Francisco mayor, an old friend. Originally from Croatia, she was a popular mayor. It was a routine visit. Her closeness to the president and the always-unsettled nature of the former Yugoslavia were the only things that made the news interesting.

National and international news also didn't offer up any obvious clues. It was still the same wars, the same destruction. He was going to have to dig, checking gray-area sites and conspiracy theories, and many of the outwardly crazier ideas that so many paranoid folks had.

They weren't always paranoid. Sometimes they were the very few who had been born with the ability to *see*, and, like Cassandra, they were cursed with not being believed.

The Challenge could only be fire related. Until Rachel turned up, he had intended to join Griff in Iceland, to spend some time with his friend before it all began again.

He itched to do something. Sparring in the boxing ring and long-distance running only went so far. Better to fulfill his role and fight.

His Skype beeped. The young image of Ondine, their water Elemental, appeared on his screen. Appearing to be in her midtwenties, Ondine was already ten years beyond that. Her age had been permanently fixed at the time of her assuming the mantle of water Elemental. Having a female to contend with as an equal was new to Phoenix.

As usual, her short, dark hair was damp. Whatever the criteria was for the choice for a new Elemental when an old one died, the chosen person always fit the station. In this case, Ondine had been associated with the water as a human, but he didn't remember the details.

"Just checking in," she said when he answered. "The dolphins and whales are agitated. Do I need to be worried? I haven't been through one of these. I don't know what I'm looking for. I feel something strange, though."

"Keep vigilant," he said, knowing nothing he could give her would be reassuring. "There is no mistaking it. It is early, but it is the time of Challenge."

"I can't wait." Sarcasm.

"Where are you?"

Her shoulders moved in a shrug. "The yacht. I've got a couple of shifters with me who say they want to help. We're going to Europe to meet up with Griffin. After that depends on Challenge. Anything I should know?"

Phoenix shook his head. "Not yet. Stay in touch."

"I will," she said and cut the connection.

A frustrated sigh accompanied his lurch out of his desk chair, sending the chair spinning.

Ondine was too damned young. He needed Trevor's insight. The old Hippocampus had a way of sorting through possibilities when Challenges came, coming up with the only possible one. It had helped mitigate the damage one of the times they had been Challenged, a time that had ended in Elemental failure. Plague had been their price of defeat, the Demonos's chosen cause of human death. The Black Death had killed more than one-third of Europe, Asia and the Middle East's population in less than ten years. At least seventy-five million people had died, a staggering number for that time period. While other plagues hit the continents in the next centuries, only that one had been caused by the Elementals' failure. Their fault, their price for losing their Challenge.

The bathroom faucet turned on and the toilet flushed. Rachel. The urge to peek into her mind was an almost overwhelming compulsion.

Rude, Phoenix.

What was it about her? Perhaps it was the fire he sensed in her, although he had not dealt with many other fire beings since his disastrous encounter those centuries ago. He pictured Rachel, dewy and slack-jawed, in his California king bed, her trim body under his thick black comforter. His body stirred even now at the remembered image, hardening against the snug jeans. He contracted with the Dhampirs when he needed a woman, but it had been…months since he had bothered. It had been decades since he'd been with a mortal. He left the womanizing to Griff, who wore the crown proudly. Griff played in the safe zone, among supernatural beings and minor deities. Among the nonhumans, being with an Elemental often earned the partner bragging rights.

Phoenix stayed out of danger. The Dhampir clans served his needs when the desire for skin contact became too great. His body itched right now, wanting the feel of her against him. He heard her pleasant voice cooing to the cat. He could get used to that voice moaning softly under him. Phoenix shook his head. Enough of that. He had a job to do.

* * * * *

Rachel entered the kitchen to find Phoenix dressed in jeans and a shirt that, judging by the quality of the cloth and the tailoring, had not come from a department store.

He was even more handsome in daylight than he was at night, wreathed in moonbeams and shadow. Dark blond pieces of his predominantly brown hair caught the light, shimmering on his head. His arms were dusted with hair, covering the strong muscles of his forearms and scattering along powerful biceps. His face wasn't perfect—his nose was a little too large and his lips were too full for a man—but his face would seem unbalanced without them. Conventionally handsome men were boring, anyway.

As they had the night before, her palms heated and she resisted an urge to rub them together, creating friction. So strange. Memories of past instances when she'd woken up with the smell of burned matches and the feeling she'd been singed. The sickness inside her she had put down to aftereffects of the fugue. So far nothing had linked her to the burns, but she had been the only one around at those times.

Her hands tingled, the redness moving up her arms in a slow crawl. Rachel's heart began beating fast. She caught a whiff of sulfur warring with her perfume.

She was in the same clothes from the night before but had put on a light coat of makeup before facing the man whose house she had landed in. She hadn't wanted to rise from the very comfortable, huge bed, but eventually hunger and curiosity had gotten her up. There was a day ahead of her, questions to answer. Danger to confront.

A memory surfaced of a hushed, urgent voice. One she'd only ever heard in her mind.

"Get out, Rachel. I will protect you."

"Rachel?"

Phoenix's eyes were narrowed, and he was following the path of red up her arms. He stepped closer and took a deep breath, looking at that moment like the bird that was his namesake. There was an overlay of a beak before it faded.

"Fire calls to fire," he muttered to himself.

Rachel's brow creased. It sounded like a chant, a benediction and also a curse, but it meant nothing to her.

"Who are your parents?" He asked it with a fierce tone, something underlying the words, but she couldn't pick anything out of his mind. He had walled his thoughts off to her with a skill she yearned to possess.

She sipped her coffee, holding on to the cup like a lifeline. "Just people. Harley and Jane Quinn."

"Not people. There is no chance at least one of them isn't something different."

She tried to smile. "I don't like those odds."

"You weren't meant to. Where are they now?"

Her shrug was careful and slow. The redness continued but she didn't feel faint, nor did she feel any sign of a fugue coming on. It was more like swallowing an energy drink, her body charging with power.

"Dead," he said finally. "It fits. You're alone. Why now? Why is it happening now?" He gripped her forearms and turned them over, seeming to note the red streaks with interest. "You smell of fire. You are more than you seem. How is this possible?"

The view out the kitchen window was an uninteresting one of the hillside and neighboring houses, but it was better than his questioning eyes.

"I don't know, Phoenix. I was leading a normal life, sort of. I was having fugue states and the doctors couldn't figure out why, but there was nothing special about me. Then the wolves and shadow people yesterday. I don't know how to answer you."

He kept one hand on her forearm and used the other to turn her face up to his. "We will have to investigate the fugues. And the way you smell of fire. As for the others…the wolves are a good place to start."

Easier than the shadow people, she supposed.

* * * * *

It might have been a state park, but the air of menace made it feel like something out of a bad movie. Maybe it was knowing there were werewolves somewhere in and *under* the park that gave it its ominous feel. Rachel had never felt this shiver of dread when seeing its name before.

The trees were close together and their leaves rustled in a melancholy tone of warning. The grass and bushes along the ground swayed and also seemed to be scornful of her. *Rachel*, they called, *you're a fool to come here*.

The parking lot was nearly deserted. There were only a handful of cars decorating the lot. Did any of the cars belong to the werewolves? They must assume human form to be able to move in the world, so presumably they could get driver's licenses and other human necessities, just like Phoenix had.

Without warning, Phoenix put his hands under her armpits and lifted her into his arms. Their forms were wedged together in the driver's seat of his car, chest to chest. He stirred against her. He rubbed her body over his in a back-and-forth motion, and then he kissed her boldly, his tongue thrusting into her mouth as if he owned it.

Rachel surrendered herself to the hard feel of him and the intimate pillage of his tongue. His thrust became gentler, teasing, using the tip of his tongue to touch hers before tracing the inside edge of her lips with it.

Finally he raised his head. His breathing was rapid and shallow.

"What did you do that for?" she asked and was annoyed at how breathlessly the question came out.

Phoenix's eyes were fixed on her breasts. Her nipples pebbled at the continued intimate rubbing, and he gently drew his thumb across first one and then the other.

The sensation was so fierce Rachel gasped. "Phoenix," she protested. "I barely know you."

Reluctantly, it seemed, he raised her and placed her back in the passenger seat. "You're weaker than they are. They are wolves. They will smell you on me and assume we are together. It will make things…easier."

"Easier for who?" she asked shakily, looking at his crotch, his penis pressing against the zipper of his faded jeans.

Phoenix's lips turned up and his eyes shone with amusement. "Not easier for me, that's for damned sure. You make me hot. Come." He climbed out of the SUV and shut and locked the doors.

Phoenix took her hand and folded his around it. "We're together, Rachel, as far as the wolves are concerned. It could save your life."

Her heart was beating so fast, all she could do was nod. She should have been scared, but all she could think about was this gorgeous, sexy…

"Three blind mice, see how they run…" Rachel walked hand in hand with him into the woods. The trees seemed to close around them, and Rachel shivered. If it weren't for the warmth of Phoenix's hand, she wasn't sure she would have the courage to go forward. She felt a low burn in her chest and let it expand outward.

Phoenix gave her a sharp look, sniffing the air.

He seemed about to say something when rustling distracted them. First it came from behind and then in front of them. Then it was all around them, directionless. A whisper started telling of horrible things. The words were one shade too low to understand, but the meaning was clear. The whispering grew, speaking of rending and tearing. Blood and guts spilled on the ground. Feasting on the remains while they were still warm.

Her shivers increased, and Phoenix put his arms around her, drawing her against him. She was hot, internally and externally. A deep shudder ripped through her, and she leaned into him, holding him close. Their bodies melded together, heat rippling between them. There was a rightness about being in his arms that was unlike anything she'd ever experienced. It spoke to her in some primal part, reaching down into her core. Sweat broke along her skin as if the heat was going to radiate out and set the trees on fire. Phoenix shimmered.

"I am the fire Elemental," he said in a low whisper, and small flames danced along his fingertips. "What are you?"

The sounds grew louder, pulling their attention away from each other. Rachel wanted to clap her hands over her ears to block them out. Phoenix pressed his head against hers so his hair draped over one ear. The flame subsided, but his heat reached something in her, something familiar. She was not scared of the flame; it was oddly compelling.

Phoenix's gaze was fixed on the shaded woods. His muscles under her hands were tense and coiled.

She turned to look at the places Phoenix was examining. Slowly she discovered she could pick out spots of brown in the green and yellow density. The brown intensified, first dappled and then coming into focus. Brown fur tipped with black. Large, shaggy wolves with pointed ears and lolling tongues.

They moved into the clearing with graceful, easy lopes. There was a leashed quality to their movements, as if they were controlling a more basic desire. She smelled damp fur and dirt mixed with the forest.

Phoenix subtly shifted to a fighting stance.

"Don't show fear." Phoenix squeezed her fingers. *"They can sense it. Don't let them see it."*

"Easy for you to say."

A wolf, more than half again bigger than the others, separated from the circle surrounding them and rushed toward Phoenix and Rachel. Phoenix watched the wolf steadily as it approached, his face giving away nothing.

Two feet from them, the wolf abruptly stopped, as if hitting a wall. One moment he was in motion and the next it was as if he had landed on an unseen marker. Without breaking eye contact with Phoenix, he reared up on his hind legs. Bones shifted and crunched. Fur fell away as arms and legs transformed from pelt to skin. His—there was no doubt it was male—torso transformed from the extremities in, creeping up his neck until the head underwent its change. The elongated nose shrank and the eyes changed from yellow to blue, shifting on his face from wolf to human location.

Rachel had thought Phoenix was a big man, but he was a dwarf in comparison to this…this giant. That was the only word Rachel could think of to describe the immense naked man standing in front of them. Looking from Phoenix to the wolf, she measured the difference between the two and estimated the wolf/man at seven feet tall. His skin was almost as brown as his pelt, and laced with scars. Thick muscles bulged on his body. There was a slash across his cheek that carried fainter slash marks next to it, but didn't mar his features.

Another wolf also shifted, this one female. Picking up a bundle on the ground, she hurried forward and pulled out a pair of shorts and a T-shirt for the behemoth. He donned them without taking his gaze from Phoenix. Somehow, his dressing seemed like an insult.

"Elemental," the wolf said, and the clipped words left no doubt he meant to be insulting. The words were followed by a growl, one echoed by the other wolves. The clearing filled with the low hum. "You are not welcome here."

"Your welcome is not needed, Fenley." Phoenix said. "Your were-cubs attacked my mortal. It is my right."

The rest of the wolves assumed human form, and the crunch that accompanied the transformations echoed in her ears. The ones who attacked her had to be among them, but she could not pick out the culprits. Even if she had been alert and not in a fugue state the night before, she doubted she would remember anything except terror.

"She is no mortal." Fenley's voice rose on a yip. "She is dangerous."

Phoenix said nothing. His hand squeeze warned her to stay silent. In truth, her mouth was so dry she wasn't sure words could have formed anyway. The giant man folded his arms in front of his enormous chest.

The standoff continued for a few minutes, with neither large man moving, just staring at each other without blinking.

Fenley dipped his head. His skin rippled and tufts of fur poked out, as if he was barely controlling his wolf. His nails alternated between human nails and the beginnings of claws, and there was movement under his face. He drew a deep breath, and the wolf vanished.

"I accept your claim, but the woman is unsafe. You must know what she is."

If Phoenix knew, that was news to Rachel. What was she if she was not human? The idea, which would have seemed outlandish yesterday, didn't seem so strange now. The echo of Phoenix's flame answered a deep compulsion in her. What would it be like to control fire?

She could feel emotion coming off the other wolves. Their glares and barely concealed snarls let her know she was not welcome here. She dared to look at one briefly and saw the same anger, hatred and odd fear that she remembered as if in a dream from last night.

Do not show emotion.

"She is my concern."

Out of the corner of her eye Rachel could see a slender boy with a shock of black hair move fractionally forward. With his free hand, Phoenix pointed in the pack's direction. A fireball erupted out of his hand and landed near the boy, setting the grass and the leaves on top of it ablaze.

Cool.

The wolf yelped and began stomping at the flames. The others watched as the boy put the fire out with his feet. Dark hair fell into the boy's eyes as he gave Phoenix a baleful look and then slunk into the group of people. Singed leaves now joined the forest smells. The burned smell in the air was familiar. Rachel's hands itched.

Neither Phoenix nor Fenley had moved. Finally, Fenley blinked, and there was a hint of yellow in his eyes. The werewolf alpha shook his head.

"We have had a cordial relationship these last seven years, Phoenix. But make no mistake, this is our city. It is time for your Challenge, and we want no part of it. That is between you and the Demonos. This woman is connected."

A mix of emotions danced across Fenley's mobile face. The woman, who appeared to be his mate, blinked slowly. Rachel recognized the gesture as something JT would do.

"Char and burn. You are correct. Challenge is upon us. However, it has nothing to do with Rachel."

"Char and burn?" Rachel asked. "Is that a Phoenix thing?"

His lips twitched.

"It's a me thing."

Deciding it was one of those things, like her old guardians saying "what the tarnation", Rachel let it go.

The female spoke for the first time. "Are you sure your Challenge has nothing to do with Rachel?"

Insects and birds chirped. The leaves on the sturdy trees rustled, and the sun glinted through their branches. Rachel's pulse was pounding so hard she was sure the others could hear it.

Part of his Challenge? What were they talking about? She needed to find out, and fast. Once again her palms itched in a sensation so fierce she wanted to throw them up and...what?

Phoenix inclined his head at the female, a seeming sign of respect. "Perhaps it does, Brienne. That makes her that much more important."

Once again a person slid forward, apparently thinking his movement could go unnoticed. A primitive part of Rachel recognized this one as one of the aggressors in the attack last night. Fury surged inside her.

The person's teeth elongated to wolf canines, and he moved closer. Rachel's hand shot out. Something wanted to erupt from it. The tips of her fingers felt as if they were going to melt. A small flame gleamed across her nails before it faded. He snapped at her, and she reacted, sending out a weak bolt of fire, thin and orange as if ultraheated. Rachel's flame singed along his flank, sending werewolf jeans smoldering. His yip of injured surprise was loud, a howl of fear more than pain.

The entire assembly froze. Rachel's mouth dropped open. Heat still scorched across her fingers. It felt familiar, as if she should have always been able to do this. She turned her heated palm up, not sure what she expected to see. A hole or a ray gun, perhaps, winking out from flesh that had just shot fire at a werewolf. There was only the rapidly fading flush that had been there a minute before.

Fenley growled, baring his teeth. Rachel's gaze shifted from the werewolf she had singed to Phoenix, who was appraising her with a curious light in his eyes.

"Leave my wolves alone, Elemental. She is not human. Take your Challenge and your woman elsewhere. This is your free warning."

"Rachel...how?" Phoenix asked, his eyes focused on a point beyond her. Blood pounded in her veins, matching the banked flame lurking inside. A force was trying to push its way to the surface and surge to life. It was familiar and strange at once.

She turned her other hand up and it seemed normal. It was just flesh over bone, as human as the rest of the people she had known up until yesterday. Now it felt like it wasn't part of her, like she was outside all of this. Was she slipping into another fugue state? No, she decided immediately, it wasn't that. Her body tingled from head to foot, like she had been shot full of vitamins. Her heart wasn't even beating fast. She should feel upset or anxious, but there was nothing but relief, as if a thing that was struggling to get free had finally asserted itself.

"I don't know," she admitted.

He seemed to have expected that answer.

"We will find out." She wasn't sure if Phoenix's words were a promise or a threat.

"I appreciate the warning, Fenley, but you are mistaken. This could be the answer. She could be critical in saving the humans."

To her surprise, Fenley laughed, a long, booming sound. "You are assuming we want the humans to be saved."

Chapter Four

Rachel didn't know why Phoenix had handed her the keys to the Mercedes SUV. The large, high-priced car felt enormous, too high and too wide. Rachel gripped the wheel tightly, afraid she was going to clip the other cars on the road. He hadn't struck her as the type of person who would want another to drive his car. Phoenix seemed lost in thought, his mind seething behind its shield. The vistas changed quickly as she drove.

"I should have known," was the only thing he had said since they got into the car. After a few attempts at small talk, which were met with single-sentence replies, Rachel fell silent and concentrated on driving, although her mind was still wandering.

"*Brakes. Now.*" Phoenix's voice was loud in her head.

Rachel stomped on the brakes and the expensive car immediately shuddered to a halt. Less than a foot away was a white car, half in and half out of the concealed driveway, its front end in the road. A loud horn sounded.

The portly man inside the older Honda was glaring at her and waving his fist, unheard oaths issuing from his thin lips. She could feel anger and hatred pouring off him as he continued to shout. There was something behind him…as if his face were a mask. A faint outline of horns showed above his head, and there was a red tint to his skin.

Shaken, Rachel looked at Phoenix, but he had his eyes closed and was mouthing words. The hefty man continued to shout. He appeared to be getting ready to leave the car and confront them, judging by his hand on the door. The image of another face was gone, replaced only by the man.

"That car wasn't there a second ago," she said, although in retrospect she couldn't be sure. "It came out of nowhere. Didn't it?"

Phoenix opened his eyes, and there was an angry look on his face. "It wasn't there a second ago." Flames flickered against his skin.

As the door of the other car opened, tendrils of smoke appeared from the cabin. Rachel would have thought it was steam, but it was too thick for that. The man smacked his hand on his car hood. There was a voice in her mind that she recognized as Phoenix's.

"Leave. Immediately."

The portly man jumped. With a look at her as if memorizing her, the man stepped back from the SUV and ran back to his car. He shook his hand as if it was burned and yowled, glaring at them. Putting the car in reverse, the strange man disappeared back up the driveway.

Rachel waited until she had maneuvered around the empty space and departed before trusting her voice to words.

"What is going on?"

Phoenix had closed his eyes again. Opening them, he gave Rachel what she could only term a sympathetic look. "Minor demon. There are many in the city. They don't usually act alone, or during the day. Haures is responsible."

The world tilted crazily, as if she were Alice and this was the looking glass. San Francisco, which had previously seemed like a pretty safe place to live, earthquakes aside, now seemed filled with unseen menace. She didn't know who or what Haures was, but she didn't like the sound of his name.

"Her name," Phoenix corrected.

She opened her mouth to speak, but Phoenix held up his hand.

"We are not safe. There is much that needs to be explored. We must get back to the house."

Rachel's cell phone rang. Rachel saw the number and flinched. "It's work."

She didn't want to answer it. She wanted to let it go to voice mail, but Phoenix gestured for her to pull over. "Take the call."

* * * * *

Rachel's face fell rapidly as she talked to a person he deemed to be from human resources. It was obvious what was happening. The question was why? This woman, this half-breed of whatever kind she was, had to be linked to the upcoming events. But just as with his Challenge, he didn't have enough information to fit the pieces together yet.

She hung up and said nothing, starting the car again. Her fingers were white on the steering wheel as she drove toward the house on the hill.

"What was their excuse for firing you?"

Rachel darted a glance at him, let out a sigh and said nothing.

Patience was a virtue. He had read it somewhere. He counted to ten and backward three times, trying to control his rising temper, before she spoke.

Rachel cleared her throat. "They made up lies, but the truth was they've wanted to get rid of me since I started blacking out. I must have left work early yesterday without knowing it. So they fired me. It's crap."

It made things simpler, but he had enough experience with women to know that she didn't want to hear that. "I know." He resisted an urge to reach over and take her hand, feel her skin against his. Would it be hot or cool? He hoped for hot. He wanted something reassuring to say but had little comfort to offer. "They're scared."

She kept driving, nursery rhymes echoing through her brain and obscuring her thoughts. He caught snippets of fear, of failure and of uncertainty.

She pulled into the expanse of driveway and opened the garage door. Finally they were in the two-car garage, empty of everything except the car. The usual yard tools, ladders, boxes of unneeded supplies were nowhere in evidence. The garage was as clean and new as the day it was built.

"I don't have family and friends," she said. "I know some people, casual friends mostly from work. I'm from Wisconsin. When I was eighteen, the people whose foster home I lived in told me to get out and never come back. They had done their duty, I figured, and wanted nothing more to do with me. There's something inside me that keeps people away." She studied her hands. "What happened out there, Phoenix? What did I do?"

"They sensed the strangeness in you." He meant both her foster parents and the wolves. "You are not human."

"Wouldn't the wolves embrace that? They're not human either. Why would they be scared of me?"

"I don't know, Rachel." He would find out.

She had fire in her. No wonder she had appealed to him. Fire called to fire, and she was without question a fire being. His urge to protect her fought with the need to explore her, to discover what she was and revel in it. And also run screaming from her. He knew what had happened last time he embraced the flame.

"Am I a dragon?" she asked and shuddered.

Phoenix flinched at the word and then tried to smile. "I doubt that very much. If you were dragon, you would know it. They don't play well with others and they are protective of their own." Whatever she was, why wasn't her clan helping her?

Her eyes went unfocused. He saw controlled fire around her but not burning her, and Rachel by the dancing red and orange, laughing.

A memory? A fantasy? Or both?

"Who or what am I? What is the strangeness in me? What is the fire?"

The connecting door to the house yawned open and a light beckoned beyond.

Phoenix pivoted and Rachel jumped when the bass voice echoed through the garage.

"You big, dumb bird," the voice said, and Phoenix recognized the air Elemental. He let his shoulders relax. "What the hell is going on?"

* * * * *

A figure appeared in the doorway.

"Come," Phoenix said to her. "Come meet Griffin."

He went to the person. The men embraced like long-time friends, but still men—arms and upper body only.

"Good to see you." Phoenix pounded the as-yet-unseen man on the back. All Rachel saw were a pair of tanned hands covered in blond hair and the outline of a sneaker.

Then Phoenix pulled back, beckoning Rachel in. She hurried through the door, wanting the protection of the hilly residence. It was only when all three of them were safely inside that she turned to the second man.

She was facing another Elemental. This one was as stunning if not even better looking than Phoenix. He was tall but not as tall as Phoenix. At a height she estimated at six foot two, he was two inches shorter than the other man. Straight dark-golden-blond hair hung past his shoulders. One long, thin braid snaked down his back. Wings poked around the sides of his body, their butter-yellow feathers appearing as soft as Phoenix's. Classically handsome features spoke of a Northern Italian or European heritage. Wearing a black cloak, he reminded her of the characters in the TV series *Highlander*. All he needed was a sword.

There was something different about Griffin, but not in the same way Phoenix was different. She caught a glimpse of cat…no…of something unique to Griffin, lurking under his surface. Now that she knew how to look, she could see the otherness in him, as well as an overlay of the striking man she saw.

"Please tell me the other Elementals are average, or ugly?"

"*Scusi*," said the new blond. "We're all fantastically good-looking. And modest."

"Rachel, this is Griffin. He's the air Elemental."

Even as they shook hands, Rachel tried to remember what the Griffin stood for. She filtered through every mythology class she'd ever taken before she remembered. Griffins were half lion, half eagle, she thought, and were supposedly exalted creatures. They drew the chariot of the sun, at least in legend.

Well, he was blond. It was fitting.

She let her gaze run over his entire body. His nose had a faint hooked quality, and he moved like a lion.

"Shouldn't you guys have to wear something that says you change into mythical creatures?" Her smile took the sting out of her words. "Nice to meet you, Griffin. Meeting not just one but two Elementals, beings I've never heard of, and getting chased and confronting a pack of werewolves and other nonhumans has certainly livened up my week."

Griffin shook his head, the blond locks flying. "I liked women better when they had to obey their lord and master," he said with a smile that wasn't quite sincere.

He seemed more hard-edged than Phoenix, a little rougher. Shouldn't it have been the reverse, if the legends were true? Griffins were noble beasts and the Phoenix bathed in fire.

"You haven't learned how to shield properly, have you, *carina?*"

"Give her a break, Griff. It's been less than a day. She's had a lot to handle."

Rachel slipped away from Phoenix. Her head had started to pound, but she wasn't sure if it was from the effort of trying to take all this in or a simple need for more coffee. "I'm sure this isn't a social call, so don't let me get in your way. Griffin, can I make you some coffee? Or don't griffins drink coffee?"

"Yes. Strong and black. Thank you."

"You share that," she said with a smile toward Phoenix.

"I see." Griffin's reply revealed little of what he was thinking.

"Why are you here?" Phoenix said after a short, uncomfortable silence. "Ondine said she was on her way to visit you."

"She is. I'll be back in Europe before she arrives. I wanted to see Rachel for myself," Griffin said. "Challenge is here. We can't afford distractions, and your woman's thoughts came across the ocean like a beacon."

Rachel busied herself with the single-cup coffeemaker, making a loud clatter as she worked. She reached out to Phoenix's mind. He let her slide in, his attention still on Griffin.

Phoenix and Griffin both sprawled on the sofa and Rachel joined them, staying close to Phoenix. His warmth made her want to press up against him, soothing her nerves with skin-to-skin contact. There was something about this air Elemental that agitated her. She didn't want to be near him.

"Any Amai sightings?" Phoenix asked Griffin. Rachel got an impression of a giant tattooed Pacific Islander with a…basket? That was odd.

Griffin shrugged. "We had an encounter. Challenge is coming. It's expected. Any sign of Haures?"

"Not yet."

Rachel felt the image of a female, she thought, with black eyes and multicolored hair. This could only be Haures, Phoenix's Demonos enemy, if she took what he was saying at face value.

It was clear the two Elementals were close, and as the talk went on for a few minutes in the way old friends remembered good times, Rachel started to relax. Phoenix's warmth was a beacon. Rachel wanted to curl around him like JT would snuggle up to her on cold nights.

"What can you tell us about your parents?" Griffin said, and his blue eyes were lasers focused on her. She blinked, unprepared for the assault.

There was a faint tingling at the base of her skull. With an effort, she focused on Phoenix. Rachel shifted, her skin tightening across her scalp.

"Not much. I have some memories from before they were killed, but it's all dim, as if there's a heavy cloth over them."

Griffin shot Phoenix a look. There was no mistaking his mistrust.

"Griffin," Phoenix said, but the other man's blue gaze was unwavering. Rachel swallowed. Something shifted down in her core, as if awakening.

"They were just people," she said, feeling the wrongness in those simple words. "There was nothing special about them."

"Wrong answer."

Suddenly Griffin yelped as the tips of his top feathers showed a line of flame. It went out as quickly as it had started. There was rightness to the flame in her. Her recognition of it went all the way to her core.

"Stop harassing Rachel or you will be out on your beaked face in no time."

The growl in Phoenix's words left no doubt of the sincerity of his threat. The scent of char caught the air, a light burn smell that delighted her. Griffin's formerly yellow wings had a thin line of dark brown along the top edges. What must it take to control fire that way? She wanted to learn the trick.

To her surprise, Griffin smiled.

"My apologies, *carina*," he said, and Phoenix growled again. "*Signorina*," Griffin amended and Phoenix sat back, a satisfied look on his face.

"They were," she insisted. "Harley and Jane Quinn. I don't remember them very well, like I said. Everything prior to the car accident is a blur, and the memories always dance away if I try and pull them too close."

"Try to remember," Phoenix said, and Rachel felt the urgency in him as well, a deep need to know. It was odd how she'd never focused on that time, the time before she'd been sent to foster care. It wasn't a blank as much as it was a slope that slid her right into the present.

"I am," she said helplessly. She reached out a hand, needing Phoenix's touch, his warmth. He called to her in a primitive way, unlike anything she'd ever felt before. The thing at the core of her beat against her skin, as if wanting to explode out. Rachel's head continued to buzz.

Then it was as if she were in a long hallway, telescoping at either end until there was no way forward or back.

The buzzing increased like a thousand angry bees were swarming around her. She couldn't hear anything past the sound in her ears. Rachel recognized that she had slipped into a fugue state, only familiar now that she was in it.

Memory tugged at her, of something important but she couldn't think what. An image of the car accident, of hiding behind a stand of trees as she watched the car burn and her parents' corpses inside and the flames all around, the flames the flames... Fire beat against her, a living thing inside her. The hallway seemed to elongate, and the bees were orange and red now, like the color of Phoenix's wings, like the dancing of a bonfire, like...

"*Rachel!*"

* * * * *

She came out of herself to a vision of Phoenix's living room that was wholly unexpected.

When had she gotten up? When had the room shifted around her? When had Phoenix's wings erupted on his back?

Both men were standing, their wings fully extended so yellow overlapped with red and orange, presenting a wall of feathers and tendons that appeared at once beautiful and deadly. Phoenix's T-shirt fell in tatters on his chest, the cloth shredded where it had once clung to his sculpted back.

There was a voice calling to her, but it wasn't Phoenix's. It felt familiar and unfamiliar at the same time, like an echo of a prior time. It wasn't the grumpy Griffin either, it was a person she knew but yet, she didn't…

"Rachel," Phoenix said urgently, this time with sound.

She cocked her head at him. She was standing in the middle of the living room. How much time had passed? The buzzing sound was retreating, but there was something wrong, something different.

Then she smelled an acrid scent, similar to what she had smelled a few moments—or had that been minutes or hours before—but it wasn't coming from Griffin. It was coming…from her.

It was coming from *her.*

Her skin felt hot, as if she had been sitting in a sun-tanning bed. Slowly, Rachel raised her hands. Relief flooded her—they were the same pink color they normally were and not the red she had so lately seen.

"How long?" she asked. Phoenix's wings fluttered, moving slowly to her and then away, as if they had a mind of their own. His fellow Elemental gave her a studied look and stepped away from Phoenix, his butter-yellow wings folding against his back until they almost disappeared.

"How long? Rachel repeated, feeling off-balance. She staggered a little, and Phoenix went to her, putting his arms around her.

"Twenty minutes," Phoenix said, and his voice had a rough quality, as if he had been shouting.

Rachel breathed out a sigh of relief—there was no evidence that she'd set anything on fire. The room held the heavy scent of char, and Griffin went to the sliding glass door and flung it open. Cooler air rushed in, gliding over her heated body.

"Interesting." Oddly, Griffin seemed more relaxed, as if whatever had just happened had made sense to him.

"Explain," Phoenix said. "What are you thinking? We know she's not dragon. They do not mate with humans." There was something else behind the word *dragon* that left Rachel wondering what the beasts did do.

Griffin's look held a wealth of shared history and experience.

The feel of Phoenix's wings was an unexpected sensual pleasure. They were warm and soft, with just a hint of danger at the tips and along the tendons. Those same muscles could break bones, but they also protected her and kept her safe.

"She is not Cherufe either." Griffin's lips curved at the look on Rachel's face. "A being of rock and magma. You're definitely not a hellhound, and if you were a Lampad you would gravitate to the evening more. Hecate always liked her maidens to come out only at night. You may be driving Phoenix mad, but for different reasons. There is only one possible explanation."

Rachel felt Phoenix tense and she grew still. While the buzzing in her ears had receded, her mind was whirling. She was on the precipice of something huge, something that would change her life irrevocably.

The thought came to her unbidden. Change it or…make it right.

"Ifrit," Griffin said, and although the word meant nothing to her, it echoed inside. "It's the only thing that makes sense."

She snorted, drawing a quick look from Phoenix. "What is an Ifrit? Wouldn't I know if I were a…a…whatever an Ifrit is? Phoenix leaned forward, his casual attitude at odds with the fierceness of his eyes. For a moment Rachel thought that they had changed color and shone with an amber cast. Then the image was gone.

Rachel tried to stay calm as the heat of anger rose in her. Phoenix's wing stroked her, soothing the jagged edges of her temper.

Unaccountably, Griffin chuckled, and Phoenix relaxed slightly.

"You're a cool one. I'll give you that." Griffin said.

"She's a hot one. Rachel, a line of flame ran from your hands up your arms and down your torso. You are fire, which explains much." Phoenix continued to hold her, stroking her arm as if soothing a scared cat.

"Fire calls to fire," Griffin said, and his tone was flat.

"It's very sexy." Phoenix's mental voice was husky, his eyes lingering on her breasts.

"Kids."

She flushed guiltily and saw a similar stain on Phoenix's cheeks. She noticed with pleasure the hardening of his strong length as his penis pressed against his jeans.

Griffin made a disgusted sound and clicked his tongue. "Phoenix, you may be twice as old as me, but at least I know how to shield my thoughts when aroused."

"You've had more practice than me."

Griffin studied her for a minute and then rose. Leaning over to where she and Phoenix were sitting, he brushed a hand over his eyes. "Rachel." He still had that flat quality to his voice. "The world is at stake. You came out of nowhere as Challenge was starting. *Che coincidenza!* as we would say in Italian. A fire being showing up at the fire Elemental's door is too neat. We haven't survived this long by being stupid."

She put aside that she knew nothing about what an Ifrit was. She would find out. Rachel turned to Phoenix. "I thought you were immortal."

"Elementals have extremely long lives, but we're not immortal. We can be killed."

His voice was so matter-of-fact, Phoenix might have been discussing a grocery list. Rachel held up her hand. "Stop. Just stop. I can't take any more. Sorry." She lowered her hand. "I do want to know. But I'm getting this in large, indigestible chunks. Could you feed it to me slower, maybe over a couple of days, at least?"

Phoenix met Griffin's eyes again.

"Do we have time?" It was a narrowly focused beam from Griffin to Phoenix, but she heard it clearly in her head.

"Say it out loud, for God's sake," she cried, clutching at her temples. "I can hear you anyway, so what's the difference? Much more of this mind speak and my head will explode."

Nobody said anything for a minute. A gentle breeze rustled the curtains of the balcony door. Down below the hill was the sound of early-afternoon traffic, thick even at this hour. Far in the distance was the sonorous horn of a barge moving across the San Francisco Bay.

Phoenix studied her and answered the question Griffin had asked him in his mind. "I don't know."

Chapter Five

Ron was sweating, but wiping the beads running down the side of his face would make his nervousness more obvious.

The being in his hotel room shimmered as it moved. It had a jerky walk, winking in and out as if it was not quite solid.

It was on two legs and resembled a person, but its skin was iridescent. The pieces of its hair that he could see were two-toned, one side blonde and the other red. It surveyed his cache of weapons, flicking a long, not-quite-human finger over the table.

Finally, it nodded.

"The firearms will do." The hiss was more pronounced in person, and Ron fought to control a primal shudder. "You will need more explosives to put along her route. You can rig a simple timer, yes?"

Ron said nothing, only nodding his head. He didn't think the being was here for conversation.

It was a good thing this job paid well. Very well.

"Good. Arrange it." The being shimmered again, fading out before becoming clear. Once again it was hooded, and Ron decided he really didn't want to see its face.

"The mayor will be here in a few days. It should be a simple thing to remove one politician, if you are as good at your task as you claim."

He didn't know why this being would want the Chicago Mayor assassinated, but again, he wasn't paid to ask questions. It was a simple enough job. He would add the explosives along her car route as requested, although he didn't see the reason why. He could take her out easily. It was simple. Too simple.

It tossed a necklace on the table. The thing clanked there, just an ordinary stone on a thick, inexpensive chain. The stone, caught in a brass frame, was not quite round, and an off-white color.

"Wear that. Always. Do not take it off, under any circumstances. Do you understand?"

Ron picked it up in confusion, fingering it. He saw out of the corner of his eye that the being was just waiting, without moving, for his answer. Instead of saying anything, Ron slipped it on, nodding in affirmation as he did so. The weight, heavier than he anticipated, fell to the middle of his chest. On instinct, he moved the chain. It disappeared under his shirt.

The being crossed to the door, and Ron knew better than to lift his eyes to watch it go. He wanted to. Every part of him wanted this thing gone.

"I will be in touch. Do not fail."

After it had left, Ron finally let out the long sigh he'd kept in, a soul-deep fear searing through him. Wiping away the sweat, he shuddered. He had decided long ago that death did not frighten him.

But this being did.

* * * * *

World events could be mind-numbing when inspected for hours on end, Phoenix decided. It had been simpler in the old times, what mortals called the Dark and Middle Ages, before so much technology and so many people.

He hadn't been mortal for a thousand years. The Dark Ages were familiar to him but, in the way of many old memories, better left in the past.

Early morning sun was coming in through the plate-glass windows when Phoenix flipped through the BBC again, bypassing American news, and then went to the Al Jazeera site, the one Americans were allowed to see, but then hacked into the site solely for Arabs. He scanned the words, trying to find the link, the connection he knew was out there, to find the disaster he had to stop.

Nothing.

JT sauntered into the room and gave Phoenix a haughty look before turning to the kitchen to eat the kibble there. Rachel gave the cat a chirpy greeting, and he smiled.

A minute later she emerged, fresh and wet-haired, two cups of coffee in her hand. The cat silently padded next to her.

Lust surged through him, hot and deep, pooling in his groin until it tightened painfully under the sweatpants he wore as a concession to his guest. He slammed his shields down, carefully concealing his thoughts from her with the practice born of a thousand years.

She had made no attempt at makeup, and her face glowed with the dewy skin of a woman grown but not of an age where it started showing. There was something timeless about her.

She joined him by the computer desk, pulling a chair in from the dining room and sitting next to him. The heat of her and the scent of her feminine musk did nothing to stop the swelling in his cock.

It was unusual for an Ifrit to mate with humans. He needed to know more. He had been surprised that Rachel hadn't asked about her parents last night, but decided it was shock and information overload. She would be asking questions soon enough.

There were some questions he would not answer. Dragons ranked high on that list. *Fire calls to fire* had nearly burned him to ash once, and he had never thought he'd succumb to its pull a second time. Rachel threatened to burn him to another kind of ash, breathe into him a different type of fire.

"Thanks," he said, gesturing to the coffee.

JT meowed before settling next to Rachel and licking his paw.

"Char and burn," he muttered. "Cats." His tone was rueful.

She grinned. "Someone had put him in a plastic bag and tied it up and left it in a dumpster. I found him before…" She shrugged. "I wasn't going to leave him after that. The Chinese say something about having to take care of something after you save it."

"If you save a man's life, you are responsible for him." Phoenix studied at the animal with new appreciation. "You lost a life there, cat."

JT licked his paw with a lack of concern, and Phoenix chuckled. Cats were Griffin's domain. They were attracted to Griff due to his nature, but they were not natural to a Phoenix. Maybe it was time to embrace new ideas in the modern world.

Rachel glanced around at the living room, and the empty sofa with a throw tossed across its back. "Did Griffin leave?"

"When it is time for Challenge for one, it is Challenge for all. He had to get back to Europe."

Rachel opened her mouth to say something, and then shut it.

"Griffin's wings never left him," Rachel said, eyeing Phoenix's naked, bare back. "Do they vanish too?"

Phoenix shook his head. "Griff always has his wings, and Sphynx never has to change to manipulate earth. Ondine and I are the ones whose outward manifestations of our station come and go. The only thing we've been able to figure out is that air and earth are all around us, but fire and water don't exist everywhere. It's a mystery."

She cocked her head at him. "I'll add it to the pile. What about you, Phoenix? I'm decently well versed in mythology, although I guess not enough. I know the phoenix stories. The fire, resurrection, phoenix tears... How much of it is true? Any of it? Or is Phoenix just a name?"

He picked up the mouse and set it back down. After a moment, he spoke. "It's a name and a power. I have fire as mine, and control over it. Of course there is a price to pay. The phoenix legends are mostly nonsense. I have never healed anyone with tears, but sometimes I get sent to the pyre to burn. Usually it's after a failure, after we have lost our battles, one or all. Sometimes it just...happens. I never know. The Phoenix wakes up from the ashes, unless we choose not to...but not always. Going to the fire is a risk."

"Oh, Phoenix," she said, tentatively touching his shoulders. He put his hands over hers and slid her arms around his body. She belonged there. It was good, it was right, like fire that burned but did not consume. "How often?"

"Not very. I assumed the mantle of the Phoenix when the last one failed to come out of the fire. That was toward the end of the Saxon reign. I did not account for time in those days, but I'm told it was around the year nine-fifty."

"That's why Griffin calls you Aleric."

"My mortal name was Aleric. Call me that." Then he smiled. "Griff is a youngster. He was born in the fifteen hundreds, so he's a little over five hundred years old. His family can be traced back to Charlemagne, but he's from Verona. Italians think they invented culture."

She leaned her head against the broad expanse of his back, and his hard muscles flexed under her cheek. "You're a thousand years old?"

"More. I was twenty-five when I assumed the office of Phoenix."

"Oh, sorry," she said. "A thousand and twenty-five, then."

"A thousand and ninety," he corrected. "Give or take a few months."

Rachel's mind stuttered to a halt. A thousand and... "An older man," she said, hoping she was shielding enough that her thoughts didn't show. She wanted to press a kiss against his spinal column and lick the salty skin. She was surprised when a deep shudder ran through Phoenix, making him ripple.

"I would like that too."

"Ah, Rachel," he said with a tone that was sad and aroused at the same time. "It would have been better if you hadn't gone into a fugue that night."

"Better for who?" she asked.

"You." In a swift motion, he pivoted and pulled her into his arms. "It would be safer for you. Not for me. I am pleased that we met. More than pleased. You entice me." He settled her on his lap and let her know with a gentle thrust of his hips what he meant.

"I see," she said with a mischievous grin. Winding her arms around his neck, she straddled him, letting his arousal settle in the cleft between her legs. Rachel was usually shy around men, but this one had made his arousal plain and it aroused her in return. Any thoughts about his age or the strangeness of their situation fled when his hardness pressed against her.

His intake of breath brought their faces close together, and Rachel could once again see that fascinating combination of colors in the flecks of his irises.

"You're so beautiful," he whispered, and then, as if talking were no longer possible, he caught her lips with his, his hand holding the back of her head as his mouth took hers.

"I'm not," she protested.

"Don't argue with an Elemental," he said and deepened the kiss, fitting his lips to hers and plunging his tongue into her mouth.

Rachel drew back after a few heated moments and went to the large plate-glass door.

The sun, yellow and round, streamed through the window. Rachel drew a breath. So many things warred inside her mind. She opened the door to rid herself of that pent-up feeling. Then she looked down, directly into glowing black eyes on the street below.

The human—or whatever—was staring up. It was tall, but from her distance Rachel couldn't tell if it was a man or a woman. Whatever it was, it appeared to be staring fixedly at the house. When he-it-she caught sight of Rachel, it tipped its head farther back and opened its mouth. Fire streamed from its mouth and nostrils, surrounding its head but not burning it. Its hair was a strange mixture of blonde on one side and red on the other.

Rachel made an involuntary yelp and heard Phoenix's cry of alarm at her mental picture as she projected without realizing she was doing so.

The being studied her for a long moment and with one strangely knuckled finger, beckoned to her. It gestured with its body, craning its neck and tilting its head away from the house. It motioned again, this time with its whole hand.

"Rachel!"

She heard Phoenix behind her, and the humanoid winked and took to the air. It had no wings, but it flew. One minute it was there, the next it was high above her, and then it was gone.

"Oh God, Aleric," she said as he reached her, putting his arms around her and drawing her back from the door. His intake of breath told her more than she wanted to know.

"Haures. Of course. It's about time."

Rachel threw the lock and stepped back from the large glass door. It didn't look nearly secure enough to hold back whatever that was.

Belatedly Rachel tasted blood on the inside of her mouth. She'd bitten her cheek. Her heart was pounding so hard she thought it might explode from her chest, and her skin was clammy to the touch.

Then she straightened. She might be out of her depth, but she was nobody's victim. She was no simpering coward to freak at the sight of someone, even if that thing did have black eyes, breathed fire and flew without wings.

She hadn't had a chance to do much digging into what she supposedly was, but the little she'd learned about Ifrits wasn't much help. They were fire beings, like Djinns or genies. It seemed they'd be more likely to be on the side of the Demonos than the Elementals. She wanted to know more about who she was, but there was frustratingly little online.

* * * * *

The sun splashed in over the door, and it caught Rachel in a beam of light, glinting off the blonde of her hair and spiking her lashes with rays. For an instant all Phoenix could do was stand there and stare at the vision she created. He wanted to pull her into his arms and carry her to the highest mountain, where she would be safe. He wanted to trace every curve of her body with his hands until she quivered with need for him. When he took her, it would be the joining of the century, soaring together as only those who are meant to be together could soar. *Fire calls to fire.* Was he ready to pay the consequences a second time?

"Be right back." He opened the door again and went through it. With a practiced move, he jumped off the balcony, down to the spot where the being had been a minute ago.

There was a faint black residue of fire on the ground. The Demonos had left its paranormal mark on the Earth in a line of black, char seeping into the cracked pavement of the hillside street.

Phoenix sniffed the air, searching for where Haures had gone. He saw her as a speck, far above them. Phoenix wondered what the purpose of the brief visit had been. Fear? Intimidation?

Taking Rachel's mettle? The Demonos and Elementals knew each other well, locked as they had been for eons in this battle of good and evil. Rachel was an X-factor. There was only one reason Haures was trying to intimidate Rachel, and that was because she meant something to Challenge. He didn't know what it was, but clearly she did. The wolves and shadow people seemed scared of Rachel. What did Rachel's fire do to the balance of Challenge?

The residue was already fading. He could follow it, but it didn't seem worth it at this stage of the game. To do so would leave Rachel defenseless. She might be part Ifrit, but she was still learning. Her fire was an uncertain thing, unpredictable and therefore useless in this battle.

Phoenix began walking back up to the house, cutting through the scrub of the property as he did so. Rachel's fear beat at him, but he noted she brought it under control, muting it to a part of her brain where she could be afraid but still function.

The woman had a lot of strength, whether she knew it or not. He had to find out exactly who she was and what had happened to cause her to be alone and unaware of her Ifrit side. The presence of the Demonos, her interest in Rachel, made this part-Ifrit more interesting than normal half-breeds.

His cock grew semi-hard picturing the lush curves of the female waiting as he approached. His breath shortened at the thought of her naked form under his. It was so easy to picture: full breasts, small waist flaring into the curve of her hips, hips that shielded the hopefully untrimmed juncture of her.

An image of the two of them entwined, him thrusting into her, shot through him. It hadn't come from his mind. He never saw himself that way, from a stranger's point of view, even if he was looking at himself in the mirror.

Good. The attraction went both ways. Good, and bad. It was a complication he didn't need, but now that it was here it was as if it had always been inevitable.

He reached the bottom of the balcony and with a small push, leaped onto its second-floor height.

She was waiting, her hand on the balcony door and a question in her eyes.

"Haures," he said with no further explanation. She raised an eyebrow and he shrugged. "Later, Rachel." He reached for her. She let him pull her into his arms without resisting, her hands coming to rest on his shoulders.

His nostrils widened and he sniffed her face and then moved lower, to the glands in her neck. He didn't stop there. He shifted, gently nudging her arms away from her body so he could smell her armpit.

His face brushed across her peaked nipples, and with a sudden movement, Phoenix took one cloth-covered nipple in his mouth, suckling through the cotton.

Then he smelled her other armpit and straightened. "You smell like fear, but fear that's under control."

"I refuse to be afraid anymore. Well…" she said in a self-deprecating tone, "at least I refuse to let it rule me. When that thing was bathed in fire, I was scared witless. But then I remember that I can do that too. That's cool. They want me to be afraid, and I won't give in to it."

He could still taste the threads of the cloth in his mouth, but mostly he tasted the hard nipple under the cloth. Rachel had nothing under the top, and the thought of pushing it aside, baring her breasts, finished the job her faint thoughts had started. Phoenix hardened in a fierce rush.

He tried to focus on what she was saying. She wouldn't let fear rule her. That was good. Right now he wanted something other than fear.

"I'm glad." He gripped her shoulders, meeting her eyes. "We all need courage, but you most of all. You've only been in this game for a few days. You need to be a queen, not a pawn, and for that you need courage."

She swallowed. "Okay, Aleric. If I'm going to show the world what I'm made of, I can't cower here. Why not make a day of it and go to Fisherman's Wharf? I could use a good tourist attraction."

Phoenix had thought she would stay holed up here, in his house. The fact that she didn't want to hide touched the warrior in him and made him want to claim her that much more.

"Perhaps we can flush out some game at the same time. I'll drive."

* * * * *

Fisherman's Wharf, one of San Francisco's largest tourist attractions, was part of the shoreline along the San Francisco Bay. Boats and barges were visible on the water, occasionally sounding their horns: some near, and some dirge-like booms further out. Even through the throng and press of constant humanity, the people assigned to show the tourists a good time on the tourist boats could be heard calling out the attractions as they went by on the choppy water. All around them people moved, ebbing past them.

Rachel almost staggered under the sudden onslaught of voices in her head. The rush filled her mind, beating on the inside of her skull like small hammers.

"Get out of my damned way."

"Fucking tourists."

"Hey, look! Ghirardelli Square! Chocolate!"

Rachel's head swam. He gestured to her head as if to tell her to shield. She started one of her nursery rhymes and was relieved when the press of human thoughts faded. This was all so new to her, and she was still getting used to the idea that she could read minds.

They parked in a metered spot and walked down to Pier 39, located between the Embarcadero and Powell Street, Rachel's favorite tourist attraction. Phoenix walked slightly behind her, keeping an eye on the people around her. In this form he didn't look like an Elemental, only a very tall, very broad-shouldered man. The blue shirt he wore was clearly tailored for him and was probably more expensive than her monthly salary. She saw him as the powerful Elemental, ready to leap into the air at the slightest menace, and also as humans saw him: a tall man with an aura of power. It was an odd sensation to see and yet not see at the same time.

Down on the water, playing among the pier, jetty boards and logs, were sea lions of all shapes and sizes, basking in the sun or just rolling around in the surf. There was a sea lion center, relatively new to the area, but she avoided it. She preferred to see the sea lions without knowing tons of facts and details.

"*Elemental.*"

It was not Phoenix's voice. Three of the seals looked at them curiously. There was an overlay, a human shadow that stretched beyond their sea lion form and onto the other animals.

Rachel glanced at Phoenix and back to the sea lions.

"*Shapeshifters. This is Ondine's domain.*"

The sea lions gave them another glance, and then, as one, the three that were more than sea creatures turned and dove into the bay.

Rachel filed the sighting away for future use.

Beyond them was the island of Alcatraz, its small hill seeming innocent. Phoenix pointed out the tourist attraction and smiled.

"Want to go?" he asked, cupping her elbow with his hand and leaning into her.

"Can't." She looked up at the board hanging above the ticket counter. To the right was the bridge leading to the boats that took tourists to the isolated former prison. "Sold out."

She'd been on the tour once. The island wasn't anything special once you landed. She learned it was the currents and the cold water that made it so hard to escape. Many had tried; almost all had failed. The lighthouse, part of the original use of the island, still operated, but otherwise it was inhabited by birds and tourists.

"Let's get something to eat," she said, knowing she sounded relieved that the tour was off the table. "I don't know about you, but I could eat an elephant."

His face pulled down as if in dismay, but humor danced in his eyes. "They're tough and sinewy. They are not worth the trouble, even for the meat they provide. How about some eggs and ham?"

She considered, and her stomach rumbled as if in response. "I'm going to be a thousand pounds, knowing you."

Phoenix put his arm around her. They fit together like two halves of a whole, or the interlocking pieces of a puzzle. There was something primal, and very male, in him. The idea of belonging to someone touched her somewhere that had been cold for years. She wanted to bathe in his fire and bathe him in return.

"Don't worry." The mirth in his eyes had been replaced by something dark and sexy. "There are ways to work off the extra pounds."

* * * * *

It was an odd assignment, Ron thought, even knowing he wasn't paid to think. He had no idea why the creature would want this couple followed or reported on. It wasn't what he had been hired to do. He had gotten a call a few hours ago, the command to track and report on a pair. He had been given a slightly grainy photograph and the news that they were currently at Fisherman's Wharf. One look at the photo and he had committed it to memory.

He wasn't sure why the photograph would be grainy. It appeared to be from a surveillance camera. That struck him as strange. It would have been easy enough to slide a digital camera under a coat and take a picture, so why bother with anything else?

I'm not paid to think, he reminded himself.

Turning his attention back to the pair, he frowned. They seemed like a typical couple, touching each other frequently, looking at each other far too much and acting for all the world like nobody else existed.

It made him sick. He wanted to rip them into little pieces and toss them into the water.

He took several deep, calming breaths, reminding himself that he was just there to do a job, nothing more. It didn't matter if he was there to kill one politician, one lover or a whole group of people. He didn't know why, and he didn't know why he cared, but the sight of the two of them together made him want to kill someone or something. No, someone. Them.

He continued to follow at a safe distance, fingering the necklace in his pocket the creature had given him as he did so. He'd been told he had to wear it at all times, even when sleeping. He'd nodded and done as asked, reluctant to ask why. He hadn't put it on yet. His employer had made it clear by his body language that there should be no other questions. He didn't know why. Just a quirk of these people. Those dealing on the other side of the law never liked curiosity. He wasn't normally curious. There was no reason he should care. He'd been asked to do much stranger things in the past.

It mattered. He didn't know why, but it did. He watched them go into a wharfside café restaurant, joining the queue for a table.

The over-tall man and woman were easy to follow, even at a distance. His fists curled as he followed them. He wanted to tear at them, rip them apart.

He stopped and took a deep breath, struggling to bring his rolling emotions under control. He was furious, needing, wanting to hurt something. Badly.

On the busy wharf, people flowed around him, some giving him dirty looks for stopping, but stepping around him even as they glared at him. He moved slightly, shifting to the edge of another café, a place where he could keep the big couple in sight without being seen himself.

Reaching into his pocket, he slipped the necklace over his head and was unaccountably soothed. His teeth bared in a snarl before he realized he was doing it.

* * * * *

A mental lance of hate and anger flowed inside Rachel's head, piercing it. On instinct she turned to Phoenix, who was standing impassively beside her as they waited for their turn. "Aleric?"

"Char and burn. I feel it."

His head came up, and he scanned the café they were in. His eyes narrowed, only his head moving. His shoulders flexed instinctively, shifting as if the wings were there.

Loathing. Deep loathing emanated from somewhere. The kind of rolling hate that was so profound there were no words for it.

The host called another patron and they moved up in line. Phoenix's head turned, and she followed his gaze to the outside as he continued to scan the crowd. She didn't know what he was looking for.

Flesh rending, a hail of bullets ripping through skin, neat puncture holes on entry, exploding wounds, blood and sinew on exit. Blood spurting from a severed carotid artery, the knife wound jagged.

The images were horrific, and Rachel squeezed her eyes shut, trying to block them out. Her fingers heated and darkness flowed through her. She focused. The images clawed at her, making her wince.

"*Shield,*" Phoenix commanded.

She had a low-level crude shield in place at the moment to dim the human noise, but this rolling emotion pierced right through that. *Three blind mice, see how they run...*

The images slowed as she blocked them with stronger white noise, but didn't stop.

She also observed the crowd, trying to find the person or people sending these images.

The host called them, and Phoenix slipped a hand under her arm to guide her. She wondered if it was also to keep her close in case of trouble. They walked to their small inside table, Phoenix continuing to scan the area as they did so.

They sat at the table, Phoenix awkwardly, his long legs and huge frame settling like a pretzel in the space.

The images were still gruesome—limbs being torn off, faces being bloodied— but her shielding helped.

He waited until the host had left.

Phoenix was beginning to focus in on one area, narrowing to the café across the street, scanning, searching…

Then, as suddenly as they started, the images stopped, winking out as if cut off by a knife.

"Damn," Phoenix said softly. "He's got a blocker."

She cocked her head, studying him.

"There are devices—both sides have them but we rarely use them—that can stop the flow of thoughts. It's as if a barrier goes up, blocking all thoughts of both the wearer and the world around him. They can't hear us and we can't hear them. Haures must have given her minion one. Unusual."

"Do you…did you…want to go out and look for him?"

Phoenix shrugged, flicking open the menu. "With the blocker, he could be anyone. He is an underling, one of many the Demonos will lure into service before this is over. There are many like him. He is of little importance."

His casual dismissal of the man rankled, and Rachel stiffened. He met her eyes, understanding flaring in their brown depths. For a few, intense moments there was nothing but the two of them, the hunger plain in his eyes.

"I am unused to humans," he said after a long pause. "I am afraid I'm a bit out of practice dealing with mortals. Especially half-Ifrit ones."

As an apology, it would have to do.

She concentrated but couldn't hear the angry thoughts. Other feelings, from happy to murderous, beat at her until Rachel put up her shield. She breathed out a sigh of relief when the mind noise faded.

Try as she might, Rachel couldn't get past the thoughts that drummed in her head, left there by the angry whoever-it-was. They ate quickly, and Rachel paid little attention to the unimpressive fare. After lunch Rachel found she had lost her taste for tourist attractions. Instead, she told him she wanted to be at his house, where it was safe. Their walk back to his car was in companionable, albeit watchful, silence. He had taken her hand without asking, and laced their fingers together. Their joined palms swung between them. She liked the warmth of his skin and his powerful body near her. It made her tingle and want to curve closer to him and feel his skin under hers.

Behind them the noise of the wharf faded as they moved into the hills of the city on their way to the parking space.

To their left, in a small alley near their car, there was a sound. That was the only warning.

"Phoenix," the voice said.

Phoenix swiveled toward the alley and his wings appeared. He barely staggered when their weight and feathers manifested on his body, poking through the expensive blue shirt. He swung her behind him, under the orange-and-red wings, gripping her hips with his hands. His shirt had slits, like panels, clearly designed to accommodate his intermittent wings. In a moment his wings had closed over her shoulders, draping down her back to right below her butt, covering her in feathers and tendons.

She had never thought wings would be warm, but these were. She wanted to stroke the tendons and feel the feathers to see if they were as soft as they looked, or if they were spiky and sharp like the points that went into the ligaments.

The alley, similar to the one Phoenix had found her in a few days ago, was darker than the dimming street around them. She strained to see the being in front of them, but the faint light as well as his wings surrounding her made details impossible.

"Haures," he acknowledged. His body was tense against hers. His wings quivered slightly. "What do you want?"

He had no fear in him. He seemed wary, his mental touch that of curiosity.

"Now, now, old friend. I wanted to see your mortal." The word *mortal* did not sound like a compliment.

Although people were moving outside the alley, not one of them checked inside it. Above them the sky was almost fully dark, and streetlights winked on one by one. It was just like with the wolves. Rachel wondered how much of her life had been an illusion, with all manner of beings and beasties moving around her while she'd been living her life unaware.

"What the hell do you want?"

" I've been waiting for you, Elemental."

The voice was female, she decided, although not like any woman she knew. She recalled that Phoenix had told her Haures was female. Her voice had the unmistakable edge of the feminine, but there was a flat quality to it, with neither music nor lilt. Rachel could only see shapes in the dim light, and all she could make out was the other woman's outline. She was tall like Rachel, but unlike Rachel had little curve to her almost elongated body. She seemed to have a faint red glow, like the corona around the sun at a full eclipse.

"We are a lot of things, Haures, but friends was never one of them."

The being sighed and moved a step closer. She was still wreathed in shadows, but red danced across her skin. The Demonos's hair appeared blonde and then red. Rachel had thought all demons had wings but did not see any stretched out behind this woman.

"I like you, Phoenix, and I am going to offer you a deal," Haures finally said. "Stay clear. Don't interfere, don't try and help the humans. It is time to finish what we started in World War II. This time we will win completely. Just let… it…happen. I promise I'll use my influence once we have won to see that your companion survives."

Phoenix had started shaking his head almost as soon as the other being started talking. "You know I can't do that. None of us can. We are Elementals."

"You will lose. It is destined. You lost before and you will lose again. This time it will be over once and for all."

Rachel shivered at the flat certainty of the words. There was so much evil in the world; it seemed as if it would inevitably win. Why did Rachel think that good always triumphed? Even if she was an Ifrit, what could she do to stop this?

Haures stepped forward, and Rachel's impression of a woman was solidified into certainty. She was humanoid but not human, female but not at all feminine. She was female in an avenging-goddess sense, in the Kali sort of way. Her eyes were huge in her head and showed no white. Her skin was fair almost to the point of being albino. Cold red fire crackled over her skin in small jets, emerging from her fingertips and then playing down her hands. It looked alive, reminding Rachel of a pilot light.

She looked at Rachel for a long, long time, clearly assessing, weighing, pondering and then dismissing.

Haures turned back to Phoenix. "Her heritage will not help you, Phoenix. She is still part mortal and she is an Ifrit. They rarely get involved."

"There is always free will," Phoenix said. "No deal, Haures. Not this time, not ever. It is the same answer I have always given, and the same answer I will always give."

A part of Rachel was fascinated by the play of flame along Haures's body. It surrounded her, running over her arms and up her neck to her head, an outline of red and orange, the fire equivalent of a police chalk body. What would it be like to have the fire at your fingertips and be able to control it? Rachel wanted to learn. She *would* learn.

Haures made a mock sigh, shrugging her thin shoulders as if in dismay. She would have been beautiful if the fire didn't dance across her skin, and if her eyes had been remotely human. "Watch your back, Elemental," she hissed. "We will see you when this is over. Perhaps then we can finish our discussion."

With a flick of her wrist, Haures dipped into the shadows and vanished.

Rachel waited until she was sure Haures was gone before breathing out a sigh of relief. Phoenix's wings vanished as quickly as they had come, but he remained motionless. She missed the warmth of feathers, and a brief flash of what they would be like draped over her body differently darted through her. The air seemed to grow dense and then clear. People were now peering into the alley, mostly rushing by, but some examining it with curiosity.

A woman checked Phoenix out with the practiced, knowing smile of a flirt. The woman showed no interest in why they were in the alley and didn't seem to feel any psychic residue clouding the scene. After a moment she moved on.

The San Francisco skyline loomed over the buildings of the alley, with the Transamerica Pyramid dominating the view. Seeing it had always made her feel like something bigger than herself. Now it just seemed to mock her as all too human.

Rachel shuddered, and Phoenix put his arm around her, drawing her close.

The mental noise started again, the din of human thoughts pounding at her. She heard other things too, beings unfamiliar to her, their thoughts foreign. The darker ones pierced through her shields, with thoughts of muggings and other human atrocities.

There were deeper thoughts under those of the humans. The ones of beings who had lived for her until recently only in stories. There were so many, so many. They seemed to be everywhere, as pervasive as the mortals. Mortals who, from what she had seen so far, seemed to exist, at least in the minds of the paranormals, one step below them on the food chain.

Phoenix steered her toward the edge of the alley. "Come. Let's get you home."

Chapter Six

The drive back to the hillside house was wreathed in the sort of silence that practically cut the air. Rachel was bursting with questions. Phoenix could see it in the fidgeting and frequent looks his way, but he kept silent. The time was best spent trying to figure out how to tell her and what to tell her. The truth, or a variant? How much could he tell her without further putting her life at risk? What should he tell her? There were no easy answers.

Phoenix said nothing until they were parked and inside. Once there, he strode to the living room and motioned her to sit on the couch.

He wanted to enclose her in his arms and comfort her with his body. He wanted much more than that, judging from the quickening of his heartbeat. She looked at him and then away. Phoenix knew that distance was a better option, but the rest of him disagreed.

His cock hardened again, begging him to plunge into her warm body. Her lithe form was so lush, so right for his hands. It would feel so good to break his long sexual fast inside her.

"It's all around fire," she said, and her voice shook a little, although he could feel her strain to keep it level. "You, me, Haures. Is that the way the world ends?"

He could not stay away. Phoenix sat next to her and let his hand move over her arm, settling on her forearm, her skin warm under his.

She smelled of fire too, as if it was smoldering inside her, as well as the unmistakable tang of woman.

He studied her and she met his eyes unflinchingly, her questions clear in their depths and the creases in her forehead. She said nothing, though, just waited.

"Fire calls to fire, Rachel. Haures and I are two sides of the coin, always opposing each other at the time of Challenge. Where you fit in, I am not sure. But you are part of this. Each element has affinity for its own kind, which explains how you reached me. You have power. I have felt it, but I haven't figured out more than that."

"My parents?" she asked.

"I don't know. There are paranormals around and the equivalent number of offspring. None frighten the Demonos like you have. None have made the wolves, the shadow people and the Demonos want to take them out of the game, until now. The dragons would scare her—they scare me—but they haven't been seen in centuries." *Thankfully.*

She swallowed. "Phoenix, this is new to me. I was tossed out of my foster home at eighteen, but I should have left before then. I wasn't wanted and I knew it. The minute the state stopped paying for me I was out on my ass. They didn't care where I went, only that I was gone. They never liked me, but I don't know why. I tried to be good, to stay out of their way and not make waves, but it didn't matter. I've had few friends. The guys who asked me out never went beyond a couple of dates. My jobs have been entry level and I haven't advanced up the ladder, despite a college education. Grocery store and department store workers are more often than not rude to me."

He put his hand in hers and gripped, pulsing his palm against hers in what he hoped was reassurance. "Did you ever consider why?"

She shrugged, the gesture jerky. "It's easy to think that I was inherently unlikable. I never thought maybe it was because I had fire in me."

"You are different, and the mortals can sense it and hate you for it. Fear you for it."

"Maybe."

He carefully shielded his mind from her. He hoped she understood he wasn't trying to be unkind. He was trying to protect her.

"I could drown in his eyes," he heard her say, and he chuckled. Rachel flushed. "That is still taking some getting used to."

"Yes." His fingers laced through hers and his grip firmed, squeezing gently. He kissed her, his lips grazing hers, and pulled her against him, tucking her head against his shoulder.

He could hear his heartbeat, slow and steady, in her mind. She radiated uncertainty, fear.

"It's crazy to let someone see who I am," she said. "You're going to see my ugly side and never want to know me again."

"I am not those people. I am not one of your mortals to be so easily scared by a few dark secrets. I have more than my share."

She sighed and relaxed a little bit more. The scent of fear and adrenaline was acrid in his nostrils. A part of him that hadn't felt anything for a long time surged to life.

"I want to know," she said. "I can feel something shifting inside me, like a dam breaking. I don't understand who or what happened, but I want to know."

He swallowed, cupping her face in his hands. "Let me in and let me see if I can discover what you really are."

Her reluctance was plain in a fearful look in her eyes. He hated that she wasn't meeting his gaze. He hated that she was afraid. But there was no way to avoid the process. They needed to do this.

"Okay." Her voice was tremulous. When she met his gaze, to his relief there was strength lurking in the blue depths.

He took both her hands in his. Then he opened his mind to hers all the way, leaving himself bare to her. Her shields went down, the small ones she had erected only recently, and the deeper, instinctive ones she had carefully locked around her innermost self.

Images. Her parents at the water. He saw the world through Rachel's child eyes, and he worked on orienting himself. That memory was only a fragment, and he went deeper, searching her mind for the answers there.

Dark memories. Images of petty crimes. Stealing a candy bar as a child. Taking toilet paper from her employer when she was so low on money she didn't know how she was going to eat after she had fed JT. Deep sexual needs, hard, fast, more than her partners could give her. A horrifying loneliness, soul deep, when she realized that nobody loved her. Nobody but the cat she had rescued from death in a dumpster, anyway.

Before he could think, he mind spoke. *"You are not alone anymore."*

She shuddered.

He went deeper. There it was. A thread, something not human. Phoenix followed it. He sensed something deeply buried, a power banked that had not yet been revealed. It licked at him like flames, like his own ability to manipulate fire under certain circumstances, but different. Very different. This was focused, somehow feminine. There was no question her gift came from the maternal side.

Images. Her mother bathed in the flames from a campfire, out in the Sierra Nevadas. Her father enjoying the view of his woman, seeing but not seeing the glow of the red fire.

Images. Lightning sparking and touching down near them, not as close as it seemed but feeling close enough to touch. Her mother laughing while her father looked on with fear, watching her reach out to the energy.

Images. A small Rachel looking up at a furious father, who was holding a scorched teddy bear.

Images. A dream this time, Rachel tossing and turning in a stormy night, dreaming, dreaming, dreaming of revenge on all the children who mocked and pointed at her. Of the foster family who only took her in because of the money, and made sure she knew that every meal she ate was begrudged. The dream took the form of the movie *Carrie*, with Rachel sending fire down the hallways and corridors of the school and into the master bedroom at home, setting everyone ablaze.

That fateful night. A ten-year-old Rachel running from the car as it erupted in flames. There was a large…something…behind them, and it spat fire at them.

Memory jumbled and she was away from the burning car, her overnight bag in one clammy hand. Inside she could see the skeletons of her immolated parents. A big winged figure, like a page from the *Arabian Nights*, was hovering out of sight of another, smaller one. She wasn't sure how he managed to be unseen, but he did. The large person spared her a look, and she heard, *"Run, Rachel, run. Now, granddaughter."*

Her feet were moving before she was aware of it. In the distance there were sirens, their sounds indicating they were getting closer. Someone must have seen the fire. She could stay, she could go back…maybe her parents were still alive…

"They are not. Run."

It was the only thing to do. Tears on her cheeks, Rachel had run. As she did so a blanket descended over her mind, something that protected her even while it took her memories.

She came out of it with a cry, still clinging to Phoenix.

* * * * *

Rachel was damp with sweat, and released one of his hands to wipe her forehead. His eyes were closed, as was his mind, and he was mouthing words, their meaning unclear.

Memories continued to crowd her, but they were distant, like a far-off dream. They were fading and hard to get to, more like sepia-toned photographs than actual memories. Without opening his eyes, Phoenix tugged her until she went into his lap. His arms closed over her. She burrowed against him, allowing the skin contact to soothe her.

Finally, he opened his eyes. His expression held understanding but no fear, and a kind of respect. His eyes were warm and liquid brown, their depths seeming to say, "I understand."

He opened his mouth to speak, but suddenly the images started again. This time, they weren't hers.

There was a Phoenix much the same as he was now, except decorated with war paint and smeared with gore and bile of other men's bodies. He was thinner and his shoulders far less massive. By the look of him, she decided this was before his change to an Elemental. He was chanting a cry of some sort, swinging a huge ax that looked as if it could dismember half the universe with one blow. He didn't look that different than he did now. He swung his ax, killing all around him. She watched as later that night he stood on the side of a volcano, shaking his head as a handsome light-skinned Egyptian man and woman stood in front of him, explaining his new station. It didn't seem that this warrior had had a choice in what he became.

The Phoenix origin story, she thought wryly. Far different than the comics.

A shift, the image fading to be replaced by a brown and dirty city, small by today's standards, with dim illumination and people bustling. They were dressed in archaic fashions that she didn't recognize. There was a pall in the air, a cloud of what she would call smog if this were modern times. The smog dimmed the sun, the rays peeking out through streaks of pale brown.

There was a river, the banks of which had trash on them. The harbor was clear, however, with many ships going in and out of a major shipway. The shape of the port and the river were familiar in a travelogue way. *"London?"*

"Yes."

Rachel searched her memory for her history lessons, trying to remember what time frame this would be. She didn't know architecture well enough to place it accurately.

"Fourteenth century."

With a small shudder, Rachel found the reference. London in the fourteenth century had been struck by bubonic plague, one of many cities to succumb to…

"The Black Death."

Things happened as if in stop motion. Mongol armies tossed their infected corpses into their warring Italian foes, who fled, taking the plague with them to Italy. It then spread into France and other ports north, including London.

Phoenix and three others she didn't recognize watched helplessly from the sky as the plague ships landed at port after port, spreading the disease. It spread throughout Europe, taking the continent down like Asia shortly before that. *"You caused it?"*

"The Demonos caused it. Challenge happens simultaneously; we all fight at the

same time. In this case all four of us failed, making a final Challenge unnecessary. We lost, and therefore the humans paid."

Rachel studied him. *"If only one of you loses then what happens?"*

"We all fight again. It is the way of Challenge. If we all win or we all lose, then there is nothing further until the next time, but if only one loses then we all fight again. If we win that final battle then all is won, but if we lose that one, as we did in the Second World War, then we have lost."

"That doesn't seem fair."

"It is the way of Challenge."

Even in telepathy, his voice was flat. She filed that away for another time, the bubbling questions put aside. The image of the Black Death still danced in front of her. Over one third of London's population sickened. Their skin blistered and blackened and corpses littered the streets, continuing to spread the disease, families torn apart. People killed animals out of fear, not realizing they kept at bay the rats that had the fleas that spread the disease. She watched as both continents lost so much of their population that it would take over a century to recover from the devastation. *"This was a Challenge?"*

"Yes."

She continued to watch, seeing the plague sweep the continents until it settled down. Always there were Phoenix and the other Elementals, hovering, watching. Then there were the Demonos, crowing their delight as human populations were decimated, leaving behind a shattered populace.

It appeared to be happening in fast motion, like a movie on an old-style projector. When Challenge was finally over and the Demonos disappeared, Phoenix gave a start and took to the air. His flight took him to the top of Mount Aconcagua, the highest mountain in the Andes. Phoenix just sat, unmoving, for an indeterminate length of time.

Active magma and licks of flame bubbled in the caldera deep inside the mountain. The color was bright red, similar to the red of his wings.

It was time to go to the fire.

He didn't hesitate. He only shrugged, rose to his feet and soared upwards.

Higher and higher he flew and then, with a sudden, swift bank, turned until he was headed straight for the lava. Rachel cringed as he got closer and closer, the heat buffeting his body. The noise of the active magma was similar to a slow-boiling pot of fudge—*bloop, bloop*. It would have been beautiful if it weren't so deadly.

If it hurt, she could not feel that emotion inside him. Perhaps after several times the pain was no longer an issue.

"Perhaps there are some things you're better off not knowing."

Burning, burning, his flesh catching fire, streaking off his body until just his skeleton remained. The feathers of his wings turned black and then fell until he was nothing but a skeleton. That too gave way, shattering in the intense heat. He was dead, ashes to ashes, dust to dust, never to be seen anymore.

But then, high above the volcano, the ash fused. First an unrecognizable lump of gray, it quickly separated into a form. His body knit back together. Skeleton, bone and tendons regrew, organs, skin and blood returned. He returned to human and then rose from the ash of his prison, his voice still the harsh caw of his bird form. Phoenix beat his wings higher and higher, away from the heat of the volcano, surging up into the night, crying out. The cry became a hoarse shout of a human, part legend and part man, until he fell from the sky, recovering himself enough to glide back into the safe house nearby, where he could finish putting himself back together.

Rachel knew that she should be scared. Fire fascinated her, called to her as if it was something she should have known all along. The knowledge of what lay in her subconscious, now coming to the forefront, and her fire abilities gave her strength. The idea of her controlling fire was wonderful and terrifying. Part of her embraced it and part of her wanted to run for the nearest mountaintop.

"If you're going to go to a peak, a volcano like Masaya would be more appropriate," Phoenix said, his voice amused.

Mary had a little lamb. She clamped down on her wayward thoughts and the background noise smoothed out. His mind receded until they were two separate minds. Mostly.

She held up her hands, and her fingertips flickered with fire. *Yes.*

"Rachel. You know it's too late to run. It was too late the moment you arrived in San Francisco."

She concentrated on the fire. She wanted it to grow and leap to life, and mingle with his to create a large flame, one that could burn down the night. Rachel swallowed as the fire receded, once again focusing on Phoenix.

"In all the lives I've led, all the centuries I've lived, I've never had a woman involved in Challenge before. For the most part the decades pass uneventfully. Sometimes there are fights, and we win or lose, and there is a punishment or a reward. Mostly we live side by side with the Demonos, and the shapeshifters and other paranormals live their lives without interference from us. We observe and occasionally direct the flow of history. We hope when we make changes it will help our cause, but it doesn't always turn out that way."

"How—" Her voice was harsh, and Rachel cleared her throat. "How do you guys live, all those years? How do you get money, places and lives?"

He chuckled. "You haven't met Sphynx. Shani, the female of the duo, aside from being an incredible fighter, has the ability to see trends far into the future. She set up trusts and intricate holdings a long time ago. Elemental, Inc. is a fully operational company, with employees and many parcels of land, bank accounts and much more. Even if we all died tomorrow, the company would continue for decades without realizing anything was wrong. The other part, the ability to function in the modern world, is trickier, especially now that the digital age is upon us. But we manage."

She swallowed again. "And me? What am I? Besides an Ifrit?"

"Your memories should start coming back, now that we have broken through the block that held them at bay." He rose, still holding her hands, and she rose with him. "Googling Ifrits won't tell you much," he said gently, nodding to the computer.

JT chose that moment to come out of the bedroom, meowing faintly. She smiled at the cat and broke contact to go pick him up. He butted her neck and kneaded her arm for several moments before pushing his paws at her to be let down.

They watched the small feline trot into the kitchen. Rachel turned to Phoenix again, knowing her question was in her eyes, even while she was keeping her mind clamped down.

He perched on the arm of the couch. "In legend, an Ifrit is a large winged creature, mostly evil, that can manipulate fire and do many other things. They are also called Djinns, and litter many folkloric tales. *The Arabian Nights*, for one. In reality, Ifrits generally keep to themselves, generally marry each other and tend to live in sparsely populated areas. The desert is the most popular spot. Many are winged; some are not. What I—what we—need to figure out is what powers you have and why you were made to forget. I think you have a relative who protected you. Your parents died fifteen years ago?"

Rachel's reply was a short flick of her chin.

"Hmm." Phoenix said.

The "hmm" was so deep with meaning that Rachel paused in the act of opening her mouth. She thought for a minute, turning things over in her mind. Then an idea, clear and sharp, hit her. It was right, and also very wrong at the same time. Wrong because if she was right, she had been in this game, without being aware of it, for longer than she had imagined. "How long have you been in San Francisco?"

He smiled grimly. "You are beginning to understand. We both are. I decided to come here seven years ago on the force of an impulse so strong it couldn't be ignored. I didn't know why, but I do now."

"Around the time I was kicked out of my foster home and made my way here." She said it flatly.

"It's tied in." He went to the window and looked out over the horizon, to the edge of the water, as far as he could see. "You're a part of this, whether you like it or not."

"Maybe I can help fix it."

He shrugged. "Maybe. Or maybe it shouldn't be fixed. I would never say this to her, but maybe Haures was right."

She stared at him. "What…what do you mean?"

"I've been alive for a thousand years. I've seen things, so many things. I've seen mankind's cruelty; I've seen things that would curl your toes. You're here. That's all I need. Maybe you're here to give me a companion after this is all over."

* * * * *

He stretched his wings, feeling the air under them. He hadn't flown for a while, content to stay at home and tend to his needs. He kept a watchful eye on Kamal and the family, but they had shown no inclination to take revenge for his actions. The council hadn't condoned it but they hadn't punished him either, and both combined made Farouk confident he had done the right thing.

Now he knew why. The mental voice was unmistakable, a hint of the woman he had once thought to marry before she had so treacherously given herself to a human. Now he understood why Kamal had acted so calm these years. He had a secret. How the daughter had escaped, Farouk had no idea, but it was inconceivable that it would be allowed to stand.

His wings creaked slightly, years of neglect in the stiff tendons. The strong leather in between needed tending after the disuse, and he had found salve to see to the material. It would have been easier if he hadn't had to hide his intentions from his family, but if his plans were revealed, his clan would be honor-bound to report him.

He had done nothing wrong, but he had been lucky to escape censure. He had righted a wrong, fixed an abomination, or thought he had. There was work yet to be done.

Not yet, he told himself. He needed a few more cycles to regain his full strength to be able to tackle the job ahead. This time, when he went to finish the job, he would make sure it was done all the way. This time, when the job was finished, the clans would see that he had done the right thing and applaud him.

This time, there would be no survivors.

Chapter Seven

"You're not serious. Elementals are supposed to save the world."

Phoenix squared his shoulders and shook his head. His mind was blocked from her, and she had no idea what he was thinking.

"It's unimportant. What is important is finding out the truth about you."

The stiffness of his body told her this was not the time to pursue this line of questioning. Unsure whether she should believe him, Rachel filed the comment away for future attention. Then the memory of the car accident drew her back. "Why don't I remember? Why don't I know?"

He turned to look at her and his big body almost filled the window, blocking the view.

"Why don't I have wings if I'm what I saw in that vision? Why don't I have more…power?" Her body heated again, and part of her wanted to be that winged creature with the power of fire at her command. She *yearned* for it, like it was a part of her she hadn't known was missing until this moment.

Phoenix shrugged, his shoulders flexing. "There was something there, interfering, maybe protecting. I'm not sure. As to your wings, not all Ifrit have them."

"Shouldn't I look more…different?"

Another shrug.

Heat warmed her face as her temper started to fray. The visions Phoenix had teased from her mind made her feel off-balance, like a wobbling top. She dashed across the room to him, her face heating with anger. "I am so confused."

Rachel did the only thing she could think of. She kissed him.

Phoenix reacted, his arms immediately closing around her. His tongue sought hers, probing, demanding a response, which she gave, meeting his desire with a hot, burning need of her own. It flared like fire between them, passion that came to life instantly.

He broke off the kiss only to nibble on her ear. His breath was warm, and she shuddered with wanting him. She had to have him. She was projecting desire and she didn't care.

He chuckled. "Come, Rachel. I want you so much. This Phoenix is hungry." His hips thrust against hers, leaving her no doubt of his fierce arousal.

"Yes. Now. Now."

"Hungry Ifrit too." His laugh was fierce and possessive, tinged with hunger. Phoenix lifted her and kissed her. His lips moved over hers until she let out a breath and opened her lips to his.

With Phoenix she was a queen. All the pent-up passion inside her could finally be expressed without fear. But her desire, her needs, were so intense she thought maybe even an immortal Phoenix couldn't deal with it.

"I can deal with it, Rachel. Give me everything. I need all you have. I have to have it," he said on a fervent whisper.

"Aleric." She leaned against him. "What I feel, it scares me."

He gathered her body into his arms, pulling her legs around his waist, and started kissing her neck. "It should scare you. I should scare you."

"You do. But I want you so much. How is it possible for me to feel both?'

He paused and ran his hand over her neck and shoulders before replying. "Because you're a half human dealing with an Elemental. You are doing better than most."

Easing her back, he put her on her feet and then rose. Even at her height he was an impressive half-foot taller than her, and her eyes widened. She touched his chest, and his skin rippled.

Concern beat through his mental signature. Rachel understood that he didn't know, once the primal part of him took over, if he'd have any gentleness in him. "Show me what you want," he demanded. "Come here." He kissed her hard.

"Rachel, once you give yourself to me, there's no going back."

She kissed his neck and wound her hand into his hair. "No stopping, Aleric. I want you so much."

"Maybe as much as I want you. Maybe. I doubt it."

He strode with her to the California king bed that dominated the bedroom, taking up almost the entire room. The soft cotton sheets were smooth against her skin. His knees made indentations on the mattress when he carefully laid her down.

Phoenix lit some candles by waving his hand toward the tapers set in old crystal holders.

Rachel leaned into his hand and there was no more talking. Uttering a low growl, Phoenix took her lips, molding his to hers before sliding his tongue into her already open mouth.

He was pulling off her shirt as he did so, only releasing her lips to motion to her to rid herself of her shirt and bra, tugging his own shirt off as he did so.

Rachel did as he asked, quickly, wanting to feel his naked skin against hers. Once she was bare to the waist, she ran her hands over his broad, muscular chest, loving the feel of his warm skin.

Then she forgot about anything except the wet feel of Phoenix's lips and tongue on her nipples. His lips were hard and fierce, drawing her into his mouth and suckling deep on her. She felt it all the way to her core, soaking her panties and making her moan.

"Rachel, next time I promise I'll make it last, but I want to be inside you right now," he said after he tore his head away from her breasts. "I've waited for so long."

"Yes." She fumbled for his zipper, and he stopped her hands.

"Better let me," he said on a groan. "I'm very...ready. Get naked."

She slid her hand over his jeans, marveling at his length and obvious erect status. "Yes, you are," she said. "So am I. I'm wet and ready for you." She undid the zipper of her jeans and slid them and her panties off simultaneously. Phoenix followed suit, shoving his jeans off his body with shaking fingers, and stepping out of them.

Phoenix's breathing grew shallow, a harsh sound in the otherwise quiet room. Flickers of candlelight danced across his face, throwing his eyes first into shadow and then into light, their blazing intensity apparent.

"Oh, God," he ground out. "Come here."

He was impressive, even in candlelight, that large, well-toned body flexing as he moved over her. She gasped at his fully erect cock and swallowed. "Wow," she said, a little in dismay.

"Trust me." He touched her, using her moisture to caress her, opening her to him.

"Now, Aleric, now," she begged, throwing her head back.

He growled again and moved so that the head of his cock was just penetrating her. Giving her a minute to adjust, he slowly pushed inside her a little at a time, letting her body get used to his bulk.

The pleasure was piercing, overwhelming, and Rachel clawed at him. Phoenix reared back and began biting her, hard nips of her skin that enflamed her. Rachel returned the nips, biting and sucking at his skin. Phoenix's eyes began to faintly glow. With a hoarse cry, he grabbed her hands and threw them above her head, stretching her out against him.

"Aleric!" she cried, feeling the surge in her body and realizing she was about to climax. "Oh God, Aleric."

"Yes!" he shouted. "Now!"

He plunged into her, all the way, and Rachel screamed. The climax that rode her was fierce and intense, filling her rippling body and mind with such concentrated pleasure she was a little scared. Then Phoenix was roaring, his hands tight on hers and his body shaking. With one final, wild shout, Phoenix came, and the intense pleasure caused Rachel to climax again.

"I bet all of San Francisco heard that," she said when she could speak.

A half-amused grunt came from his lips. Moving slightly, he released her hands and leaned on his elbows to meet her eyes. "Probably. I was shielding but I may have…lost control there at the end." He was still breathing heavily, perspiration dotting his forehead and chest.

"Good." She put her arms around his waist and held him.

With a sigh, Phoenix lowered himself beside her, his head next to hers. His brown curls spilled over the pillow, and Rachel reached up and idly twined one over her index finger. "A thousand years," he murmured.

She moved, propping her head up with her hand. "A thousand years for what? No sex?"

He chuckled, the sound muffled by the expensive cotton sheets. "Hell no. I'm not designed that way. I have an understanding with the Dhampirs, and they supply what I need when I need it."

She added Dhampir to the checklist of paranormals to google when the morning came.

He traced circles on her back absentmindedly. The sweat had cooled, leaving her slightly chilled.

Except where Phoenix touched her. Fire danced under her skin at the caress of his fingers, and she grew moist again. No lover had ever affected her this way.

Then again, no lover she'd ever had before was a thousand-year-old incarnation of one of the oldest supposed myths of the human race. It was probably fair to assume Phoenix had had a great deal of time to hone his skills. And being the Elemental related to fire—of course he would set her body ablaze.

His hand stilled and then he was pressing a kiss at the base of her neck. Rachel shivered, feeling the kiss all the way down to her toes. "You didn't mind my skills a little while ago."

Damn it. She had to learn to shield fully. "I didn't, Aleric. I'm still adjusting."

"Good." The bed yielded to his body as he stretched out fully. Placing another kiss on her neck, he looked deeply into her eyes, stroking her hair.

Rachel immediately warmed up, her body heating.

"Shielding is white noise, Rachel. The easiest way is to make up a nonsense song or string of words that you can use to mask your thoughts."

"Like my nursery rhyme."

"That works. Practice it until you can maintain it while you are doing other things. You should have a few, just in case." Tracing her cheek with his thumb, he put his fingers under her jaw and lifted her head to his. "What you need to do is make it so it's automatically part of your mind. You need to keep it running at all times, even if it's subconscious. That way if you need it, you can instantly shield."

She put her hand over his and laced her fingers with his. "I'll try," she promised. "I can't say I'll be perfect tomorrow."

"You're mine now, Rachel," he said suddenly, meeting her eyes. "Mine." He said it again, fiercely.

She saw a fire in his eyes she had no idea how she had inspired.

"Don't you know?" An image of the intense physical release he had felt shot through her, and she first trembled and then laughed.

"Mine," he said again and pulled her close, tilting her face to his.

* * * * *

Finally. Finally. Finally Ron was going to get to do something. He had been itching to do something, and finally the being had given him another task.

It wasn't much. It wasn't nearly as much as he wanted to do, or what he understood his ultimate task to be, but it was something. Something to tide him over until the actual day came when he would get to use his guns. Hopefully guns plural, anyway. This would be a small something, but it would cause grief and destruction.

It was a pity he had to make it look like an accident. That was what the being had said. It had to look like an accident *to humans.*

He knew he was a little too curious. Things were strange, and his well-honed sense of preservation was screaming that he was in over his head. Part of him wanted to leave the job behind and hide in South America. A job was a job, though, and this one paid well. Paying jobs didn't come along every day, and if he ran on one, it would get around fast. Besides, he had a feeling if he tried to run, he would be found and punished. He shivered at the thought of what form his punishment might take. So he stayed. Even if it meant lurking for far longer than he liked. Get in, do the job, get out. That was how he operated.

It would be simple to do. Newspaper was easy to get, and once it caught, it would take the rags he'd bought at the thrift store with it. All he had to do was scatter it strategically around the apartment, make sure some candles were burning so it would look like they had caused it, light the newspaper and rags until they were blazing and get out.

He studied the address. It was just an apartment, with no apparent riches to recommend it. He wasn't even allowed to loot it first. Just a lower middle-class apartment on the second floor of a block of apartments, near BART and shops but otherwise boring. He had no idea why the being would want to burn this place down, but she was. The reasons why didn't matter.

Time to get started. Ron rubbed his hands together in glee. He loved fires.

Chapter Eight

Phoenix's frown deepened as he flipped between channels on his huge wall-mounted plasma TV.

Rachel had thought he would be in the bed next to her, and was perversely disappointed that his side was already cold when she woke. Seeing another person there was a rarity, and she had wanted to enjoy the sight of his beautiful body sprawled out, naked.

Instead he was in a pair of drawstring shorts, his chest bare. His wavy hair was messy and had clearly not seen a comb yet that day.

She could tell the minute he became aware of her. His mind cleared, but his shields were still down, and both his mind and his body greeted her.

"Whatcha doing?" she asked, sitting down beside him.

"Clues," he said simply. "We need clues."

He put a hand on her knee, kissed her absently and turned his attention back to the TV. Bloomberg, then MSNBC, then *Headline News* flew past on the screen before he went to the smaller channels, a ritual he was repeating over and over again. The talking heads spoke of civil unrest in the Turkic republics, famine in Africa, the instability of the euro, the usual fare. Nothing that seemed to command his attention.

She had no idea how he was managing to sort through anything with the speed he was pressing the remote.

He repeated the process with the remote, going through the national and then the local channels.

The newscaster was talking about the visit of the Chicago mayor. Rachel pointed to the channel, her hand on his arm to stop his progress. "What about that?"

He frowned. "I don't think she would have any impact one way or the other. We're looking for something big, either human or natural, that has something to do with fire and my test."

Phoenix began his rapid flipping again. The story shifted, the flash of a picture of a fire catching their attention.

"In local news, a fire that burned an apartment building in the early-morning hours does not appear to have been arson."

She recognized that building. The char and black of the fire had mostly been confined to the second-floor apartment, which, from the brief news footage they were showing, appeared to be a total loss.

The newscaster was talking, but Rachel wasn't hearing it. They had gotten her basic stuff out of the apartment, but she'd left plenty behind with the intent of going back later and either getting it or taking up residence there again and resuming her normal life.

No chance of that now. No chance of either.

She was aware that Phoenix was staring at her, but her gaze was fixed on the TV screen. Gone, all gone. From the footage it didn't seem as if anything was left. Nothing left to get. Nothing left of her life.

Finally, he cleared his throat. "I'm sorry."

She was frozen. The news had moved on, talking about the 49ers and other local sports while she sat there, her mind a whirl.

"Rachel."

It was as if she were underwater. What if she had been there? What if JT had been there? What if she had been trapped in her bed, unable to escape the flames? What if, what if, what if?

"Rachel!"

His voice was loud and harsh, He gripped her shoulders and shook her.

"Rachel!"

His eyes were shadowed with worry and fear. Deeper, in the place he let few

Claire Davon

see, was a searing panic that he was trying to keep from her.

"You weren't there, Rachel. You're here. You and JT are safe."

"What if?" She verbalized what her mind was screaming. With a shudder, she collapsed against him.

"Life is like that, Rachel. It's an infinite series of 'what ifs'. But it didn't happen. The fire is a warning, that is clear, but you weren't there. I'm sorry about your belongings, but they were just things."

Tears came, tears of anger and fear. "It was *my* stuff," she said through the clog in her throat, and hiccupped.

* * * * *

It wouldn't be the last time she lost things, Phoenix thought grimly, feeling her body warm against his.

He continued to hold her, saying nothing, letting her cry. The tears weren't just about her lost items. They were about everything she had lost and was continuing to lose. Tests were like that.

Tests like being Phoenix and going to the fire. It stripped you down to nothing and rebuilt you. If you survived the flames.

Her cell phone rang, startling both of them. It was a strange beep, unfamiliar to them both. Rachel dug in her purse and pulled out the blatting device.

"It's an urgent call," she said unnecessarily. "Probably the police. My phone was on vibrate, but they must have used an emergency beacon."

Fire. It couldn't be a coincidence that she was an Ifrit, linked by legend and modern-day truth to fire. There was no way that arson fire in her apartment was anything other than a warning from Haures.

The wolves had wanted her out of the picture too, trying to warn her off before she got involved. Why?

There had never been partners involved in Challenge before. It had always been the four Elementals against the Demonos. The paranormals, gods and other nonhumans mostly stayed on the sidelines. In the opinion of nonhumans, this war, the test, was between the two sets of powerful immortals and didn't affect them. They would endure. The Demonos and Elementals employed humans, but in low-level tasks or, in the case of the Elementals, at their company.

Rachel was sniffling, but her voice was steady as she relayed information to the police. Phoenix smiled, remembering her heated passion under him. It had been a long time since he'd had a sexual encounter so satisfying. What would it be like when she had control over her fire? His mind danced with the possibilities the same way fire could dance over their bodies, alight but not consumed, heating but not burning. Alive.

He had learned not to get attached to things or to people. They were all transitory. Elementals had to be prepared to move at a moment's notice. He had left more things behind than he could remember. Pets were gone in a blink of an eye, and an unnecessary complication. Humans lived longer, but not long enough. They were there, and then they were gone. Only the nonhumans stayed around long enough to form attachments, but most of them preferred to keep their distance from the Elementals. Links were rare. It had been centuries since he'd cared about anyone other than his fellow Elementals. The last time he had allowed a woman in, it had almost killed him.

Ifrits were few and kept to themselves. It would be vital to find out more. Perhaps as vital as facing Challenge.

"They'll be over to take a statement later. He said there was no sign of an accelerant, nothing that immediately shouted arson. He asked me if I could have fallen asleep with a cigarette, a lit candle...or gotten drunk and passed out with those things. Well, he didn't say the last part, but I could read it in his thoughts."

Phoenix paused the DVR. He rose and went to her.

"I...can we get out of here for a while? Go somewhere quiet?"

"Good idea. The police can wait. They will suspect your involvement but will have no way and no true desire to pursue it. They will never solve the fire and will write it off as an accident. Haures has a way of ensuring that."

"You think it was Haures?"

"I know it was. Come. Let's go."

* * * * *

After a brief stop at a shopping mall to pick up supplies, Phoenix concentrated and was pleased when his wings appeared. They didn't often cooperate. He handed Rachel the backpack, and she slung it over her shoulders. He soared with Rachel high into the clouds, catching a fast-moving current. Soon they were over Washington State and into the Olympic Mountains. After circling, he picked Mount Storm King, a low peak that was not that interesting to tourists. There was a faint dusting of snow at this elevation.

He found a spot that was very difficult for people to climb to, and landed about halfway up.

Pulling out a bottle of wine, Phoenix uncorked the wine and poured each of them a healthy measure into two small plastic cups Rachel had removed from the pack.

She cocked an eyebrow at Phoenix. "Are you sure you should be drinking this? Don't drink and fly, isn't that what they say?"

He leaned over and kissed her. "Remember, I metabolize alcohol in seconds," he said. "I do like the taste of wine, though. Saxons didn't worry about the quality. After a battle we wanted to get drunk, and fast." He was quiet a minute. "My Challenge is always fire related. It could be war, bombs, explosions, not necessarily traditional fire. There aren't any wars that concern me, although that could change in an instant. There haven't been any more than the usual terrorist threats. No significant world leaders have been assassinated. Nonetheless, we have all felt it. Challenge is here."

He handed her the cup of wine, and she curled her fingers around it.

An idea erupted into her head before her nursery rhyme cut off contact. He set his cup down and studied her with a quizzical expression, waiting for her to speak, hands and wings folded to show he was being patient.

"Gavrilo Princip," she said suddenly.

"Bless you," he said with a smile that faded when he saw her bleak expression.

"Gavrilo Princip," she said again, her hands shaking. She carefully placed her cup down next to his as if she was afraid she would spill the wine and turned to Phoenix. He plucked desolation and fear from her mind.

"I don't understand," he admitted.

"He's the guy who assassinated Archduke Franz Ferdinand of Austria and triggered World War I." After Phoenix turned up his palms, she continued. "My foster father was a huge World War I buff, so I know a lot about that war. When he deigned to talk to me, the most comfortable topic was his obsession with the First World War. It seemed a small thing, but there were so many alliances and treaties that a small assassination of an unimportant duke dragged the entire world into war. Haures doesn't need to bomb countries or assassinate our president or the British prime minister. She just has to find the right combination of people who have ties to other countries that will bring the world to its knees."

Phoenix stared at her. "Right. I know who he is, now that you reminded me. That's interesting," he said slowly. He was quiet for several moments. "It makes sense. It makes a great deal of sense. It ties into World War II, our last great defeat."

He got up, brushing the snow off his butt with his wings. The small ledge they were on didn't leave him much room, but he began pacing anyway, folding his hands in front and his wings at his back. The slits of the shirt opened with his movements and the breeze caught his feathers, making them ripple.

He was almost physically sick at the idea this could easily have slipped past him. It was so sly, so subtle that it could have been far too late by the time Phoenix figured out what was going on. Challenge was supposed to be more overt. Haures had gotten clever since the last time.

He'd underestimated the Demonos and miscalculated Challenge. After the Demonos had defeated the Elementals during World War II, he hadn't thought it would come this quickly. He hadn't expected Haures to be so subtle.

If not for a honey blonde, she might have gotten away with it.

With such a tight shield, Rachel couldn't hear him. Cautiously checking her mind for any sign she was aware of what he was doing, Phoenix was relieved when she seemed worried, but unaware. He sent a quick, tight beam to Griffin with the new information and heard the faint acknowledgment.

"You said the Black Plague was a Challenge. And the Second World War," she said slowly. "What happened?"

"The Second World War was one of the greatest Challenges we have ever faced. That's what makes this timing odd. It's too soon. Challenges come when they come, and there is no rhyme or reason—none that we can fathom, anyway—but there is usually more than a century between the major ones. This is only a few decades. None of us expected a Challenge this quickly."

She doubted that people born seventy years ago would think of this as "only" a few decades, but she let it pass. "You lost that one? But the Allies beat the Axis. How can you call that a defeat?"

He made a twisting motion with his lips.

"Elementals do not count wins and losses as humans do. Hippocampus lost his individual Challenge, and we lost the final one that we had to fight after his loss. It is estimated that eighty million people died as a result of that war. Yes, the Allies ultimately prevailed, but the human cost was so high. The Demonos destroyed much as a result of our failure. That is what we call a loss. The final outcome is irrelevant for our purposes, although I am glad the Allies were the winners. Think of all the people who would die this time. We cannot lose."

Rachel was silent for a moment. "You're right. We have to win. Maybe," she mused thoughtfully. "Maybe this test and those tests were linked. There is always talk of World War III. Maybe this is a continuation of those."

He cocked his head. "It's possible." Putting a hand out, he gently caressed her cheek with his index finger. Her shudder and the dilation of her eyes thrilled him. Hardening in a rush, Phoenix pulled her against him and folded his wings around her. "Clothes off," he murmured. She stripped off the parka and then the simple jeans and sweater underneath.

Rachel sighed. He could feel the warmth of her breath on his neck, and she relaxed into him. He sat down and maneuvered her onto his lap, urging her legs open so she straddled his cock, only his jeans and the barrier of her underwear separating them.

"Hmm, Aleric," she murmured, pressing small kisses along his neck. "All for me?" Her breathing began coming in short gasps as he thrust against her, letting her feel the weight and heaviness of his desire.

His answer was a grunt as he slid his hands around the front of her body. Closing his wings tighter around her to keep out the chill, Phoenix unbuttoned her emerald-green blouse and slid her breasts free. Even through the bra he could see that her nipples had peaked, and the sight made Phoenix's cock harden further.

Using his wings to brace her, ran his thumbs over the erect nipples. Rachel's body rippled, and she threw her head back against his wing. He caught her with a band of feathers and held her head still even as he bent to suckle deeply from her ruby-colored nipples. Surrounded by red areolas, they were made for a man's touch. For a Phoenix's touch.

He cupped a breast in each hand and hefted them so they stood straight up, directly in front of his mouth. Phoenix pushed them as close together as he could and then ran his tongue from one nipple to the other, circling each in turn until they were wet. Rachel rocked against him, clutching at his head, every movement of her groin against his sweet torture. The dampness of her arousal was apparent even through cloth. He moaned at the sweetness of the passion she showed.

Their cries echoed off the mountain. The sounds lingered in the air as if ghosts surrounded them, mimicking their passion.

Bearing her down to the snow, his wings protecting her from the cold, Phoenix shoved his jeans to his knees and rubbed his underwear-clad cock against her body. Kneeling, he moved a hand to the waistband of her panties and slid under it. She was damp and slick, her body open to him. He moved a finger inside her and caressed her both within and without. To his surprise, not only his body but his wings were shaking from the force of his arousal.

"Oh, Aleric, please, now, Aleric. Now."

Without removing either of their underwear, Phoenix pushed hers aside, then slid his cock out and into her. She was welcoming, her arousal easing the way for his big penis. A fire circle erupted around them in the snow, close enough to feel the heat but far enough not to burn her. The snow under the circle began to melt. She pushed with her fire sense, and the wall of flames grew higher, dancing around them. Their combined power would have thrilled him if he weren't already beyond the point of no return.

Then there was no thinking as their bodies moved together.

Rachel moaned, meeting his thrusts. She clutched at his shoulders, drawing his upper body down to her and wrapping her arms around him. He shuddered, rapidly losing control of his body gloved in her soft warmth. He kissed her deeply, his tongue thrusting into her mouth.

Phoenix freed one hand and inserted it under her underwear. Finding her clit, he circled it with his index finger, and Rachel jerked.

"Come for me," he ordered, circling faster until Rachel screamed and moisture flooded his penis. Phoenix let slip the frayed remains of his control then and surged into her. Crying out, throwing his head back, he tensed almost to the breaking point and spilled into her, his voice harsh and birdlike as it echoed in the cool mountain air.

A long time later, after their breathing settled back to normal, Phoenix gently rearranged Rachel's clothes and put his pants back on. Then he gathered her in his arms and let his wings furl behind him. The fire circle cooled and the flames winked out. A circle of melted snow surrounded them, revealing hard dirt and small rocks.

Her gaze flicked to the fire circle, and Phoenix grinned sheepishly. "I wanted to show off a little. You made it spectacular."

Rachel smiled. "I liked it."

"We should get back. We have a lot to do."

* * * * *

JT was meowing insistently when they got back to the house. Leaving Phoenix in the living room, Rachel picked up the small feline and took him into the kitchen. Feeding JT his favorite ham treat and giving him lots of attention helped soothe Rachel's mind as she turned over the new idea. Finally, JT grew tired of being petted and sauntered off. He trotted regally to the corner where Phoenix had set up a cat bed for him, kneading it for a minute before settling into it and promptly falling asleep.

They needed a whiteboard, she thought absently, turning to the kitchen sink to wash her hands. Something like what police used when they were trying to solve a crime. They could hang it on the wall or put it in the living room. Then, as threads came together, they could arrange and rearrange them easily.

Suddenly, her mind filled with dark, bloody visions. Visions of stabbing, of arteries being severed and blood flying. Visions of death in violent ways: beheading, garroting, quartering.

Rachel staggered, and the water that was still spraying out from the faucet hit the sink and splashed onto her face. The visions were stark and brutal, with dirt and horses, and blood everywhere. She recognized the visions as those Phoenix had shown her from his time before becoming the Elemental, when he was just Aleric. A quick probe showed that he was thinking of nothing more than smug male satisfaction in pleasing a woman. But if not him, where had they come from?

She had bent to turn off the water when a different set of visions hit her. Fires burning, bodies stacked everywhere and being put to the flame. Rats. People with boils on their faces and covering their bodies. People shutting their doors to strangers for fear that the disease—the Black Death as it would later be known—would spread to them. The stench of fear was everywhere, overlaid by the thick, acrid smoke of burning bodies.

"This is what your lover did," a voice said. *"This is what the Phoenix is."*

Rachel knew that female voice, although she had only heard it once before. In mental communication it had same flat tone she spoke with. There was only one person it could be.

"I know, Haures. Phoenix has already shown me this."

"Of course. We have much to discuss."

Rachel mentally shrugged and tried for an indifferent emotion. She might be new to her powers, but she would be damned if she showed that to the Demonos.

Could she summon anger? Rachel tried for it, found it and brought it out. Using the black emotion to coat her mind, she turned her attention back to Haures.

"I know what you are, and I know what Phoenix is. Get out of my head and leave me alone."

A tinkling laugh surprised her. It was followed by an image of Kali. Rachel didn't think that was Haures's form, but it was a compelling one nonetheless. Kali, the Hindu goddess. Kali, sometimes associated with change and destruction.

"Do you? Do you know what your lover is, really? Do you know who is good and who is evil, Ifrit? Do you? There are many more tests they failed besides the Black Death and World War II. Has he told you about them? The other failed Challenges? Stay out of this, Ifrit. You do not know the truth. You will survive the scouring. This is of no concern to you."

More images, dark, black and vile. Blood, so much blood. Phoenix killing, one on one, by hand, strangling people, knifing them under the ribs, shooting them. Phoenix looking almost unrecognizable as he dispatched people with his powerful body alone. Images flipped quickly, like an old-time projector movie, each more terrible than the next.

"Stay away from her." The voice was gravelly, harsh and wholly masculine.

Rachel blinked in surprise. It was not a voice she recognized, but it was somehow familiar. The images halted, stuttering to a stop. Then they receded, as if being sucked back into a vortex. The blackness of Haures as Kali lost some of its edge, wavering.

That had not been Phoenix's mental voice, or any of the Elementals she'd met yet.

"Stay away from my granddaughter."

It was the same voice. But…granddaughter?

The Kali image brightened again before it wavered and disappeared. *"I'll be back,"* Haures promised. Then she vanished, winking out like the Cheshire cat. The only thing left behind was the tinkling laugh, incongruous against the fierceness of the goddess's image.

The unfamiliar mind touched hers, a questing tendril. It probed her, finding and sampling her fire power. The mind felt familiar, something she had known a long time ago but had forgotten in the weight of life's memories.

An image of the same being she had seen the day of her parents' death came to her. He was tall, with a dusky tint to his skin and leathery wings, smaller than Phoenix's but no less impressive.

"I'll be there soon. Be careful."

* * * * *

When Rachel re-entered the living room, Phoenix had the TV and the computer on. Pages of notes were strewn across the desk haphazardly. Several browser windows were cascaded, and he was flicking between websites.

"The police left you a message," he said, nodding to a piece of paper on the coffee table. "They want you to call them again to discuss the fire." His focus went back to the computer, and it took him a moment to realize she hadn't said anything. "Char and burn. Rachel?" he asked when she didn't answer.

Finally her eyes focused on him and beyond, to the papers on the desk. "I'll call them. Did you…" She stopped. Heaving a sigh, she started again. "Did you find anything good?"

"Lots of information. Many possibilities," Phoenix said. "Too much to make any sense of yet. We need to a whiteboard, or some of that whiteboard paint, so we can make notes and find the patterns."

"Good."

Her mind was closed to him. Closed, locked and barred. It was locked in a way he hadn't known she could do. As impressed as he was with her ability to shield, the complete lack of feedback alarmed him. He probed a little bit but couldn't find a quick entry. She would tell him. She couldn't keep secrets for long.

"I'm separating the ideas into a few piles." He frowned at the screen and jotted down a note from a political conspiracy website. "International figures and domestic. I'm going to focus mostly on domestic leaders, politicians and businesspeople, because of what you said. I don't want to give up on the international mortals completely, though, because we never know where the link may be."

Rachel picked up the piece of paper with the police message and put it back down again. She wandered to the window, looked out, turned away and walked back to the center of the room.

"Rachel, is everything all right?" He didn't think she regretted the sex. He prided himself on the fact that he had left her satisfied. It wasn't that, but she was so locked down he had no idea what to think.

Finally she focused on him and shrugged unconvincingly. "It's fine," she said, with a slight tremor in her voice. She rubbed her forehead. "I'm just feeling all of it. My life has been turned so upside down. It's weird to think I'm a fire power, with the arson, and that your Challenge could be World War III. It's just… wow…"

She was lying. Her voice rose slightly, giving away the falsehood. "Come look at what I have so far," he said, holding out a hand to her. She walked to him but didn't accept the intimacy, stepping around the hand to his desk.

That could not be tolerated. With a deft touch he sent a questing probe into her mind and saw the Great Wall of China. Without betraying his presence, there was no easy way in. Where had she learned to shield that well, that quickly? There was something different about her, some shield that hadn't been there before, adding to what she was already discovering.

He had written down all the current world leaders, from the obvious like the US president and the Russian leader to the heads of small countries in Africa and South America. Each was on a separate piece of paper, which Phoenix and Rachel would transfer to the whiteboard.

"Do you want to call the police?"

Her current frame of mind made it hard for him to tell how she was feeling about the loss of her possessions and the message that the arson had sent.

"I will in a few minutes. They don't care. I don't have renter's insurance so there's really nothing to do. There wasn't much in there, not much to lose."

He wanted to reach out and shake her to get some emotion back in her voice. "You're right." His tone was rough, but he was unable to stop himself. "But they will be suspicious if they don't hear from you. You have to deal with it."

"Is that what you do? Is that what you call what you do? Is that what you call the aftermath of the tests when you lose? Dealing with it?"

The verbal attack, so unexpected, made him blink. Phoenix reached out and there it was, anger tinged with something dark, something not of her mind. It was gone before he could grip it, but he understood what had happened. "What did Haures say? How did she get to you?"

Rachel shuddered. She moved away again, putting distance between their bodies. He hated the space as much as he hated the closed mind that she presented to him. He detested that she mistrusted him so easily, and that anger made him primal. He shouldn't blame her, but the savage warrior part of him wanted to rend something.

"I don't want to talk about it right now. Later. What about that person we felt at Fisherman's Wharf? Do you think he could be the one who burned my apartment down? You said they had a—what did you call it, a blocker?"

Phoenix's hands curled and flexed with the urge to shake her. "More than likely," he said, and she relaxed as he accepted the change of subject. "Blockers are rare. We need to find him or her."

She laced her hands together, her expression distant. "What do blockers do?"

He wanted to pull her body against him and force the truth out of her. Alternatively, he could kiss her until her eyes went blind with desire. The urge, dark and hungry, beat at him under his skin. Fire danced on him, threatening to spread, before it died away. Rachel's gaze followed the flame, a look of longing on her face.

He settled for moving to her, stopping a foot away from her place at the window, trying to see the same view she was seeing. Her mind had never been so closed. Phoenix tried to see past the wall to what was inside her, but her wall was frustratingly smooth. "Blockers are similar to shields, but for those with no ability. They take away the mental signals the person emits, that daily chatter you hear, and show a blank wall to anyone who probes."

"Nice to have."

He let out a low, harsh sound. "You don't need it. You're a blank wall right now."

She rounded on him. "Am I?"

There was no question she wanted a fight. Her fists curled and she breathed heavily, as if she had run a long race. The primal part of him wanted to give her that fight. He wanted to tangle with her until their bodies were slick with sweat, and then give her another kind of fight. A mutual one. Fire playing along their skins while they moved together, him buried so deep inside her they were one person.

Her wall slipped, showing visions of death, mayhem and destruction. There was also hurt, anger and fear behind the wall before she slammed it down again.

"It was awful," she said on a cry, her composure evaporating. "It was so dark, so awful. I hate it, I hate it!" Her wall shattered, her hatred now a tangible thing. A fire arrow of anger launched on the mental plane toward Haures from Rachel. There was a hoarse shout in the distance as the arrow had found its mark. It singed across their minds before it died away.

Rachel had a triumphant, self-satisfied smile on her face. Then her brows knitted.

"What?" she said, her smile slowly fading. "I found her and warned her. I used my power. Isn't that a good thing?"

"Hate and anger are powerful weapons," he said, choosing his words carefully. "But they leave you vulnerable." And yet, he had felt them far too many times. Why should it be different for her?

Because you don't want her to slip into darkness.

"Oh hell," she said. Her anger dissipated. When she turned to him again, the darkness was gone from her face. "How very *Star Wars* Yoda of you. 'Luke, don't give in to hate. That leads to the Dark Side.'"

Phoenix held her gaze until she looked away. "Where do you think *Star Wars* got it from?"

Tears were running down her face and she made no move to check them. They fell over her cheeks, onto her chin and down her neck before disappearing into her shirt. "I don't know if I can do it."

He yanked her into his arms, more roughly than he had intended. Her body was stiff for a moment and then she yielded, collapsing against him. "You can do it. You are strong. You can be stronger."

She said nothing, clutching at him. He let her cry, wanting all the dark energy washed out of her. Her body was supple in his arms. The burn of desire started again, more quickly than he could have believed.

Eventually her tears slowed. "Why didn't he help me?"

Phoenix said nothing.

"The Ifrit. In my visions, my grandfather, I think. He looked like something out of *Arabian Nights*. He was big and menacing and had wings. He could have helped me."

"I don't know, Rachel." The thought of her grandfather tugged at him. Her family. He wanted to know more about them.

"Why didn't he help me? Why didn't he stop it? Why can't I remember?"

Although they were rhetorical questions, it was safer to answer. "You had a block on your memories, and with it your fire. I think it was designed to dissipate, perhaps at a certain age, like now. Perhaps that is why you were having fugues as your fire began to manifest. We need to know. It's important."

From far off, he heard an unfamiliar voice. *"I am coming. Soon."*

Chapter Nine

Ron writhed in his bed, the nightmare vivid. Death. Destruction. Mayhem. Excellent.

Then a winged man, and a guy who looked like a lion, a couple that had catlike qualities, and the last, a freaky fish person who appeared to have gills, collectively appeared. They fought on the opposite side and stopped the war, driving back forces that would have taken over the entire known world at that time, and changed the course of history. There would have been bloodshed everywhere, the victors killing most of those who didn't look like them, and keeping only a few as short-lived slaves. Half the world would have fallen to their blades, if not for the do-gooders who stopped it.

The blood would have been beautiful. The massacres would have been epic. The humans' world would have descended into chaos, all progress halted.

The voice of his customer echoed in his mind. *"Pity we lost that one. The Elementals won that time. They won't win this one."*

Ron bolted upright, shaking his covers off, the dream lingering. He wasn't sure if the dream was real or not, but he discovered he was grasping the necklace the being had given him when he/she/it had hired him.

He wanted to rend, to destroy something. He wanted to kill.

Ron flipped on a light in the living room of the subletted apartment. To calm his edgy nerves, he checked each of the weapons he had acquired over the last weeks and found all of them to be in perfect working order, just like they had been yesterday.

It soothed him to know his guns would fire flawlessly. He checked the bombs and the grenades and was pleased to know all was in order. Perfect.

This jangled emotion wasn't common to him. Ron prided himself on being cool under all circumstances, no matter what shit storm was going on around him. The anger he was feeling was almost visceral, primal in a deep-seated way he never allowed himself to feel.

It would be unwise to go out in the early-morning hours and find a transient to kill. It would be satisfying, but it would be a mistake. He wasn't paid to do anything more than the tasks handed to him. The being had made it very clear that he was to do exactly as instructed, and no more.

Killing a transient was out. Unfortunately. He would be able to kill soon enough. The need to take a life beat against his skull, begging to be released. Who would know? If one more person died, who was to know that hadn't been part of the plan? That it hadn't been necessary? He didn't think his employer would mind a few extra bodies, as long as the goal was accomplished.

An image of the couple he had followed the other day swam into his mind.

Them. Assholes.

Now he recognized the man as the same one from his dream/nightmare. The fucker who had spread his wings and stopped the primitive arrows from reaching their destination. That had been part of the reason the tide had turned against the warring tribes, and that failure had made their resolve nosedive, shattering their ranks.

The abnormal thing was good-looking too, if you went past the wings. He hadn't had them the day Ron saw him, and Ron wasn't sure what the deal was. He had wanted to be handsome like that jerk when he was younger, but he had been doomed to be small and nondescript. It had taken years to be glad for that plainness.

Who the fuck had wings, anyway? The anger surfaced again. Ron took several deep breaths to calm himself. A thing like that didn't deserve to live. It wasn't human.

The girl, that woman with him, she was clearly into the freak. She had been giving him that doe-eyed look, the one that said, "Oh fuck me, please fuck me now." He could tell by the look in the guy's eyes that he was thinking the same thing.

Ron's cock sprang to life. Sex would be amazing right now. He could find a hooker to fuck, make it rough. Maybe kill her.

No, damn it, he couldn't kill anyone. He couldn't bring attention to himself now.

Torching the place had been fun, but not enough. He didn't understand why the being wanted it burned...or maybe he did know. It had to have been the place of the freak's woman, he knew, and Ron smiled in satisfaction.

In the end, she could die. She deserved it for hanging out with that thing. He could make sure she went down when the politician did. A twofer. A searing hate went through him at the thought of the woman, hate he rarely allowed himself to feel.

She would die. That was all there was to it.

Yeah. That would satisfy him.

Too bad he had to wait.

* * * * *

Rachel was trying to make sense of their notes the next morning when Phoenix came padding out of his bedroom, dressed only in faded black sweatpants. His hair was tousled and there was the beginning of a five o'clock shadow on his jaw.

She turned back to the notes she wanted to transfer to the whiteboard, her mind still a jangle of emotions. She could feel his similar feelings. He wanted to do something, to act, not write names on boards. He wanted to lay a stream of fire on wood until it erupted into flames and they basked in the red-orange glow.

"Does that make any sense to you?" Phoenix said, his voice rough but with a smoky edge. She understood. The itch along her skin and in the center of her palms let her know that her fire too yearned to break free.

Rachel shook her head. "We need to get it all up where we can see it. There're too many possibilities." She pointed to one sheaf of paper, a printout of the countries in Eastern Europe. "You seem to be concentrating on Eastern Europe. Any reason?"

He shrugged. "Just a hunch. Nothing really concrete. There's always turbulence in those regions. The others feel it too. Griff and Sphynx and Hip…"

"You don't talk much about Hippocampus. He's your water Elemental, right? Stuck with a name like that, I might spend all my time on the water too."

If he smiled, it was a faint, fleeting turn of the lips before it was gone. "Hippocampus means sea horse in this context, but the confusion with the human name for brain case decided it for Ondine. She said she didn't want to go around being called something that was located in the temporal lobe. When she assumed the mantle of the water Elemental ten years ago, she insisted on being called 'Ondine' instead of 'Hippocampus'. The name took some getting used to, but it still fits. She was—I guess *is*—a marine biologist. She's new to the Elementals. We're all still getting used to each other. I told you this. Our old Hippocampus died ten years ago. Sharks got him. We think."

"It still doesn't seem real that you guys can be killed. You seem impervious to harm."

His Adam's apple worked as he swallowed. "It's rare but it happens. None of us are the Elementals who began this journey, except for Sphynx. They were there at the beginning, I think. Hip was torn apart, so shredded there was no way to repair the damage. It was…gruesome. The only explanation we could think of at the time that they had been provoked by blood in the water, which was weird because Hip had a good relationship with the sharks. The water Elemental always has a connection with the life in the sea. But the sharks were there, and his body was fragmented. We were so unprepared for a new Challenge that it didn't occur to us that it could be anything besides a strange accident, but now I wonder." He spread his hands. There was fire at his fingertips. "Lara, the new Hippocampus—rather, Ondine was given the role immediately, to her surprise. We don't know how we are chosen. She hasn't completely adjusted to this role."

Rachel snorted. "I can understand that."

"We should have known it was something more. That was devastating. Sphynx usually knows these things. They're the senior Elemental among us. They always have been. They've been alive for…I don't know. Maybe as long as humans have been. They're a paired couple, and together they are the earth Elemental. Their separate names are Masud and Shani. You will need to know that for the future."

His eyes grew distant, as if he was seeing something far beyond him. The fire faded from his hands. She wanted to go to him and soothe the ache that the old Hip's death had clearly left.

It didn't seem right that they could be killed. Still, Phoenix was only a thousand years old, so there had to have been one before him. Then she laughed at herself, her body moving with the quick sound. "Only" a thousand years old. Her life was measured in decades, and the centuries Phoenix had lived seemed like a wonderful luxury. "Can the Demonos be killed?"

"They can, but like us, not easily. Many paranormals can kill those like us, especially the gods and demigods, but we don't go around killing each other. The object is to win Challenge, and by extension, defeat the Demonos."

"Have you ever killed a Demonos?"

"Of course. Casualties happen." He paused. "Hippocampus's failure in our last Challenge started the events that led to World War II. He was killed ten years ago, but he was never the same after our devastating loss."

There were circles under his eyes. His shoulders drooped, making his chest slightly concave despite the muscles. Although the early morning was uncharacteristically bright, the rays of sun streaming through the large sliding door, he appeared shadowed, as if the day weighed heavily on him.

She put her hands on his chest. He raised his eyes to hers, hurt and pain in them. He made a muffled sound and closed his arms around her, pulling her against him.

"He was my friend," Phoenix said finally, and his voice broke. "The three of us—me, him and Griff—went all around the world. We were a merry trio for centuries. When Hip died, we all felt it scream across our minds. He winked out,

like a door slammed shut. Gone. It is horrible when any of us die, but Hip…"
He shuddered.

She held him, murmuring soothing words against his neck and stroking his skin until the shudders slowed and then stopped. "Well." She met his eyes. The shadows had lifted and she was glad for that. "We just have to make sure it doesn't happen again. Come on, let's see about these notes."

He breathed out. Gathering up the papers, he squared the corners and fanned through them. He took the notes and flipped to a fresh page, writing with a back-slanting script.

"You're left-handed."

Phoenix grinned, and if it was a pale shade of his normal smile, she opted not to notice. "I'm ambidextrous. It's useful in a battle. I can use both equally."

She arched her eyebrows. "Can I see those?" She took the notes from his hands and studied them again. "We can start with eliminating countries. It might narrow the list down." Rachel grabbed some clean sheets and wrote the different continent groups—Europe, Asia, South America, North America, Australia and Africa—putting them on the floor in a row.

Phoenix stared at the papers and said nothing.

"It could be any of them," he said after several heartbeats. "Or it could be none of them. We think that Challenge may be designed to upset alliances and send the world into another World War, but we don't really know." He pointed to the Europe paper. "Each one of these countries has a reason to get involved in a conflict, given the right set of circumstances." He then toed the Australia paper. "They are isolated, but who is to say that they wouldn't react if threatened? We just don't know."

Knowing her dismay was plain on her face, Rachel looked at each of the papers with the continent names on them, wishing she knew more about global politics.

"How did you face Challenge in the past?"

His gaze moved to her. "When it happens, we will know."

"But you're here. I'm here. The shadow people and wolves freaked out.

Doesn't it make sense that your Challenge, whatever that means, is here in San Francisco?"

He shook his head. "It's not that simple, Rachel. Challenge has taken place all over the globe. It doesn't have to be here just because we are. It could be anywhere."

It seemed to Rachel that he was making it too complicated, but she remained silent. She would learn more about the world, she vowed, if they got through this.

JT picked that moment to rub against Rachel, meowing up at her. He dropped a toy at her feet, giving her an imploring stare. They played fetch for a few minutes, and Rachel caught Phoenix smiling at the catch and return. He might not like cats, but he didn't seem to mind this one.

Finally JT tired of the game and, leaving the toy halfway across the living room, licked his torso a few times before plopping down on the edge of the rug. She smiled at Phoenix, her mood lightened. He was expressionless except for a crinkle of amusement around his eyes.

"Hey, any chance he is…" Her voice trailed off, and she jerked a thumb to her cat.

Phoenix followed her motion with his eyes. "Paranormal?" he asked. He shrugged, shaking his head at the same time. "Sometimes a cat is just a cat."

Disappointed, Rachel turned back to the task at hand. Joining him at the computer, she studied the pieces of paper on the floor. The names of continents and countries seemed to mock her.

From what little she knew about the world there was any number of ways that things could explode. They would need to study further. Phoenix was right. There were too many possibilities.

"Let's see what we can find out online," he said. "Perhaps we can track down some likely candidates. We may have to arrange for an overseas trip."

She glanced at his back muscles and then at him.

After a slow grin, he shook his head. "That's far even for me, and complicated by a passenger. Modern air travel is a wonderful invention." Then he rose. "I will go get our supplies. Wait for me. Lock the door."

* * * * *

Once Phoenix left, Rachel paced for a few moments. There were infinite possibilities. Then everything went still. Even JT seemed to make no sound. There was a silence filled with ominous nothingness, and then a rush of air. Suddenly, Rachel was no longer alone.

Now there was a woman with her. She glided—there was no other word for it—into the room, looking around the open space as she moved.

She wasn't tall, maybe five feet, with one of those small forms that made men want to protect and care for her. The unknown person's hair was black and her skin so fair it resembled porcelain. Her mouth didn't quite close, and through her lips Rachel could see the tips of her canines.

Rachel realized she was in the same room as a vampire.

One that could walk in daylight. Foggy daylight, yes, but daylight nonetheless.

A vampire. In daylight.

And Phoenix wasn't there.

She shot a frantic beam to Phoenix while turning to the vampire, her face impassive. His reply was instantaneous.

"I'm on my way. Stay calm but be careful. Arella is very powerful."

"Noted."

"Can I offer you a, um—" Rachel fumbled, realizing how her offer of a drink might sound. "What can I do for you, Arella?" She was pleased that her knowledge of the vampire's name wiped the look of superiority off Arella's face, if only briefly. Rachel's dislike of Arella was instant, rage bubbling up from deep in her psyche. Her palms itched and she welcomed the sensation. Heat curled along her spine, radiating up and through her bones. Rachel let it come.

The deceptively slender vampire picked up a wrapped chocolate from a bowl on an end table. Studying it, she frowned slightly and then shrugged and unwrapped it and slid it into her mouth. "I wanted to meet Phoenix's secret weapon. His Ifrit."

There was a tendril of exploration, a foray against her shield. Without moving, Rachel visualized an impenetrable wall and felt Arella's raid end when it reached that barrier.

After a moment Arella laughed, a brittle, tinkling sound laced with an edge of menace. Rachel tried to look unaffected.

"I thought that was you a few days ago trying to get me outside my apartment, but Aleric told me it was the shadow people. So hard to tell in the dark. Did you burn my place down?"

Arella shuddered. Rachel realized that would be unlikely. She didn't know what was true or not true about real-life vampires, but they couldn't like fire.

Good.

Arella looked Rachel all the way up and all the way down, and her face said, *You are nothing to me.* "When you began manifesting, we saw the danger. The shadow people acted. The wolves acted. We waited. That was a mistake." She made a gesture that spoke somehow of futility. "Now it's too late."

Rachel found her wall was so thorough she couldn't let Phoenix in either. The silence was complete. The only person in her mind was her. She'd gotten used to hearing a low level of mental noise and missed the ambient sound. Hoping he was already in the air, she backed away from the vampire. "I don't trust you."

"You are not as dumb as I thought, then."

How had Arella known that Phoenix wouldn't be there? How had she picked a time when the half Ifrit, half mortal would be alone? Rachel knew the answer to that. They were being watched. She searched for a conversational gambit, knowing she needed to delay the vampire. "I thought vampires couldn't walk in daylight."

Her tinkling laugh came again, like glass down Rachel's back. "Only very old vampires. Ones that have enough supernatural blood to change into something beyond vampire."

If Arella's words were designed to remind Rachel that she was young, weak and mortal, they worked. JT meowed and lifted his head. Rachel willed the cat to stay quiet.

"Why are you here? An all-powerful vampire shouldn't bother with little me."

Arella crossed to the middle of the room, assessing the surroundings. The plate-glass door was closed and locked, but Rachel didn't think that would stop much. Sunlight, muted by rolling fog, made a weak foray through the door, mottling the floor and furnishings with its narrow yellow beams. The computer was flickering, its LED screen showing the last country they had stopped on in their investigation.

Rachel didn't want Papua New Guinea to be the last place she thought of. Briefly, she dropped her shield and called to Phoenix again.

"Hurry."

The tendril shot forward, trying to seek an entry. Rachel slammed her shield back down and felt the silence. This time she embraced it.

"We have never cared about the war between the Elementals and the Demonos. What happens to humans means little to us. Humans force us into the shadows, take away our dark and destroy our kind. This Challenge is different. We get to take our reward if you lose. In which case, we win." She turned and faced Rachel fully, and Rachel saw the red tinting her eyes. Rachel didn't see veins carrying blood under the skin. She hadn't considered until that moment how unnatural it was not to see a jugular beating.

Arella was in front of Rachel, so close they shared breath. Rachel hadn't seen her move.

"We have been promised things. A certain number of willing humans. Food. Control. We don't need or want humans for anything other than blood. A plentiful supply means freedom."

"No half-Ifrit female is going to stop this." She grabbed Rachel with a strength ten times that of a mortal. "I've never tried Ifrit blood. Your mortal blood will dilute it, but I am sure you will be delicious."

Rachel struggled. Arella held her with a grip that no amount of struggling could break. Arella's eyes were fully red, and there was a dark compulsion in them that made Rachel want to give in. Power welled up in her, dancing along the edge of her consciousness. She reached for it, but it eluded her grasp. Frustrated, she struggled to calm her mind. The fire was there, but it shied away from her like a feral animal.

Three things happened, almost at the same time.

From his place on the carpet, JT screeched, a bloodcurdling howl she hadn't known the cat was capable of. With ears flat, the small feline launched at the vampire holding his mistress, raking his claws across Arella's arm.

Arella shrieked but didn't let go. JT's trajectory landed him past the pair about three feet away, where he crouched, hissing fiercely, his eyes big and wild, his ears flat and fur up in a spike across his back.

"Damn cat!"

"JT, go!"

Rachel's attention was briefly divided between her pet and the vampire. JT fled, diving under the sofa, still hissing. Arella's skin was open but there was no blood. Nothing oozed from the cut. The incongruity made Rachel shiver even as Arella turned her red eyes to Rachel again.

The front door burst open and the plate-glass door shattered. Huge forms came through both the open door and shattered window.

To her surprise, neither one of the beings was Phoenix. There was so much sensory overload that her fire fled again. Rachel tried to focus, struggling against the grip Arella still held her with.

The form in the doorway resolved into one of the werewolves. Fenley, a numb Rachel decided, judging from the size. The wolf ran at Arella and knocked her off Rachel, sending Rachel to the floor. The hard wood hit her back, making her breath come out in a rush. The fire leaped inside her.

Rachel saw the tableau unfolding. The fire ran in her blood like flames licking at wood. Flames. Wood. Oh, it would be so marvelous to light the wood on fire and watch it burn.

An Ifrit, the one who had called her granddaughter in her memories, also went for Arella, swiping with a leather wing at the vampire. The thwack of connection was loud, and Arella staggered. She snarled, and her canines fully descended.

The blow would have been enough to cause deep skin reddening and bruising on a human, but Arella had no blood. The lines of tendons and wing were visible against her skin, telling Rachel how fierce a blow it had been.

Rachel clambered backward and jumped to her feet. She looked at the scene, trying to determine how she could best help. Fire beat at her, suddenly wanting, needing to come out. She could feel it dance across her veins and redden her skin. *Oh yes.*

Backed into a corner, Arella snarled again, crouched into a defensive position.

Fenley snarled back, foam gathering in his huge canine jaws. The Ifrit, like something out of a fairy tale, joined him, forming a barrier between Arella and the rest of the room. Flames licked out from the Ifrit's fingers, and Rachel saw that Arella had seen them as well, judging from the nervous way she moistened her lips.

Arella feinted, but the Ifrit's wings blocked her approach into the room. She appeared to study her options and then backed away.

"Unfair odds," the vampire said, her voice cool.

There was a loud screeching sound, and another being came hurtling through the broken door.

Fire glowing around his skin, Phoenix flew in, in a smaller bird form Rachel had only seen in visions. He swept across the coffee table, knocking the few small ornaments from their resting places. They crashed to the ground. He went for Arella, ducking around the two huge beings, and latched on to her shoulders, pulling her up with his talons. His wings beat at her, smacking into Arella's back.

His strength was astonishing for a large bird. The flames that flickered around his edges didn't seem to burn, but they danced over him and onto Arella. She shrieked, her eyes widening in the kind of primal fear that neither of the other beings had inspired. The fire left black marks where it touched the vampire.

Phoenix pulled her off the floor, his wings beating, the weight seemingly nothing to him. His orange-and-red coloring was darker than Rachel had seen, and his small bird eyes were wild.

Arella shot a glance at the other beings, as if for help. Fenley and the Ifrit simply stepped back, relinquishing the fight to Phoenix. He began changing, lengthening, turning into his human form without losing his hold on Arella. With gratitude, Rachel saw his familiar features emerge. Then he dropped Arella.

Phoenix also landed, his now-human feet making contact with the polished wood of his living-room floor. His wings slowed as her Ifrit grandfather cornered Arella. Fenley snarled, once, when Arella tried to move.

The flames retreated but didn't vanish, shimmering around Phoenix's body. His eyes were still wild. Rachel focused, yearning for her fire, trying to draw the power forward.

After a moment, she smiled. "Glad you're here."

* * * * *

Phoenix didn't take his eyes off Arella.

The vampire had risen from being dumped on the floor and now held herself regal again, pointedly dusting herself off. She stood as high as her small stature would allow, her expression haughty.

Phoenix wanted to rip her apart. He wanted to summon massive flames, set the vampire on fire and watch her burn into ashes. It would be satisfying to tear her limb from limb, or use a broadsword from his mortal time and take her apart in sections. He visualized the severed limbs, the separation of her head from her body, her eyes losing focus and going blank. It would have been more rewarding if there had been gouts of blood darkening the landscape. A mental shove shot the whole dark vision at Arella.

Phoenix turned to Rachel. Flames licked over her fingers and spread up her arm. As with his fire, it didn't burn her. Arella tried for the door again. The Ifrit cut her off and she snarled but stopped moving.

"I think she would look good caged in flames, don't you, my Elemental?" Rachel asked.

Arella cried out, and Phoenix smiled without warmth.

"I'll start." He flung out both hands, fingers splayed. Flame shot from his fingers and surrounded Arella in a rough circle. He waited. Rachel opened her palms, her movements less certain. Flames, lighter in color than his, joined his fire and also circled Arella until she had bars of fire around her. She turned in all directions quickly, trying to avoid the flames.

It gave Phoenix satisfaction to see Arella shudder, her body rippling. If a vampire could have paled, she would have. It made the warrior in him glad. Rachel smiled. There was little human in that smile.

Phoenix waited. Rachel studied Arella appraisingly and then looked down at her fingers.

Fenley had shifted to human and stood blocking the door, his giant form filling the frame. His face was impassive, but his arms were folded, and he was standing on the balls of his feet, clearly ready to move again.

The unknown Ifrit, who had to be a relative of Rachel's, folded his wings behind him. He bore little resemblance to Rachel, but something in the way he held himself reminded Phoenix of his woman.

"Where are your friends?" Phoenix jerked his chin at Arella. "You don't travel without your posse, especially in daylight."

Arella sniffed. "I didn't need reinforcements to take her." She stood still now, her eyes wide as she made her body as small as possible, recoiling from the fire. Phoenix felt her terror and he wanted to amplify it, make her cringe and cower. Part of that desire was coming from Rachel. The warrior in him gloried at the thought.

There was a taint of falsehood over Arella's statement. She lifted a hand as if to test the cage and drew back when she touched the flame, yelping as her finger blackened.

"You would risk all of us," Fenley rumbled, a hint of wolf growl still in his voice. "The vampires want the humans gone."

Phoenix cocked his head at the man/wolf. "And the wolves?" Rachel frowned, clearly remembering the harsh words exchanged in the park.

Fenley's shrug was eloquent. "I have rethought my position, Elemental. We need humans. Without our interaction, we become only wolves. One generation, maybe two, and there would be no werewolves. It's not an easy life, but it's our life. The younglings…they got a little overzealous."

"Haures will have something to say about that," Phoenix said, keeping his tone neutral.

Fenley's smile showed a hint of muzzle before it became human again.

"Haures does not rule the wolves. We thought your Rachel was a threat, and we acted. Whether she is or not remains to be seen, but I believe that we were wrong. Our actions will not be dictated by the Demonos." He inclined his head to Phoenix.

"Does that mean you're on our side?" Rachel asked. He wanted to wrap this woman in thick cotton and put her somewhere safe at the same time he wanted her to stand by his side and rain down fire on their enemies.

The wolf made a gesture that could be taken for assent. "Paranormals usually stay neutral," he replied. "However, I do not believe that is an option anymore. I will aid your Elemental, as much as I am able."

"Take a message back to your clan." Phoenix walked to Arella. The cage of flame faded. The vampire cowered, her eyes darting between the three huge paranormals. Her gaze landed on Rachel. Phoenix saw deep hatred there mixed with fear. She had underestimated his half Ifrit.

Summoning his fire again, Phoenix concentrated, focusing on a spot two feet in front of Arella. Judging the space between the ceiling and the ground, he created a firenado, stopping it a foot before either surface. It hovered there, a whirl of tightly coiled fire, small flames licking out.

Arella's eyes widened in fear again. Her head turned, taking in first the fire tornado and then Phoenix's implacable face. "I could summon more of these and send them into your den, daywalker." Phoenix's voice was conversational. "I could burn you out so no evidence of your kind remained." He shifted, and the firenado moved fractionally toward the vampire.

The room was heating up from the intensity of the firenado, but nobody moved. Except JT, who meowed and ran for the other side of the room, where it was cooler.

Everyone studied the tight spiral of fire death. The fury that beat through Phoenix made him want to turn the power on Arella and burn her to a cinder.

"Tell the other vampires there is to be no interference. Don't side with us; don't side with the Demonos. Whatever happens, happens. But that is between us and the other side."

"You will lose," she shouted, her voice harsh and raw. She paused, and it seemed as if she collected herself with an effort. Her face smoothed out and she pulled herself straight, still eyeing the red gleam of the fire column.

"We may lose," Phoenix agreed. "We may win. It is between us. Don't try to interfere again or there will be a reckoning."

Arella locked eyes with Rachel, and her expression was ugly. "I hate halflings."

Phoenix waited. When she said nothing else, Phoenix moved the firenado still closer. "Your choice, vampire."

Rachel opened her mouth and then shrugged. She cocked her head at Arella, whose expression was disdainful. "It might hurt to be called a halfling if I didn't know you had to have been 'made' at some point," Rachel said. "However long ago, you were once human. Essentially, you are a halfling too. At least I have fire. You only have fangs." Her lips curled, her desire to strike again clear.

Arella frowned at that, seeming to be taken by surprise. There was a long silence. Finally, her chest heaved in annoyance. "We will stay out of your business for now. You will lose. Then your fire powers will mean nothing." Phoenix waited until Arella shifted, looking down at her feet. "We will leave you alone." Still, he waited. Arella's face twisted. "And we will leave your woman alone." The words were a rasp, as if torn from her throat.

With a clap of Phoenix's broad hands, the firenado vanished.

Arella breathed a sigh of relief before she smoothed her face out. She pushed past Phoenix, and he let her go.

His voice stopped her when she reached the shattered plate-glass door. "When I say char and burn, there are times when I mean it literally. Whether we win or lose Challenge, Arella, if you come after Rachel again, you are a dead vampire. Your entire clan will die if you lay a hand on her. That is a guarantee. I will incinerate it all until nothing is left of you but ashes on the wind."

The only indication that she'd heard was a slight flinch of her body. Picking through the glass, Arella stood on her tiptoes at the edge of the balcony, and then, in a blur of speed, she was gone.

Once the house was clear of their unwanted visitor, Phoenix turned to the unfamiliar man.

He knew who the Ifrit in front of him had to be, but was unable to determine a name. The other man said nothing, but his gaze never left Rachel.

"I believe introductions are in order," Phoenix said.

Chapter Ten

"Kamal," the Ifrit said and held out his hand to Phoenix. "Rachel's grandfather."

Phoenix took her grandfather's hand while Rachel's mind whirled. She'd seen him in her visions, and now here he was in the flesh.

Almost without realizing it, Rachel put up the same high wall she had retreated behind when Arella had tried to penetrate her shield. The others wouldn't need telepathy to know she was upset. Her silence and stiff body screamed that emotion to the world.

"Grandfather," she said, and her voice was ragged. The man had identified himself as Kamal. Her grandfather.

"Habibti," he said and his eyes were soft. His wings fluttered and he folded them behind his back. Letting go of Phoenix's hand, he gripped Rachel's shoulders.

She stood still, not retreating or accepting his touch. He had almond-shaped eyes, high cheekbones and a strong jawline. Small horns were on his forehead. If she had to guess, she would have thought he was from somewhere in the Middle East—Egypt perhaps, or Saudi Arabia.

He equaled Phoenix in height and didn't look any older than the Elemental. He seemed like her contemporary rather than her ancestor, and she wondered how long Ifrits lived.

Long enough to have more than a decade or two with an immortal Elemental?

That was a crazy thought. They were lovers, but Phoenix hadn't said that he wanted permanence. Maybe having a longer life span than humans would make a difference.

"You have your mother's eyes." Kamal said and seemed to register Rachel's stoic stance. Then he stepped back and gave Phoenix a once-over again.

Fenley was still protecting the door, his arms folded. After a moment, he moved enough to allow entry through the shattered pieces of wood that stood where a door once had been. "I must go. Be careful. Not all wolves agree with my decision. I am their alpha and they obey, but I may face my own battle soon. Many still feel that this is not our concern. It's possible they will act even if it means expulsion from my pack. I will be keeping watch, but my assistance will not always be available."

Phoenix tilted his head toward Fenley. "Thank you. I am in your debt."

"I will collect." His voice was flat and cool.

Rachel went to Fenley, holding out her arms. "Thank you," she said, and her eyes were moist.

The werewolf hugged her briefly, his body stiff.

"I will have my son Artur watch things. It can be his penance."

She grinned. "He'll love that."

Fenley's shrug told her it didn't matter what Artur thought. With a wave, the giant took his leave, stepping through the debris as if it meant nothing to him.

Rachel looked at the plate-glass door, now just a series of shards on the floor. "We're going to need a handyman."

JT came slinking out from across the room, his belly so low to the floor she couldn't see space between the cat and the wood. "My hero," she said, scooping the feline up. He let her hold him, but like the wolf, was rigid in her arms. "I'll put him in the kitchen. He'll be safe there."

Both men followed her movements until she had put the cat away and rejoined them. The silence was thick with questions.

She stood next to Phoenix and touched his shoulder. His heat was still high, radiating off him, matching hers. The skin over the muscles of his arms had droplets of sweat on it. She wanted to lick the sweat off him—slowly. He slid his hand into hers, lacing their fingers together.

She lowered her shields, carefully. Her mind stayed alert, ready to put it up again if needed.

"You have questions," Kamal said in a neutral voice.

To her surprise, his hands were trembling. She heard the ambient chatter of human minds again, the low-level hum of regular mental noise. It comforted her. *"How quickly we become used to things that would have been unimaginable days ago."*

Phoenix's mind was there inside hers, as if he had been waiting for her wall to come down. His probe held concern, anger and dismay.

"I'm okay," Rachel said.

"Arella is alive because of that."

The picture he'd painted of a burned Arella was at the forefront of his mind. She saw the Saxon warrior, his face painted and a loud war cry on his lips, wielding ferocious blows with his ax. She was glad that she had such a protector, but she also needed to be able to rely on herself. She was not helpless. Her fingers tingled at the remembered feeling of fire.

Naked. She wanted to be naked with him, astride his body, taking her pleasure until they both shrieked in fulfillment. It took her an effort to yank her mind away from the images. She couldn't remember feeling so alive.

Finally she focused on her grandfather, similar and yet not similar to her. He resembled old paintings from Sinbad and other fantastic fairy tales. He had called her *habibti*, which—after a moment's reflection and a little subtle mind-probe—she decided was an endearment. She'd heard it before, in the memories locked away in her subconscious. It was a puzzle. She'd never been mistaken for anything other than Caucasian. Her eyes, her hair, her skin all screamed Anglo-Saxon.

"I have lots of questions," she said when the silence lengthened.

Kamal's expression was smooth, but his mind behind his shields seemed tumultuous and chaotic.

"In the end, though, I really only have one. Why? Why didn't you help me? Why did you leave me to grow up with a foster family that hated me?" She let the hurt and pain of being alone lace through her mental signature, knowing her grandfather would feel it as well.

A shadow passed over his eyes, and he sagged a little. The moments stretched on before he took a deep breath and answered.

"It was the only way to keep you safe. Farouk thought you were dead. In order for him to continue to think so, I could not be a part of your life. They were sent money every month. They were supposed to tell me if you showed any signs…" He trailed off. Turning his attention to the broken door, Kamal's lips twisted.

"How long?" he asked, and his face was bleak. "How long have you been on your own?"

She swallowed, feeling his pain wash over her. Sorrow, an old wound, rode through her mind until Rachel nearly staggered under the weight of it.

"Seven years," she said, each word like a dagger. "They kicked me out when I was eighteen."

The string of curses was unlike anything she had heard before, and Rachel made a mental note to learn what they meant. *Ebn el-mara* she particularly liked, which she plucked out of his mind as meaning "son of a bitch". She tucked it away for future use.

"They did not tell me this." His tone told Rachel that there would be an accounting. It wouldn't go well for her former foster family. The fire side of her was glad about that. She touched each finger in turn with her thumb, wanting to "help" with that particular discussion.

"Char and burn," Phoenix said. "Why are you here now?"

The scent of their combined fire bands and Phoenix's firenado had left a faint smell of flame in the air, but it was rapidly dissipating in the wind. Rachel missed the smell as it faded. Part of her wanted to go up into a forested area and see what it was like to watch trees burn. It would be amazing.

"Rachel."

Kamal ignored Phoenix's question, focusing on Rachel.

"You know nothing of your heritage. That is my fault. You know nothing of your mother." Rachel got an image of a woman resembling Kamal in her mind, then one of her father, blond and fair, like her. Her mother looked Ifrit, complete with wings and a dusky tint to her skin. Rachel also saw her as her father saw her, overlaid with a lighter color that made her seem exotic but not otherworldly.

Her father would only have seen the human side. Had he known? Had he been aware that his bride was something other than human? Had he known his daughter was something other than human as well?

"He knew," Kamal said. "He couldn't see it but he knew. They were happy, as these things are accounted for."

The strangeness of it caught Rachel. She wasn't human. She. Wasn't. Human. She had fire powers and a grandfather who was something that in old fables would have come out of a lantern. A pop song about genies and bottles danced in her mind, blurring her thoughts as effectively as her nursery rhymes.

"How did they die?" Phoenix asked.

She wanted to tear the clothes off him and plunge him into her. She wanted to take him and have him take her again and again. It was so powerful, heat rose along her skin and between her legs, a different fire than the previous one.

"In time, love. There will be time."

She shot Phoenix a heavy-lidded look before she returned her attention to her grandfather. The presence of the Ifrit was making her feel off-balance. She was humming from her skeleton through her nerve endings and to the top of her head.

Phoenix shook his head when Kamal would have stepped forward. The Ifrit froze where he was standing. "We are a very private race." There was a heaviness in Kamal's tone and a slump in his shoulders. "Bushra's choice to marry a human caused a fury in all the families. The other clans predicted failure, and our clan was shunned. Your grandmother and I visited rarely, by mutual decision. We were hoping the furor would die away. Do you remember those visits?"

Did she? The only time she could recall seeing him was the last time, in the fiery aftermath of the car accident, when he told her to run.

Rachel concentrated. A flash memory of the large, winged man giving her a present briefly danced across her mind. She teased the memory forward, letting it slide through until it surfaced. "You gave me…a…jack-in-the-box?"

A small smile lingered on his lips. "It was at the bazaar and it seemed like a good idea."

Brief slices of memory came to her, small moments in time. "I remember a little. It's like all my memories have a heavy blanket over them and don't want to come out from under the covers."

"I did that. After Farouk killed your parents, I blocked your memories so you could pass for human. I suppressed your Ifrit side. My intention was…" He shook his head and gave her a sorrowful look. "You were supposed to remember before this. You should have had your memories and your fire by now. I lost track of time. I'm sorry."

"How did they die?" Phoenix asked again.

"We thought that Farouk had given up as the years passed." He sighed, as if the memories pained him. "What I didn't know is that every time Yadira or I visited—" Rachel decided Yadira was her grandmother, "—he was watching. Waiting…"

"To kill us?"

"Not all. Just your father and you."

A smoky scent rose from Phoenix's feathers when they ruffled in agitation. "Her father and Rachel."

"Yes. Farouk was going to take your mother back, force her to marry him. We are a traditional race. She was a disgrace to the Ifrit, but he wanted her. You could not live."

"Here I am, though."

"Do you remember anything about the car accident?"

Rachel searched her mind and finally shook her head. "Just that you were there, telling me to run."

"You did as you were told. That is why you are alive today."

She made a dismissive sound. "I ran."

"Exactly. Farouk shot your father through the window and accidentally hit your mother, to his dismay. He thought he had gotten you as well, but I clouded his mind so he didn't see you escape. If your mother had not been dead, she would not have burned. We do not burn except in death. He would have come to check, to make sure you were dead, but the human police came before he could. Since you never surfaced, he assumed he had eliminated you as well."

Frustrated, Rachel gave Kamal a mental push of anger and saw him wince.

"Don't let your emotions rule you." Phoenix dipped his wings toward her.

"Fuck you."

In that way they did, Phoenix's wings made a sucking noise and then they vanished, disappearing from his body until only smooth skin remained on his back. Something in Rachel calmed when they went. No further vampires were going to come rampaging through the broken door.

Her grandfather took a step toward her. "It's easier if I show you. May I?"

Phoenix looked at Rachel. After a moment's hesitation, her mind roiling with the idea of being so invaded, Rachel nodded. Better to know than not to.

Phoenix looked unconvinced, but he released Rachel and stepped back.

Her grandfather's breath was warm, with a slight hint of cigarette smoke. He smelled of cloves and cinnamon. "Open your mind."

She gazed into brown eyes covered by thick, ungroomed eyebrows. Her breath exhaled in a rush, and she tried not only to keep her wall down but allow Kamal into her thoughts.

He put his hands on either side of her head, his index fingers on her temples.

Instantly her mind wanted to reject the invasion, but she forced herself to breathe deeply until there was only the touch of his thoughts in hers. It was as reassuring a presence as his scent. She understood that he had been there before.

Images.

They expanded, bombarding her with sights and feelings, rushing into her like a movie stuck on fast-forward. Rachel cried out in panic and the movie pulled back. The speed slowed. Kamal lifted his hands, and she met his eyes.

"Apologies."

He put his hands back on her temples, and the images started again.

A brief whirl. Ifrit life in Saudi Arabia. They were isolated from humans, interacting with mortals only when necessary, but maintaining enough of a presence in modern-day life that they were written off as unremarkable. To be a mystery would have made some mortals want to solve it, but if they were just everyday people, then they could glide through life unnoticed. Humans had perceived her grandparents and mother as big but human when they interacted.

Faces. The other families. So few. Small clans of small families, scattered throughout the world but mostly concentrated in the Middle East, each one a self-contained unit, but all within the larger Ifrit culture.

It was a private nation. One that was secretive at its core but with the outward-facing look of normalcy. Their strangeness was concealed as with all paranormals, hidden from humanity. Their long lives meant they needed to move around periodically, before humans became suspicious. Unless they were far away from human civilization, they could never settle down for life.

"How long will I live?" Perhaps a long-lived Ifrit could hold the interest of an immortal Phoenix.

Her grandfather shrugged and answered mentally. *"I am three hundred and sixty years old."*

"Cool."

Memories tugged at her and she let them come. Mother reaching into her crib, Father beaming next to her. This woman looked unlike Rachel, and yet Rachel had the feel of her, in that way that children look like both their parents. Even the baby Rachel could see her mother as two people, the one with a dusky complexion and leathery wings and the overlay that her father and the others saw.

The same woman and man, showing Rachel how to ride a bike.

The man… Oh, now he was mad. Dad was yelling at her, gesturing toward the fireplace, where a roaring fire was going. The windows were open and a gentle breeze lifted the curtains. It didn't look cold enough for a fire.

"Fire? That young?"

"It is strong in our family," Kamal said with a touch of pride. "All Ifrit have some ability, but ours dates back to before recorded time. We are one of the strongest." He glanced at Phoenix. "Fire calls to fire," Kamal said.

She had heard Phoenix say that before. Fire called to fire. She was fire. She was *fire*. She commanded the same element Phoenix did. She could use it, manipulate it. She had power. Rachel felt dizzy with the knowledge.

More memories, still fuzzy, like a dream. She was barely walking and had touched the stove while the gas burner was on. Instead of burning her, the flame had crept up her arm, delighting the girl.

"The fire that took my apartment…"

"You wouldn't have burned. Fire is your friend, not your enemy. As we saw." He indicated the spot where Arella had been.

"Yes," Rachel said slowly, her mind whirling.

"Rachel." Phoenix's voice was harsh. "Challenge. This is no coincidence."

Kamal inclined his head. "I agree. After Farouk killed your parents, it was difficult to accept that he was not punished. For your sake, I did not press it. You were alive, and that was what mattered. Some hailed him as a hero."

Her lip curled and rage built in her. The Ifrit, the one who had done this, lived while her parents were dead. If Farouk had been standing in front of them, she would have gone for him.

"I rarely have help," Phoenix continued, putting distance between them. "Challenge is between the Elementals and the Demonos. I thought the prophecy was a myth."

Rachel shook her head. "Prophecy?"

She heard it in her head, a singsong coupling of words. *"Fire calls to fire. Air will glide with air. Water swims together. Earth is always there."* It wasn't much of a rhyme, but something about the way the words echoed in her brain gave them a deeper meaning than the simple links.

Kamal's expression was shuttered. "We have never taken a side. This war does not concern us. It is far beyond our understanding. It is the same with most paranormals." He nodded to Rachel, who stared at him without comprehension. "Win or lose, Elementals or Demonos, the paranormals survive."

"We live in this world," Rachel protested.

"You would survive even a full-scale human annihilation. All half-breeds are immune to the slaughter."

"We live in this world!" Rachel couldn't stop the dismay in her voice.

To Rachel's surprise, Kamal smiled at her. "You take after your mother."

"What happened to Farouk? Where is he?" Picking up a blank sheet of the paper that had been fluttering around the floor, Phoenix wrote the name Farouk on there with a question mark and flicked it down onto the floor in its own pile.

Kamal's expression grew uneasy. "That is why I am here. He is on his way. We discovered he has been missing for a few days, and I came immediately."

A strange feeling dug into her spine, like a spike making its slow way up her body. "Could he be part of this?"

Kamal made a motion with his hand like a seesaw, back and forth. "It is possible. He is very family-oriented, proud of being a pure Ifrit. His loyalty is to his family, himself, and then the Ifrit clan. He has already killed once."

Twice, Rachel thought to herself.

Phoenix's eyes clouded. He quickly scrawled *Ifrit* on another blank page and sent it down to the same pile.

Kamal's wings quivered slightly, but she couldn't tell if they were shaking in silent amusement or anger. Before she could say anything more, Kamal spoke again.

"It has always been understood that we do not interfere."

"Why?" Her voice was as tight as her lips.

Kamal shook his head. "There are many things we don't know, and many more we don't need to know. It has worked for thousands of years—for all of us. We have a saying: 'avoid that which requires an apology'. As long as we stay neutral, we need not apologize. We are not going to, what is the saying, *rock the boat* now."

Rachel found her fury growing again. "Dammit, Grandfather, these are people we're talking about." Heat rose in her cheeks, reminding Rachel of the vampire's lack of blood. Rachel shivered.

"Your Phoenix may have been human once, but he hasn't been human for over a millennium." Kamal's gaze took in her thin lips, the high color in her cheeks, and her stiff body. He sighed. "Habibti, I will take care of you, but I should not interfere further. However, you are my granddaughter. I won't let what happened to your mother happen to you." He glanced over at the papers on the desk and floor and tipped his wing to them. "If Farouk comes, I will be waiting." He shrugged in a way that she usually did. "I can tell you this. Your research, everything is meaningless."

Phoenix stiffened, and if he had still had his wings, she thought they would have bristled.

"This is good stuff," Rachel said indignantly.

"It is good research for your other Elementals. Their Challenges have also started, as you must be aware. The Sphynx left India a little while ago."

"Some paranormals have tried to stop Rachel, but other than that, we haven't found many signs of Challenge," Phoenix said.

He turned the wing to Phoenix. "The signs started when you moved here. When Farouk killed Rachel's parents. You were drawn here, to San Francisco, for Rachel, but also for something else." Phoenix frowned at him. "You were summoned to your Challenge."

"Of course."

"The reason you can't find a link to your Challenge, the reason you haven't been able to determine where it is, is because it's right here."

Rachel nodded, realizing her instincts had been right before. She had known, somehow, that Challenge could only happen in one place. "Who? How?"

Kamal shook his head. "I don't know. It's coming, though, and soon. It's human. That is why you can't find it." He turned to Rachel. "Habibti, you have great power in you. Use it wisely." He gripped Rachel's shoulders again and kissed her forehead before he stepped back. He paused and then held a hand out to Phoenix. Phoenix took the proffered hand and pumped it once. Kamal took another step back, toward the broken door. "I must go, but I will be watching. Phoenix, take care of her. Good luck."

Rachel wanted to argue, but after a look at her grandfather, she let it drop. Feeling strange and uncertain, she went to him. The big man looked down at her from his superior height, his face gentle.

After a moment, he held out his arms. Rachel stepped into his embrace and hugged him. Her hands landed on his leathery wings. The heat of him against her skin and the cinnamon/clove scent permeated her nostrils as they hugged.

His large chest sighed out a breath. "I love you, habibti. You are my only living descendant." He pulled back and Rachel tilted her head up to him. "I will protect you." He gave Phoenix a stern look. "You will protect her as well, or you will have me to answer to."

Phoenix smiled, but it was a ruthless smile. "She is mine to protect, Ifrit." There was an undercurrent in his voice.

Kamal released Rachel and stepped back again. "I see how it is. I am glad." He raised a hand in farewell and his wings followed. Phoenix's wings were soft and feathered, and Kamal's more like dragon wings. Rachel was mesmerized by the difference in their anatomy. "Farewell, Elemental. Farewell, granddaughter."

After he left, Phoenix looked at Rachel thoughtfully. "I have underestimated you."

She smiled wanly. "The good news is that they had a reason to warn me off. Even if we don't understand it." She moved to Phoenix. "The bad news is that I need to learn how to use my powers."

She touched him, their skins still warm from the dance of the flames. The fire called to her, and she moved into his arms. They went around her in an instant, pulling her close.

His mind was barred deftly, with a durable wall. Emotions danced around the edges of the barrier. She touched it with her own and felt him yield, but his true mind was still shuttered. "Aleric?"

"Ah..." He pressed his lips to hers, his mind still closed. "I am glad you are with me. I am glad we are together."

She blinked once, remembering JT giving her the "eyes" that cats did when they were happy. It wasn't a declaration of love, but it would do. "I'm glad we are too."

There was something beating in his mind, but she couldn't pick it out.

"When all this is done, after Challenge, we will have a different conversation."

"Aleric." It would be enough. She would make it be enough. He was too much of a warrior to do anything else.

He kissed her again, a fierce warrior's claiming, taking her tongue. She yielded in his arms, meeting his passion with her own fierce need, her body quickening.

"I haven't had a companion since I became the Phoenix," he murmured, cupping her face in his hands. Something lingered, a wisp of green scales, but that wasn't the entire truth. She would find out, in time. For now, it didn't seem to matter. "If we survive this, if we win this battle, there will be much to say. Will you be there?"

"Always." As long as always was.

"Good." He studied the shattered door regretfully. "I'd love tear your clothes off, but this house is a hazard. We need Elementals, Inc. to come in and deal with this."

She winked at him. "There is always later." She hoped there would be a lot of laters.

Chapter Eleven

Kamal's words stayed with Phoenix throughout the day, even as the house was repaired by handymen, courtesy of the San Francisco branch of the company.

Your threat is right here.

Of course it was. There was always a purpose to the Challenges, a rhythm, a pattern to the test. Thankfully he hadn't followed any of the leads, which he realized now were nothing but empty roads. They weren't entirely false. For some they rang true, but not for him. His Challenge was right here in San Francisco.

He'd been played by the Demonos, who was cleverer than he'd remembered. He'd been lured into looking outside the obvious, thinking it too apparent. He'd thought his starting point was San Francisco, not his ending point as well.

Phoenix eased out of bed, careful not to wake Rachel, and began to pace the living room. His wings had not manifested; danger was not imminent.

JT came out, blinking, and meowed at him. Phoenix scratched the cat's ears and the feline purred before pulling away to go to his cat bed to curl up.

Phoenix flipped on a light, barely registering the repaired living room and the giant whiteboard standing in the corner. Efficiency was expected of the employees who worked for Elementals, Inc., and this house was no exception.

Sifting through the notes, he found the article he'd been half remembering in his dreams.

Chicago Mayor Visits San Francisco.

The Chicago mayor was of Croatian descent, a country with a longstanding distrust of Serbians. Perhaps there was an Eastern Europe connection after all. He wrote the mayor's name and the date of the trip on the board with three lines under it for emphasis. As his mind cleared, he felt the rightness of this path.

It was an innocuous visit on its surface, just a mayor visiting another city. There was nothing special to tie it in to Challenge. Mayors made public appearances all the time. Even with the unrest in the region she was originally from, he had focused more on other areas such as the Ukraine. The Ukraine had had its own share of troubles with Russia, and Phoenix would have thought a threat could emanate from there. This didn't seem big enough to register. It was a dignitary visiting an old friend. Nothing more.

Phoenix cursed under his breath. Rachel had mentioned this visit twice, and he had ignored it both times. Russia was unstable, its annexation of a portion of Ukraine still reverberating. Eastern Europe and the Turkic republics were always in unrest. If there was an incident during this visit, the outcome could be grave. All it would take was a push from the Demonos during the aftermath, the suggestion that America had done this on purpose, and it could inflame the region. In this day of modern warfare, splinter groups didn't need more than a few nukes to wreak havoc. Suicide bombers had shown that when people were willing to sacrifice their lives, it was hard to stop them.

Phoenix had little faith in mankind's ability to see through the falsehoods spun by the Demonos. He had little faith in humans, period. For that matter, he didn't have much faith in anyone except his fellow Elementals.

Rachel stood in the doorway. Her eyes flicked to him, a question in them. They hadn't started putting their notes on the board, and the mayor's name stood out.

"This is it? This is what Grandfather meant?"

An oath formed on Phoenix's lips but he did not verbalize it. He nodded. "I think so."

"When?" She walked to him and stood beside him, gesturing to the crumpled newspaper headline in his hands.

Phoenix wrote the date from the article on the board.

"A week? Okay. That doesn't give us much time." She paused. "I knew a Croatian lady once. We were friends for a while. She hated Serbians. I remember when that other Chicago mayor was found guilty of corruption, she told me, and she was serious, 'What do you expect from a Serb?'"

He tried to respond, but he failed. His Challenge had almost been lost before it began. The lines of Rachel's face pulled into a frown. His silence had gone on too long.

She shook her head in a motion similar to that of a person shaking off water droplets. Finally she managed a smile that seemed as insincere as the one he'd turned on her. "We found it. It's not too late."

Phoenix pulled her to him. The printout fluttered to the floor.

"Hey," she said. "This isn't like you." She tapped him gently with her fists against his back. "Why so glum?"

"I would have missed it."

"You didn't." Her fists spread back into hands, her palms warm. The feel of her skin was a balm to his senses.

"We didn't," he corrected. "Your grandfather didn't."

Rachel smiled. "That's why we have friends. Even Elementals need them."

With a jolt, Phoenix grasped he was being manipulated. The wave of helplessness coated him, urging him to lose his Challenge. He was an Elemental. He would be better off without humans.

At a millennium old, having faced the Phoenix fire several times, sometimes Phoenix had been tempted to let life go. Sometimes he wanted to rest and see if there was anything after this. Mostly, though, just to finally put an end to the struggle.

That had all changed. He didn't want to give up the fight. Not now. It wasn't the time to tell her, but he had fallen in love. That it was her, this combination of untested fire power and human, was unexpected. He had always thought that if he ever gave his heart away, it would be to a goddess or another, more sophisticated paranormal. Instead love came in the form of this half-Ifrit, untried and unproven. It was proof that in the end, Elemental or no, he still had a human heart. He had given it to Rachel. He wouldn't tell her, not until Challenge was over. That would be the proper time.

Phoenix shifted and straightened. Rachel's posture was tense, her brow furrowed.

"You will not win." Haures's mental voice was harsh.

There was a laugh in his mind, and the Demonos retreated.

"We will see," Phoenix said, sending an arrow of red-hot anger out.

* * * * *

"We will see, Aleric," Rachel said, repeating his words out loud. "We will do more than see; we will win."

Phoenix's despair shot through Rachel, lodging hooks in her core. Icy tendrils of worry slipped through her veins. She needed him—not just physically, but to rise to his Challenge. Taking his shoulders, she shook him. "I need you, Aleric. The world needs you. Let me be scared while you are the big, tough guy saving the planet."

He chuckled, and his face lit up, telling her it was real. "It's not the planet I save, it's humans."

"Them too."

"Rachel." His voice was gentle. "If we don't, if we fail…"

"You won't fail."

"If we do, you will still be safe. Only humans are affected."

"I'm part human. You used to be human." She busied herself with writing information on the whiteboard. She didn't know how to fix Phoenix or the Challenge, other than with what she could offer. She hoped it was enough.

"I haven't been human since Roman Europe marked the date in three numbers."

She paused in her writing. She would never see the things he had seen. She would never experience the things he had experienced, except through his memories. He might look no more than thirty, but he was older than everything around her. "You were human once," she said. "You are here to protect humans. You can't give up now. You can't." She turned from the whiteboard, marker still in hand.

Finally, he sighed. "I'm not going to give up. I have thought recently that it would be fine if there were no humans. I get tired of protecting people who don't know I exist and who would try to destroy me if they knew what I was. But that's changed. I'm not going to give up. If all else fails, you are worth it."

Rachel flushed. "You've known hundreds of women…"

He put a hand up and she stuttered to a halt. "I have had lovers, yes. I told you I contract with the Dhampirs when I want a bedmate." He paused. "I was unmarried when I became an Elemental. In my centuries as the Phoenix, only once have I had what we would consider a true mate. It was early in my tenure. I made the mistake of thinking that all fire beings were compatible. After all, fire calls to fire."

Her hand stilled. This was the piece that had been missing, the one he had concealed from her this entire time. The flush Rachel felt had nothing to do with desire. "Will you tell me?"

He came up behind her and slipped his arms around her, curling his fingers over her belly and rocking her gently. "I wanted, and had, many women when I was human. Warriors are like that. When I became the Phoenix, I was so absorbed in my new powers that I didn't think about sex for a while. Until she came along."

Rachel again had an impression of size, of something majestic and…scaly. She tilted her head, trying to capture the impression in her mind.

She couldn't see Phoenix's eyes, and she turned in his arms. They were clouded, the memories skittering in his mind like jagged shards, apparently still painful after many centuries.

Rachel waited, her hands on his forearms, at a loss for what to do. Wanting to move, she instead waited, forcing herself to keep still.

"As I said, it was early in my tenure as Phoenix. Elementals do not leave instructions behind for the ones who follow, which has been a problem with Ondine. We have to figure out the station as we go. I was fortunate in that I had almost a century from the time I became Phoenix to the time we faced Challenge." He paused. "At the time it felt as if I was being Challenged. But it was not. Just the folly of a young man who should have known better. There were a different

Griffin and Hippocampus at that time, and neither understood. Sphynx may have, but they did not interfere. Even back then, they were impossibly old."

Rachel finally stroked his face, and Phoenix pressed his cheek into her touch. She sighed, glad that he had accepted her caress.

"You said fire calls to fire, and I feel that pull of kindred spirits. Is it like that for all fire beings?" If so, she hated them all. Phoenix was hers and nobody else's.

His smile was grim with a hint of feral savagery.

"On the contrary, Rachel. Most fire beings come down on the other side. They tend to align with the Demonos. Even among your race, the Ifrits have been tales told to scare children rather than delight them."

Her brow furrowed. "But the rhyme…" She ground to a halt.

"After her, I thought that rhyme was a bunch of nonsense. I decided there was no such thing as prophecy."

The sun dappled over their bodies. Its fire was the ultimate power, and Rachel gloried in the touch of its rays.

"She was a dragon?" Rachel said, and Phoenix nodded.

"Green. The dragons come in many colors, but they are aligned either with gem colors or metals. They use those elements as the source of their power. As I learned later, green dragons are relatively weak in comparison to the metal dragons. Emeralds are not as powerful as gold." He passed a hand over his eyes.

Rachel swallowed. "I would think even a weak dragon would be powerful." She thought back. "We haven't seen or felt any dragons, right?"

"Dragons are rare. They will surface when it suits them. She approached me as a human, but of course I could see the dragon in her." His eyes were troubled. His mind roiled. She wanted to embrace him with her body, cut off the tale, but she did not. Rachel suspected she would get one chance at this, and wanted— needed—to hear this.

"It excited me," he admitted. "She excited me, this centuries-old dragon, and I was stupid enough to think that I could hold her. She preferred her dragon form but stayed human appearing for a little while. I loved her, so I thought, and I told her so repeatedly. She was so exotic, so different from anything I'd ever experienced. The Griffin back then had told me the prophecy, and I thought it was a sign. Fire calls to fire—surely this was meant to be. I was so arrogant."

He passed a hand in front of his eyes.

"Of course she didn't love me. Dragons are different in ways you can't understand. She was a shifter, but even shifter dragons have minds unlike our own. They are terrifying. I was a young Phoenix back then and thought I would be enough. Until she tried to roast me."

Rachel caught the image of a large green-scaled body, three times as big as a human, flame searing from her as the more agile, smaller bird Phoenix danced away.

"I escaped and never believed the prophecy again. She vanished into the sky, and I haven't seen her since. Dragons slumber for centuries sometimes." He gripped her body and looked into her eyes.

"Dhampirs were my companions after that. They were safer. I thought I didn't want a mate, especially a fire one, ever again. I didn't realize something was missing. I didn't realize the prophecy was true. I stayed clear of fire beings of any sort. When you got close, I felt the call. Now I understand. Fire calls to fire."

He pressed a kiss to her neck. She sighed and relaxed against him, feeling his warmth against her back stirring the heat within her. She would have no chance against this dragon, but if she ever saw the green-scaled thing, she would go toe–to–toe with her for hurting her Phoenix. That the dragon had had Phoenix's love sent a needle of jealousy through Rachel. The desire for revenge sent red lights dancing through her mind, and heat erupted along her spinal column. She could almost see it, her Ifrit side manifesting flame through her body. She would bob and weave, dodging the dragon's clumsy blasts while she shot at the dragon from crevasses the dragon couldn't reach.

"I would love to meet her," Rachel murmured. To her delight, Phoenix laughed.

"A short time ago my money would have been on her." He tucked a strand of her hair behind her ear. "Now the odds have shifted. Ah, Rachel," he said, and his tone was mournful, "I would stay in the bedroom and make sweet love to you all day long."

She heard the unspoken "but" and said nothing, letting him continue.

"We have a week. We need to make a plan before it's too late." His gaze was now fixed on the whiteboard. "We don't have much to go on. We know there's at least one, and maybe more. The one we do know about has a blocker, so we won't be able to find him mentally."

"We'll figure it out." She sounded too optimistic, but she wanted to banish the shadows still lurking around him. "Are you sure the person we felt at the wharf is the guy we want?"

"Nothing else makes sense. We will find him. Thank you. I'm glad you are part human. You remind me of what it means to live."

Rachel flushed again. "Come on." She pulled away and tugged on his hand. "We've got work to do."

* * * * *

Ron woke with a start to see his employer standing in his room. Struggling to control his fear, he rose from the bed, trying to look casual.

"Is everything ready?" Her voice was deep and rumbling.

Sometimes Ron wished he could get a really good look at the being. Other times he was glad he couldn't. Like now.

"I have what I need. I will be laying them down tonight, before the sweeps start. They will never find them." The sick feeling inside him grew. "I am good at what I do."

He thought he caught a glimpse of blonde and red hair, and there seemed to be no white in its eyes. Concealed by the hood as it was, he couldn't be sure. "That is why you were hired. And the weapons?"

The sturdy wood furniture was covered now with a tablecloth, but several handguns and semiautomatic rifles lay under it. He would leave most of the weapons behind after the assassinations, but it wouldn't matter. Ron would be gone, vanished into South America with his huge payoff, never to surface in

North America again. That was part of the deal.

Ron was aware that he was in over his head, involved in something far bigger than he had ever known, and it unnerved him.

Not that he would let the taller person in the room know that. Fear was not a welcome emotion in any job. Deep in his gut, he thought that to show fear to this creature would be the last thing he did. He would get through this final job and be gone.

The being pulled back the tablecloth and examined the weapons with a casual interest, flicking a hand that didn't look human over the firepower. In the darkness, Ron couldn't pinpoint exactly what was wrong. Once again he decided didn't want to look too closely.

"Very good," his employer said, and threw the cover back over the table, once again concealing the weapons. Ron caught a brief glimpse of elongated nails, almost talons, and suppressed a shudder.

"Do not fail." The words were such a clear warning that Ron finally allowed himself that shudder.

"You didn't hire me to fail."

"Exactly."

Ron blinked. In the space of his eyelids going down and reopening, the creature was gone.

He allowed himself to moan loudly, and went to the refrigerator to pull out a cheap bottle of vodka. Pouring himself a generous portion, he drank down the bitter alcohol quickly, his hands shaking.

He had no feelings one way or another about person he was about to assassinate. People died all the time, and life was never designed to be fair. All politicians were corrupt. A job was a job. This job, however, had turned weird. Something curled in the pit of his stomach like a bad meal, making him want to vomit.

This will soon be over, he told himself.

Not soon enough.

The suburbs of Brazil might work, he thought. Someplace where he could hire a few men to protect him. Somewhere where drugs and booze were cheap and women cheaper. If not Brazil, maybe Ecuador or Colombia.

Someplace far away from the being and any reminder of this weird, off-kilter experience.

This job couldn't be over fast enough.

* * * * *

"Did you find anything?"

Rachel studied Phoenix's laptop screen. The Internet view of San Francisco's downtown streets showed the route the Chicago mayor was going to take on her trip. Only two miles long, it went through some of the city's densest streets. After some local visits to the tourist attractions and a few meetings with transplant constituents and a round of courtesy meetings, she was going to travel with her old friend the San Francisco mayor to lunch at the Palace Hotel. It was all arranged, the plans available to anyone who wanted to ask. The routes had been posted online, as well as ways to avoid the roadblocks.

"We have several possibilities. The cars coming and going, and also the hotel," Phoenix said. "I can't sense anything because of the damned blocker. We're going to have to check on foot."

She traced the streets with her gaze, following the designated route. "Aren't they clearing the way?"

"They will block cars for fifteen minutes before and after the mayor goes by, and the streets around the hotel will be blocked off for the duration."

"What about the hotel?"

"They are securing two floors around the dining room. There will be rooftop officers there, and they will sweep the local buildings the day of the lunch."

Rachel slid into Phoenix's lap, although he was still focused on the computer screen. "Isn't that a lot of manpower for a few politicians? That's more like what happens when the president is in town."

He accepted her weight, shifting his legs to brace both of them. "The cops think it's strange too. There haven't been any threats to warrant this level of security, but they are not paid to question orders."

"Even humans know when something is weird."

He shrugged, his body language indifferent.

"Oh, the arrogance of Elementals."

Phoenix laughed, the movement rippling against her body. "Rachel, you are good for me." He nuzzled her neck.

"Right back atcha, pal." She arched her neck to accept his caress. "What's the plan, then? Do we go to the mayor?" Phoenix shook his head. "Right. They wouldn't believe us for a second." She considered. "You could convince them…"

"I don't control minds."

Rachel gave him a bemused smile.

"Clouding their minds is different from controlling them. We eliminate what they don't believe they are seeing. I can't control humans. If we could, this war would be a lot uglier."

"And quicker." Rachel shuddered as the full implication of what she had been suggesting sank into her. If they could control minds, who knew what chaos that would cause? "You're right. I wasn't thinking."

"You are new to this."

"So what next, oh wise one?"

He turned her toward him and kissed her before replying. "We walk. We explore. It's a beautiful day for a stroll."

* * * * *

Rachel spotted Brienne, Fenley's alpha female coleader, walking by them. With nothing more than a brief nod, Brienne tilted her eyes to the right. Artur, the cub who had so recently tried to attack Rachel, was also there.

"*They are here to help. They will not interfere, but they will watch,*" Phoenix said, nodding to the wolves.

"*Seems to be a theme,*" Rachel replied, with a hint of acidity in her tone.

The lunchtime crowd was thick, and they moved through it with some difficulty. Phoenix walked, but his gaze moved around the street and the people, checking the buildings as they passed, examining sightlines and prospective threats. "There are too many possibilities," he muttered.

After a nod from Phoenix, Artur vanished into the crowd. Although still a teenager, the cub was going to be big like his father. It was in the broad shoulders and long legs of his still-filling-out frame. Someday he would be a factor, and maybe even battle his father for supremacy of the wolf pack.

If humanity survived this. Rachel stopped for a moment. There would be a future for the paranormals, for the ones living outside the world, whatever the outcome. It was the humans who would perish if they failed.

"Wouldn't Haures stand out? Or does she also seem normal to humans?"

He shrugged, his eyes going from one side of the street to the other slowly, as if he was scanning it with some sort of infrared. She wondered if that was an ability he had.

"She can appear as a human would. She chooses to let humans see her otherness, but they don't understand. This is San Francisco. A tall, blonde-and-red-haired woman with black eyes wouldn't be that unusual here."

Rachel laughed, a deep sound that was too loud for her surroundings.

After a moment he joined her, and for that brief span Rachel forgot her troubles. She breathed in his presence like air. Her new abilities made her fingers twitch. A piece of burning paper wouldn't cause too much trouble, would it? She focused on one lying on the street and raised her hand.

"Rachel Quinn, stop at once."

Her lips tugged up at the corners, but she lowered her limb. An almost tangible fire burned within her.

The Palace Hotel, where the political lunch would occur, was on the corner of Market and Montgomery Streets. It was a four-star place known for housing politicians and dignitaries over its long hundred-and-fifty-year life. It was stately and imposing, like you would expect an esteemed hotel to look.

She had never been inside. There had never been an occasion for her to enter the hotel. None of her limited pool of friends stayed there, and the meals that were served were far beyond her tiny budget.

"Would Haures do something as obvious as stay there?" She was curious to see the inside and discover how the other half lived.

He shook his head. "She prefers the dark. The fringes. It makes her more frightening. She's somewhere near enough that she can get here fast, but not so close that humans see her regularly."

"How does she fly? I have never seen wings."

He shrugged and seemed to flex the wings that he didn't currently have. "You're right. She has no wings. I don't know. I believe it's air currents, or the chemistry of her body. There are a lot of things we don't understand about who we are, even after all these years."

He studied the hotel, ignoring the pedestrians who pushed past them, some muttering obscenities. None very loudly, as Phoenix's imposing bulk deterred most casual rudeness.

"The hotel isn't important. It's just a way station. I doubt they intend to let the mayor arrive here. There's got to be something else. Someone else." He started scanning the other buildings again.

"I thought paranormals couldn't help?"

"We cannot aid our fellow Elementals, but others are not bound by that. There have been Challenges where we have had assistance, like we have now." He pointed to the two wolves gathered in a nearby doorway.

"Most shapeshifters and other paranormals are neutral, choosing neither side. This does not concern them. You've heard them say this. Some align with one side or the other, but they rarely assist directly."

"Then it's definitely our human, the one with the blocker." When he nodded, she sighed. She'd gotten used to being able to hear the thoughts of others and didn't know how she could have lived any other way. Focusing, she picked out individual thoughts, hearing the everyday chatter of the people on the street.

"Late. I'm late. Damn the elevator."

"Eggs…milk…bread…vodka…"

"Fuck the fucking fuckers. You're all in my fucking way."

Ears ringing with the intensity of the thoughts, Rachel threw up her shields again and all mind noise stopped. She'd put up the wall that blocked everything, including Phoenix, and eased it down. The thoughts started again, but muted. Phoenix was studying her with a peculiar expression. "The wall I put up, is that like a blocker?"

He took her hand. "It would be, if a human had any power to hear you, but few do. There are some, a handful of true humans, who have that power, but they are rare. A blocker is most effective against paranormals. Your wall is natural. There are only a few blockers, and they are coveted by both of our sides. A blocker also bolsters weaker paranormals against stronger minds. I wonder who designed it, back in the day." His voice was thoughtful. "It's a rare and useful tool. Come. Let's have lunch."

* * * * *

She was aware of Phoenix's observation while they were eating. It was a nice lunch, very civilized. Phoenix had chosen from a fixed-price menu, and Rachel allowed him to take the lead. Now she ate dessert, a decadent chocolate confection.

Apart from the opulent furnishings, there wasn't much to see. The clientele was a mix of San Francisco elite and out-of-town tourists, as evidenced by their wide-eyed awe at the old, prestigious hotel.

Rachel saw Phoenix's gaze move from one window to the next She realized he was studying the sightlines from each one. After a moment, she decided he was calculating the trajectories and then picturing that flight as if he were currently winged. He was determining which buildings would be likely candidates for a sniper.

"Wouldn't the humans also have protected against that?" She gestured to the windows, finishing the thought process in his mind. "Check the local hotels, I mean."

"I am sure they have, but not all of these buildings are hotels. There are businesses and residences and, of course, underground."

"Won't they check that too?"

"They are human. They can't think of everything."

"So condescending."

He shrugged. "It's true. No matter how much security they set up, they don't have the wherewithal to deal with us."

"Can we find it? Or him? Or her? Or them? Stop this?"

"That's the idea. I have seen humans killed thousands of different ways, many by my hand. We paranormals engage in petty squabbles sometimes just for the sheer pleasure of fighting, when ennui has taken hold. The truth is if someone wants you dead, you will be dead. If that's what Haures wanted, she would have killed you. You could not have stopped it, and neither could your grandfather. If the death of the mayor was all she wanted, it would already have happened. It's the timing that appears to make the difference here."

Rachel shivered. "Why didn't she kill me? My powers had not yet manifested and I would have been easy to pick off. Why the scare tactics?"

His brown eyes met hers. She toyed with a fork, and he mimicked the motion. She sent out a small, questing probe and discovered that their minds were lightly linked, but his was well shielded. There was uncertainty in his eyes, but the reason for the emotion lay behind his shield. She probed a little deeper, trying to slip around his defense.

"Stupid people eating. They're all so fucking stupid. They better leave a big tip."

Startled by the thoughts, Rachel looked around. Her gaze landed on the waiter, and she decided that the petty anger was coming from the man, an anger revealed when she had let slip her basic shield to try and probe Phoenix's mind more deeply. The waiter rushed over. Nothing of the emotions roiling through his mind showed on his face.

"May I get you something?" he asked, all obsequious manners.

She resisted an urge to laugh loudly. Rachel asked for coffee.

A quick glance at Phoenix told her he'd heard the thoughts as well. "Everyone is petty. Sometimes it's better to be among the clouds."

She let her last question lurk uppermost in her mind.

"I don't know why Haures didn't kill you. She's clever, and never straightforward, and she always has a reason for acting the way she does. You were a sitting duck until your powers surfaced. I don't know, Rachel. I don't know if it's that she deemed you important, or if you are just a red herring." He grinned, his teeth flashing. "Maybe she thought a girlfriend would distract me from my Challenge. In that, she was right."

He projected an image to her of them making love on the mountainside, and Rachel flushed. Desire curled deep within her, and she wished they were alone, naked, somewhere outside, their bodies slick with sweat and oiled with essences from their lovemaking. Her flush deepened at the knowing look on Phoenix's face.

"Come, let's continue our mission. I would like to get you home, so…"

Her mind finished the sentence for him, and she shot back her own image of licking him, visualizing the action from her point of view—a tangle of legs and hair, his flesh jutting in between.

Phoenix's eyes darkened.

They finished dessert and he called for the check. His actions were graceful, the mark of a man who knew how to move easily in cultured circles. She wondered again how the Elementals got by in this world. What did they do when they weren't preparing for their Challenges? Or were they always preparing for their Challenges? Phoenix presented a black credit card to the obsequious waiter with unkind thoughts, his manner betraying nothing of what they had heard.

They rose and exited the hotel together, the waiter bowing low to the Elemental. Despite the waiter's foul thoughts, Phoenix must have left a generous tip, she decided. He linked his hand with hers. He was already scanning the buildings again, his eyes flitting from one window to another.

Brienne was outside, and she only shook her head at Phoenix's raised eyebrow.

"I had hoped to find him before the mayor's visit, but time is short," Phoenix said. "We may have to do it on the wing. If we have no power to hear the human, we may have to trap him on the day of the event, and stop him in the act."

"That seems risky. Shouldn't we find him before he tries to kill the mayor?"

"There's nothing we can tell the police that they won't already know. Saying to them that an assassin guided by a Demonos is going to try to kill someone will get us thrown in jail."

Rachel found an image in her mind of holding out her hand and melting a prison door lock. Her palms itched. She found the image more satisfying than she had imagined. "Jail couldn't hold us," she said, tossing the image at Phoenix.

He grinned, giving her a narrowed look of passion. Brienne coughed and he turned to the wolf.

"There is no alternative. We have to stop the assassin's plan at its source. It is risky to wait until we can flush him out, but unless we get lucky, we have no choice."

* * * * *

Them! From his higher vantage point at his apartment window, Ron saw the pair from the wharf strolling down Market Street, hand in hand, acting as if they were tourists.

They were there to find him. They would stop him if they could.

He could take the woman out. Ron calculated the range from the window, and then aimed an imaginary rifle. He had the perfect one on the table. He could feel it in his hands, could see through the scope as he aimed and fired at the blonde. He could almost see her head shatter into a cloud of blood and bone, exploding all over the sidewalk and the foul man next to her.

It would be satisfying to see her die. He wanted to do it now. He wanted to make it personal. He wanted to run down there with a knife, stab it into her back, pierce her lungs and watch her life ebb away before him. He wanted to watch the big man look on helplessly as she died, knowing Ron was better than him, because Ron took his love.

The being's words came back to him.

No killing before you finish your job.

Ron sighed and let the curtain fall back.

He couldn't kill anyone yet. But after the job was done…

After the job was done, she would die.

* * * * *

The easiest way to his destination was across the ocean, but he was weaker, out of flying practice. Without the resources of his clan, he had little money and nowhere to lie low. So he flew, first up across northern Africa to southern Europe across the Mediterranean. He stopped when he got tired, landing in remote places to avoid being detected. Humans didn't concern him, but others like him, especially others of his race, were a worry. He could take most of them with his superior height and fighting prowess, but he didn't want to draw attention to himself.

His wings were tiring. It was time to land for the night and find some wild food before he settled down into a place half concealed by dusk and half by his power to cloud humans.

Soon enough, he would be in San Francisco. Then, he would accomplish his task.

He found a promising location near a forest. Forests weren't his favorite place. There were too many trees, but they provided cover and food. Wild game would do tonight. He was in the mood to roast something. If it were still living when he did so, that would be better.

Soon enough. Soon he would finish what he had begun fifteen years ago. The abomination would not survive a second time.

Chapter Twelve

Fire. Phoenix was bathed in fire. His skin melted and his organs exploded, bursting out from the heat of the volcano. Thrihnukagigur had been the volcano he'd been compelled to that time, one of the many volcanoes in Iceland. He'd descended into the magma chamber, found the seam and flown into the heart of the volcano, deep under the earth. The heat and ash burned his face even before he'd plunged into the magma, before it stripped all humanity from him.

Even after so many times going to the fire, he still crumpled when the fire claimed him. There was nobody to witness his fear, no one to taste the terror and dread that were part of him every time he went to the fire of the Phoenix resurrection.

He was never sure when he was going to get called to the pyre. It always occurred after they lost a Challenge, but the compulsion could happen at any time.

The last time, after World War II, was still seared inside him. The volcano, an active tourist spot, was benign on the surface, like all Iceland volcanoes, capped with snow and frost. But inside, deep beyond the reach of humans, bubbled the monster that would be his punishment.

Once Phoenix had thought to resist the compulsion. He had decided he simply would not go to Mount Pinatubo in the Philippines, despite the picture in his mind. He ignored his wings when they appeared on his back, and fought the need to fly. Stubbornly, he had tried to go about his day-to-day business in the small cabin he had occupied at that time. Suddenly he had simply taken off, his wings launching him into the air despite his grabbing on to anything in the cabin he could to stay earthbound. He had flown to the volcano anyway, his wings directing him where the picture in his mind told him to go. The plunge into the middle of the volcano had been swift and merciless, as if in punishment for his defiance. Flakes of hot ash were all around him as he plummeted, down into the split in the earth, seeing tendrils of red-hot magma and then the bubbling center of the caldera, lazily burping its contents.

It was the first and last time he had fought the fire.

The resurrection seemed to hurt more than normal, each organ and piece of flesh coming back on his body deliberately painful. He lay on the lip of the volcano, first just ash and then the makings of a man, until finally he knit back together into the form of the smaller Phoenix and soared, a harsh cry on his lips, high into the sky and away from the scene of his resuscitation.

It never changed, the dance with the flames. The only thing that was different was the choice of volcano, and of course the ever-present question about whether this would be the time he didn't resurrect. It was how the Phoenix went, if he wasn't killed by a Demonos. The last Phoenix had gone into Anyuyskiy volcano in Russia, now dormant, but back then a still-active option. From what Aleric had learned, the other Elementals knew instantly when the Phoenix perished. His mind signature became birdlike and then, with a heavy cry, vanished.

Aleric had been compelled to go there, a destination that was close at hand due to the battles he was fighting. He didn't know why or anything other than that he had to go to the mountain. He had been met there by a strange couple, who told him what he now was. He hadn't believed them until the wings erupted on his back. From one second to the next, his life changed.

Phoenix turned in his sleep and felt the soothing touch of Rachel in his mind, her hands also on his body.

"If you lost, there would be no reason to send you to the fire anymore. Lose, Phoenix. Give up the fight. Life will be pleasant without people," Haures said.

Rachel's mind was with him again, stronger, dipping into his mind like a cool drink of water.

"Just walk away, Phoenix," Haures continued. *"Look what your life can be."*

They were standing together on a steppe in Russia again, not too far from the original place where he had first taken the mantle of the Phoenix. Rachel, a strong, powerful Rachel, looked at him with approval and desire, squeezing his hand. All around them was first rock and then, beyond that, trees.

They both had wings. His usual red-orange wings were on his naked back. Rachel also had wings, smaller and a little more leathery in consistency, similar to the wings her grandfather had.

Rachel had been restored to her Ifrit heritage. She was a worthy partner for an Elemental.

Former Elemental. In this world, there was no longer a need for Elementals.

He reached out with his mind and felt no human signatures. Even in the wilds of deep Russia, he should be able to hear people, but all he heard were the mental echoes of other beings. There were halflings like Rachel, but nothing pure human.

This was the aftermath of the Challenges, in which the Elementals had lost everything. It was a world free of people and their destructive ways. A world where paranormals did not have to hide.

In this age of modern man, he had assumed the final battle would be nuclear, but he sensed no radiation. Supernatural beings would survive, but he had expected that the infrastructure of the world would be destroyed along with humans.

"There is another way. Humans design the most interesting things in labs." Haures spoke again, and this time her tone was almost gleeful.

His dream self nodded, as if it made sense. It did, in a dreadful way. If there was something, a virus or disease, that could destroy only people, then the world would be left as it was, minus *Homo sapiens.*

If it could be done, they would be finished with this endless battle and would be left to live out the rest of their lives in peace. He did not know if, after the Elementals had discharged their appointed jobs, they would remain immortal. He didn't know why Challenge occurred. Sphynx was committed to solving the mystery, but they had so far been unsuccessful. Phoenix didn't know if the sides of "good" and "evil" would vanish if there was ever a time when there was no need for a Challenge. All these years he had fought when the time called for it, large battles and small, doing his duty when he was told to. He had grown so weary of it sometimes his teeth ached.

He could walk away. He could leave San Francisco tonight and let the events play out as Haures wanted them to. He could let whatever the Demonos set into motion occur. Abdicate his appointed responsibility. Take Rachel and enjoy life.

It would be so easy to let it happen. He owed humans nothing.

"No, Aleric. No!" Rachel's voice was shrill.

It was a cry of anguish and fury, and it pierced through his dream. He came awake to Rachel shaking him ferociously. Her hair was tangled as if she had woken from a sound sleep. Her naked body had goose bumps on it. The look on her face was part worry and part absolute rage. "Wake up, Aleric. Wake up."

He grunted to indicate his conscious state, but she kept shaking him.

"Wake up. Wake *up*."

* * * * *

Rachel wanted to shake him and go on shaking him. She had woken from an exhausted sleep to agitation in Phoenix's mind and a strange feeling of wrongness. His shields had been up but distress leaked under the barrier. Fear, terror and, finally, the desire to forget all about being the Phoenix and walk away boiled within him. There had been a subtle push encouraging him to do just that. Without a doubt Haures had a hand in that push.

"I'm awake, Rachel."

"Are you?" She flipped on the sleek black nightstand light, which lit the room with weak illumination. Shadows danced on the walls as she turned to him. JT shook awake, seemed to see that the others were not paying him any attention and put his head down to go back to sleep, meowing once as if annoyed at being woken.

"Char and burn! I'm awake." Phoenix threw the covers off and rose, naked, from the bed. With an agitated stride, he crossed the room to the blind-covered window and pulled the shade up so the sky was revealed.

His wings hadn't appeared. Whatever the late-night disturbance was hadn't been enough to trigger the signal that sensed danger. A bone-deep relief shot through her that whatever this was did not call for wings.

Pushing his hands through his already messy brown hair, Phoenix studied the sky.

"How much of it did you feel?"

With a lack of modesty that would have shocked her a few days ago, Rachel also got out of bed, similarly naked, and joined him by the window. "Just impressions." She pointed to the cityscape beyond the window. "Are we expecting guests?"

He shook his head but didn't take his eyes off the window. After a few moments, Rachel let her hand fall. "No. I...no." He continued to peer out, and then finally turned to meet her eyes.

The shadows on the wall were matched by the ones on his face. Dismayed, Rachel put her arm around his back. His muscles were tense and bunched under her fingers.

"It would be so easy," he said.

"Don't you dare."

"Why not, Rachel? What are we fighting for? Humans are cruel, and weak, and they hate—so much hate. If we let it happen, didn't fight it, maybe there would be peace."

"You would hate yourself."

"I would have you."

She let out a breath, and opened her mouth to speak. Then she shut it and let the silence play out, telling him without words where that idea would lead.

He locked his eyes on hers but she didn't flinch. Finally he sighed as her meaning became clear. "I know. You have a strong sense of right and wrong. You are right and I am wrong."

He wrapped his arms around her and pulled her so close she could feel the shift of small muscles in his arms and torso. Her head was pressed against his collarbone and neck, and she could feel the beat of his jugular under her cheek.

"Thank you for making me remember why I fight. I won't let the human race down. I won't let you down. It is hard sometimes, remembering why we do this."

She pressed a kiss against his unshaven cheek. His small sigh told her the touch was welcome. "You do it because it is the right thing to do. Haures wants to destroy your volition so she can take you down without a fight. I know that people can be petty and awful. I have been on the receiving end of it. There is a lot of good that humanity has done. Look at the cities. Look at the Internet. Medicine. Science—we can see everything from atoms that make up things to the stars in the sky. Bicycles. Wicker baskets. Parachutes. Vaccines. We can go places and see things today that people in your original time could never have dreamed of. We've been to the moon. We have machines on Mars showing us that planet. Humans are flawed, but we bring so much to the world. We are worth saving."

"*They* are worth saving. You are not human."

A flush crawled up her cheeks at his pointed reminder. "Part of me will always be human. I was born and raised human. So were you."

He pulled back and pressed a kiss to her forehead. "You remind me of something I had almost forgotten. Thank you."

He kissed her. His body curved protectively around hers, deep emotions searing through him. Being able to hear thoughts was sometimes unpleasant, as she discovered every time she touched another's mind. There were petty, brutal things in many people. Casual cruelty locked away in what they believed was a safe haven. But there was beauty, too, and emotions that were never as perfect as songs and stories might portray. They were flawed, as all things were.

Just like people were damaged and beautiful, all at the same time. Most of humanity she had encountered had not been kind to her, and another person might have let the end happen. "We will do this," she said. "You and me, together. We will stop this."

"We will," he agreed. "Let's hope the others do as well."

For a moment she had forgotten there were four Challenges to complete, or five if they had to face a final group Challenge. "What happens if some win or some lose?"

He pulled her back onto the bed, away from the window. His casual nudity sparked a slow burn in her, making her want to smooth her hands over the hair-roughened skin of his thighs.

"When I lost my Challenge in the six hundreds, my fire Demonos foe burned the Library of Alexandria prior to the larger Challenge. He was a different demon back then, but I have forgotten his name."

She let out a slow whistle. "The Elementals were responsible for the burning of the Library of Alexandria?"

He flexed his fingers inside their joined hands. "He did the burning—took great delight in it too. It wasn't as bad as the legends say, but it was a tragedy. Many of the important works had been moved prior to the final burning, but there is no question that a great body of human knowledge vanished in that fire. Every time we fail, it sets humanity back again. The big Challenges do the most damage, causing horrible decimation to the population. When we lose all Challenges, or the final one, the aftermath is devastation. But the human race endures."

"Is this time different?"

He shrugged. "I don't know."

She kissed him, fear curling through her. If they failed, if even one of them failed, the consequences would be dire.

"I fear…" He paused, searching for the words. "If one or more of us loses and we have a final Challenge, I fear the consequences."

"I wish we knew why this happened," she said with a frustrated groan.

"I have wondered that so many times. There's something else involved, something controlling the Challenges. But we don't know what, and we don't know why. I was a worshipper of old gods when I was made into the Phoenix. My faith has come and gone in the centuries, but I know there has to be something bigger that created this. There is a reason for our tests. There is a reason we were created and that we have counterparts. There is something that…wakes up every so often. Something that doesn't calculate time like we do. I don't know the answers. I just know that we have to succeed, or we all fail." He brushed a kiss over her hands. "There are many gods. But none of them are the ones who created this."

"Have you met your old gods?"

He chuckled, but his eyes were serious. "Charlemagne had begun converting Europe to Christianity a century before, but we were far away from his influence. I was a follower of what they now call old German paganism. Woden was my primary god, but I also worshiped Donar, who people more commonly call Thor in these times. I've met many gods, including him. They are, for the most part, an arrogant bunch. There are so many different pantheons, and each think they are the ultimate pantheon. I was star-struck when I met Donar. I was still young."

There was a story in his mind, an indication that the meeting didn't go the way the young Aleric had expected it to. "Does Donar like the way he is portrayed in the movies?"

He rolled his eyes. "Griff sees him periodically in Iceland. He is angry they get his name wrong and will complain to anyone who will listen that he doesn't have a hammer. He does command lightning, much the same way Zeus does. As with most legends, his is mostly nonsense."

"Why aren't they a part of this?" She wondered what it would be like to meet a god. After a moment's reflection, Rachel decided she could live for a long time without sighting one. Her experience with the few paranormals she had seen so far had been mixed.

He shrugged. "The gods prefer to live their lives without caring about humans. Most of them are indifferent to the battle. You will have to meet them eventually."

Deciding she'd had enough history lessons, Rachel kissed Phoenix with a bold smack of her lips against his. "I want to make love to you, Aleric. I want to hold you and touch you and sense you inside me."

He growled. "Come here, woman."

He touched her hair, sliding his cheek over the short strands before moving to nuzzle her ear. She shivered at the puff of air. His teeth nipped lightly on her earlobe and he hardened against her belly. The fact that he was so much bigger than her gave her a sense of being cherished. Secure.

Phoenix urged her all the way down onto the bed and straddled her. He met her eyes and the mind link settled between them lightly, like a loose garment. She saw as if in double, up to his body and down, like a ghost image, herself in a different kind of reflection.

"I love that you are so much woman, without all the trappings of today's modern female." He feathered his hand through the hair at the juncture of her thighs.

Her passion for him, and fortunately his for her, never seemed to abate. "I love that you love it," she managed, tendrils of need curling through her. She smoothed her hands over his shoulders and down his chest, his short chest hairs tickling her palms, and then back around to his powerful lats, made stronger by the need to support his wings. He flexed, the muscles rippling under her hands. His cock, full and hard, pointed toward her.

"Touch me," he said in a growl. "Now."

She obeyed, her hands sliding between his legs. The angle made it awkward, so within the mind link she told him what she wanted.

He grinned.

"Oh, yes." Even in the mind link, his voice was low and husky.

Phoenix pivoted until his body was over hers with his head near her legs and his pelvis over her head. His breath washed hot on her body, first on her thighs and then where his hand had been a minute ago. With her tongue just darting out, she tasted his tip and heard him gasp. He did the same, moving the curls to find her clitoris and lick it in return.

There was the ghost sensation again, partly hers and partly the desire pounding through Phoenix. It enhanced her passion, making her want it now.

She tipped her head slightly and engulfed his tip with her mouth, licking just behind the head. He was big, too big to take it all in, so she settled for taking him halfway down and wrapping her hand around his base. She mouthed and tongued him, and Phoenix stiffened further. A few drops of precome leaked from him and she took them in her mouth gladly.

Phoenix bit her clit. She jumped.

Then he began licking her, licking and tasting and taking small bites. He moved down, opening her lower lips and probing inside. The wetness coated her from inside her body, aided by him.

Rachel gasped, losing the rhythm on his cock, and he pushed deeper inside her mouth.

"Come for me," he demanded.

She shuddered, her world narrowing down to his mouth on her body. He licked her clit in a circular motion, around and around. She pulled her mouth free of his cock, afraid what she would do in the moment.

Then she was soaring, the orgasm stripping her of sense and reason. Her body coiled and arched, and she screamed her release. It seemed to go on forever.

Before the ecstasy had subsided, he moved again, pulling free of her hand. He pushed her open, wider. There was intensity in his gaze as he feasted his eyes on her body.

"So beautiful."

Without further words he took her, sliding his cock within her ready body. She welcomed him, his hands on her inner thighs, keeping her legs wide. He plunged so deep it was like they were one, all the way to his root.

He settled between her thighs, his body keeping her open to his. She let her legs splay out, allowing him access to everything she had.

"Look at me."

She did as he commanded and saw the love and need within him. He thrust once, twice, a claiming that went all the way to their souls.

* * * * *

Phoenix moved again, taking her hands in his and pushing them onto the bed, their joined fingers linked near her head. His primal need, the drive to own her, to put his final claim on her, to tell the world that she was his and only his made him roar, his eyes wild.

He thrust again. His body stiffened, and his mind opened to hers as the orgasm took him. It was primitive and it was raw and it was all the way. It started at his base and rippled to the back of his skull. It pounded through him and triggered her. She cried out and arched up into him. Release took both of them in a mutual outpouring.

Whatever the rest of the week held, this moment was perfect.

Chapter Thirteen

The day of the Chicago mayor's visit to San Francisco didn't feel any different.

All around the city, people were rising and beginning their days. Human minds chattered and hummed as they stirred into wakefulness, some by the natural rising of the sun and others more rudely, by clock or phone alarms. Soon the daily crush of commuters would begin, clogging the city with their mass. The mental waves were relatively quiet now, but that would change in a few short hours.

Around the world, Phoenix knew the others were also fighting their battles. He could sense their dramas playing out around the world. Their minds and bodies were occupied by their tasks, and their foes, just as he was. It had happened again and again in his time as Phoenix, and this one was no different.

But it was.

Rachel made all the difference. The woman whom he loved, his fire maiden, changed everything.

A familiar tingle on his back was his only warning. Phoenix jumped off the bed to a standing position right before his wings appeared. They exploded on his body, lengthening and unfurling. They reached toward the ceiling, a stance of readiness. This told him more than words ever could that their instincts had been right about this time and this day.

If Rachel had been sleeping, she wasn't any longer. She leaned up in the bed and admired his form, complete with red-and-orange wings.

Her eyes glittered. Within her mind he sensed fear but also a ripening excitement, as if she was ready for the battle. "It is time." She swept her gaze first over his naked body and then over the wings. "This is real."

"Yes."

JT meowed at them, not seeming at all fazed by the red-and-orange wings now on Phoenix's back. He gave Rachel a pitiful glance and jumped off the bed. His soft paw pads made no sound as they carried him out of the room, but it was clear he was heading for his food bowl. Rachel rose from the bed.

"I'll feed him and shower and then I guess we should go."

If something went wrong, Phoenix had made arrangements for Rachel and JT to be taken care of. If she survived the upcoming battle but Phoenix didn't, Rachel would have the power of Elementals, Inc. at her disposal. If neither of them made it, he had left instructions about the care of JT. If they got through this, he would be sure to introduce Rachel to the idea of being a part of their company. He had been happy to leave the company to Sphynx and their employees, but that would change. Things would be different, if there was a future for them.

It was still new to him, caring about anything other than his job and the Elementals. And they had been good friendships, those with his fellow protectors. But there were walls between them. There were things unspoken that would likely never be said. With Rachel he had brought down his walls and let another being in. If it wasn't all the way yet, that would come in time. If they had time.

He heard the shower go on. He found her desire to have things in their proper place humorous. As if clean hair and proper grooming could stave off the beginning of Apocalypse. It had taken him a long time to learn the value of cleanliness. It hadn't been natural to the fighter who lived for battles.

When she came out, naked and with wet hair, he wanted to toss her back on the bed and make sweet love to her. He wanted to bury himself in her body and forget the task at hand. It would be so good. She could ride them both to completion and he could see her body arch above him as she came. So good.

Then, with regret, he pointed to the front door. "Let's eat out."

She looked at his wings and then back at him. The expression of puzzlement and concern told him she wasn't yet used to the idea that humans couldn't see the paranormal.

"They won't see my wings."

"What about Haures? And her helper?"

"If we're in the open, we might be able to draw her minion out."

The corner of her mouth curved up in what he decided was an attempt to smile. Her shield was down. Dread, anxiety and a deep fear of the unknown beat inside her. But there was also a thrill that she could put her newfound fire talents to the test. It was a warrior's thrill, the idea that combat was upon them. Whatever happened today would help shape their destiny and the destiny of all mankind.

"How are the others doing?"

He didn't pretend to misunderstand. "They are also engaged in their Challenges."

"Hence, you can't help each other."

"We never can." He pulled the shirt on and buttoned it. His wings slipped through the slits and settled along his back, folded until they almost appeared like a large muscle group. "It is the way of it."

"I'll get dressed," she said.

* * * * *

Phoenix's tablet told them that the mayor and the caravan would begin their journey at eleven in the morning. Streets had already been cordoned off for blocks around the hotel, and the sidewalks cleared of foot traffic.

Rachel was still amazed that nobody could see anything different about Phoenix, although humans gave him a wide berth. Mortals might not have the same senses as paranormals, but they also weren't entirely blind to the idea that something odd was in their midst.

The sidewalk café, several blocks from the hotel, was quiet between the morning breakfast rush and lunch. They could see the cordons a few blocks away, and police sirens chirped from time to time, as if in reminder of the increased security. "What happens now?"

He took a sip of his coffee, for all intents and purposes casual. But his gaze darted around, assessing, weighing the situation.

Their breakfast was simple, croissants and coffee, and their check already lay in front of them. Rachel had felt the relief of the waiter when Phoenix had asked for it concurrent with the small meal.

"Thank God," the waiter had thought. *"They aren't going to stick around."*

Money was under the sugar bowl, the cost of the meal covered in case they had to make a quick getaway.

The buzz and hubbub of human mental energy swelled around them, but Rachel had a very strong shield up against the ambient noise. She didn't put up the complete wall she'd learned the day Arella attacked, as it kept Phoenix and others out too. They would need the communication.

"He must have a room somewhere where he can see the caravan," Phoenix said. "I think…" He trailed off, his brows furrowing and his forehead wrinkling. Rachel had a quick glimpse of what he'd be like if he ever grew old. "There are bombs. Her human is close. I can sense his scent on them, and their fire gives me the power to feel them." He gestured to his fingertips, and for a brief moment, flames danced on them. "Bombs are easy."

He seemed disappointed, as if he had expected something more complex from Haures and her underlings.

She picked the position of several of the concealed bombs out of his mind. While she knew little about them, these didn't look strong enough to kill someone in a heavily protected car. They were crude, slapped together with a simple timer. She understood what Phoenix thought—these didn't seem sophisticated enough for a plot designed by a centuries-old Demonos.

"What do we do?" She also sipped her coffee and picked at the croissant. It was delicious and flaky, but tasted like crumbs in her mouth. Still, she forced herself to eat it. *You might need the strength,* she told herself.

"I stop this." He said nothing else, and his mind was maddeningly blank. "I am trying to see if I can trace him through the signature on the bombs, but I still can't pick him out. That blocker is too strong."

Rachel breathed out a sigh of relief. There was no more thought in his mind of walking away and leaving humanity to its fate. There was only the desire to protect—her first, the other Elementals second. And distantly, more as a simple task to complete, the need to stop this plot and do his part to save humanity.

"What do I do?"

"You wait." He gripped her hand. "I should have taken you somewhere safe, but I can't help thinking that without you this doesn't work. Do not put yourself in danger. You wait. I'm the Elemental."

Like hell I wait, she thought privately, where he couldn't hear her.

"I'll deal with the bombs." He paused. "I can defuse them."

"He'll have a backup plan. He'll have guns." Rachel shuddered.

"I don't want you in danger."

"Too late for that." Her tone was emphatic.

Fenley and her grandfather approached them, threading through the café until they stood in front of the small table. Both of their faces bore grim expressions. Their gazes darted around from the café to the street beyond and back again.

Phoenix and Rachel took in their expressions. She raised an eyebrow. There was no surprise in his mind, only satisfaction and relief.

"There is little time," Fenley said without preamble. He ignored the dismayed looks of the people at the table next to them when he wedged his huge body close to Phoenix. "We have been watching your human. We know where his traps are. Where he is."

Kamal, the man she was still getting used to as her grandfather, was watching her, his look unreadable.

"I thought you wouldn't help," Rachel said, her relief clear in her voice.

Fenley's mate Brienne stood a short distance away. She was as slight and sleek as she had been the day they met the wolf pack. She motioned to the busy street. Her muscles moved under her skin, and Rachel remembered that Brienne was stronger than she appeared.

If they survived this, she was going to take up kickboxing or karate and get tough. Rachel wanted to be strong now. All she had was fire.

Unprepared or not, the battle was here.

Fenley had cuts and bruises on him, ones Rachel didn't remember seeing before or after her daytime visit from Arella.

Fenley half smiled and shook himself, a motion that made his huge frame heave. "The pack had a discussion. I won."

"Your pack defied you?" Phoenix frowned.

"It is the way of the pack. Tests are issued, and the winner leads. My win. My rules. Not all agree, but all obey."

In the distance they heard the caravan. Through others' eyes, Rachel could see the flags of the black cars making their slow way down the city streets to the hotel.

"Let's go." Phoenix rose from the table, rocking it slightly, and gestured to Rachel. Fenley and Kamal had already made their exit over the small fence that separated the café from the street. The big men were attracting attention. They were striking, even if you couldn't see the wings or claws.

"I wouldn't mind a piece of that."

It had come from a man sitting alone at a table. He met Rachel's eyes and then shifted his gaze to Fenley as if to say, "Your man? Lucky you."

She shook her head, a small smile tugging up. She pointed to the exiting Phoenix, and the man grinned his approval.

Once outside, they gathered in the relative calm of a nearby doorway.

"I will help Rachel," her grandfather said. "You must collect the bombs and take them into the air or they will cause much damage."

Phoenix said nothing further. Good. There would be no *allowing* in this scenario. She would not stand idly by while they fought this Challenge. It was her Challenge too.

"I can melt them down." Phoenix gestured to his wings and the fire faintly visible on his fingertips.

"Too many. It would take too long. We know where they are. We will help," Fenley said.

She had an image of wolves in the sewers under the city, wolves lurking in alleys, sniffing, tracking.

Fenley handed Phoenix a sack. "Come. There is little time."

Phoenix gave Kamal a penetrating stare. "Keep her safe."

The elder Ifrit nodded. "I will do my best. I want her by my side in case Farouk shows up. Are you ready?" he asked Rachel.

There. Rachel concentrated. There was a presence, a malevolent mind, hovering in…

It was as if the entire tableau was revealed before her. Looking through the wolf pack eyes, she saw the man who had eluded them. She knew where he was and where the bombs were. They were oddly placed, and even if they all blew up, they would not be close enough to kill the mayor.

The assassin was a small man, very unassuming. If she'd walked past him on the street, she wouldn't have noticed him. The apartment building was two blocks away, but with a clean line of sight to the parade route as they turned the corner to Market Street. There was something around his neck, likely the blocker that had concealed him from their thoughts. Rachel made a mental note to thank the wolves for their visual aid later.

"I have him," she said, projecting his location to the others.

"We see him now," Phoenix said. "His device does not protect him from being seen with eyes." He turned to Fenley. "We will have to come in from behind. The street is cordoned off in front."

Rachel breathed out. "Go get the bombs. Grandfather and I will deal with the assassin."

There was no sign of Haures. She was the key piece. There had to be something wrong. Haures was Phoenix's Challenger, and there was no way she wasn't part of this. Where was she?

She shot the question to Phoenix, who concentrated for a second and then furrowed his brows.

"I don't know. I can't feel her."

"Something is wrong. This—" he gestured to the street and pointed toward where the caravan was, "—this doesn't feel right, but it doesn't feel wrong either."

Fenley nodded, and Brienne approached them. "The threat is real. We have been watching." Her voice was high, almost a yip. Brienne was struggling to hold on to her human form.

"I owe you," Phoenix said to Fenley, a ring of an oath in his words.

"Go." Rachel kissed him and shoved him lightly. "It will all be for nothing if we don't."

Phoenix shot a look at the other men. "Ifrit, my Rachel is in your hands. I am depending on you. Fenley, let's go."

* * * * *

Fenley's mate ran point several feet in front of them. "We both have put our women in danger today."

Fenley appeared unfazed. "It is what wolves do. She is an equal partner, in her way. And…there are times when there is no option. I would rather keep her safe, but the world will not be safe if you fail."

"Plan?" Phoenix asked.

Fenley pointed to a small alcove. "We have marked the places where the bombs are. The human was easy to track. He smelled…wrong…and he reeked of Demonos."

The bomb, planted in the alcove, was easy to find once you knew where to look. Phoenix carefully pried it loose, noting there were five minutes listed on the timer, and placed it in the bag.

"How many?"

"We counted ten. We are collecting them as well."

"Be careful," Phoenix said.

Fenley gave him a grim nod. "We are aware of the risks, Elemental."

Humans were around them, their minds mostly showing annoyance at the inconvenience of the blocked streets, few caring who was causing it. The caravan was getting closer. Phoenix spared some mental energy and clouded the minds of the surrounding spectators and police, making himself and Fenley completely invisible. It was going to be difficult to keep focus on all his tasks, but it was necessary to do this in order to move through the barriers.

The second bomb was on the bottom of a manhole cover, and it took Phoenix a few precious seconds to get it loose.

"Are we going to have enough time?" he asked.

He saw eyes in the shadows. Fenley had summoned reinforcements.

"We can get a few. Keep going."

Three…four… The wolves brought him four—the human-looking teenagers who had originally taunted Rachel were Fenley's designated helpers. He wished he could melt the bombs down as he went, but they would run out of time before he was finished. He needed all of them. Now.

The caravan continued to move, rounding another corner, coming into sight of the hotel where Rachel had shown him the assassin lying in wait. He prayed she was going to be there in time.

The car continued to move. Nine bombs, the ninth behind a pipe. Two minutes.

The tenth was on the bottom of a barrier, and Phoenix wondered how the assassin had gotten it there. A small wolf was already retrieving it.

Fenley nodded at the sack. "That's all of them. Go, Phoenix. Go now."

One minute. Phoenix soared into the sky, the burlap sack containing his deadly cargo dangling from his shoulder.

Finally he spotted Haures pursuing him, still a distance away. *"You will not win."*

"You are wrong."

Phoenix shifted to his faster bird form, fire dancing along his body, and flew higher, trying to get to the cloud cover where the bombs could explode without doing harm to those on the ground.

Haures came in at an angle, the Demonos getting closer to the smaller bird Phoenix with every moment.

Twenty seconds.

Phoenix could feel the timer countdown like a second heartbeat.

Fifteen seconds.

He calculated the time and the trajectory, and decided he needed a few more seconds.

Twelve.

Haures was almost upon him, and Phoenix plunged through the clouds, using the white cover to execute a hard shift to the right.

Ten seconds.

Nine.

Haures was there. She had correctly judged his change in flight. They had known each other too long.

Eight.

Phoenix turned, made a dive, sending fire streaking behind him. Surprise shot across his mind, an indication that Haures had been taken unawares. He shifted back to human as he flew, hoping the change would startle Haures.

Six.

With Haures right on his tail, Phoenix slung the bag off his shoulder and, with a desperate heave, hurled it high, higher, watching it soar up and then start down.

Five.

Haures sent a bolt of fire toward him. It flew past him and continued on, disappearing into a cloud. Phoenix turned around and gathered fire between his hands, sending it toward his foe. She dodged it easily, pivoting to one side. The bag sailed past them, an arc slowed by wind currents.

Four.

Three.

Haures became a blur, managed to get by him, and grabbed for the bag. She snagged it through one of the pieces of the rough cloth. Phoenix's heart plummeted, but to his surprise she released it. It fell slowly. Then she turned back to the hovering Elemental. Phoenix judged the distance between the bag containing the bombs and the ground and let out a breath. They were high enough that the detonation would do no harm to those below. There was nothing Haures could do.

Two.

"It won't matter, Phoenix. You will not succeed."

One.

He dove down, watching the bag, ready to try a desperate burst of flame if the bag dropped too fast. It seemed to spin as if alive. He could hear the bombs ignite and tore upwards.

Boom!

The bag exploded, burlap and pieces of plastic burning in all directions. Both Phoenix and Haures moved out of range, the shrapnel missing them by inches.

Haures hovered a few feet away, smug and stationary. It had to take a lot of energy to float there, but she showed no sign of strain.

Flames licked over his body in a halo, making the world seem red and orange.

"Silly Phoenix. The bombs were just a diversion. Oh, they would have worked, and it would have been glorious, but we knew you would find them."

He frowned.

"My assassin is in place, and he will kill the mayor. I win."

"You have not yet won. I defeated your bombs and my friends will stop your assassin."

"You know what happens if you lose. If one fails they all fail. Then you will have to go to final Challenge, no matter what happens with the other Elementals. You have already lost."

It was just bluster. "Rachel and her grandfather are going to stop your man."

He reached out to Rachel and saw that she and her grandfather were moving up the back stairs of the targeted building. Kamal was in front of her, his wings brushing the narrow hallway. He could feel Rachel's tension and also her stoic determination. She would do this. His love would succeed.

He was wasting time talking to Haures. Phoenix turned to go, his wings spreading as he prepared for flight.

"They will not. They will die."

As if blinders had been removed from his eyes, Phoenix he understood. It had been a ruse to get him, the stronger Elemental, away from the assassin. Kamal was strong, but not as strong as Phoenix. Without the ability to see the man's mind, they were flying blind, unable to have any advantage except strength. He thought he understood, until Haures began to chuckle.

"You are easily tricked, my old friend. Love has made you blind. Love has made you weak."

"You will not win," he repeated, even as he turned and began his descent to the distant earth.

Haures fell on him from behind, dragging him backward, her hands more like claws, digging into him. A fireball emerged from her body, singeing his wing feathers.

Turning, Phoenix directed a gout of fire at her from his fingers. It missed, and she swiped a claw at his back.

The mayor had been a target, but not the only target. Phoenix cursed himself for his blindness. All the time the other paranormals had been strange around Rachel, he thought that was because of her buried Ifrit talents. Instead, she was more a part of this than he had imagined.

"That's right, Phoenix. You finally understand. Defeating my assassin will delay the inevitable, but it won't stop it."

"Rachel. Rachel is also a target."

"You will be too late."

With a sinking feeling, he knew Haures was right.

* * * * *

The building was dark, the back stairwell unlit. Rachel tried to sense the gunman and saw the man through the wolf's eyes, standing in a third-floor window, regarding the crowd. Rachel saw a gun but not a rifle and decided she was seeing a memory of the man and not a current picture.

"We have to hurry." Kamal pointed to the third-floor stairwell door. "This is locked."

An added layer of protection. She was going to shove it open, but Kamal aimed his fingers at the lock and it exploded into flame and melted.

Her fingers itched. "Cool," she said on a smile. "I've got to practice that."

He opened the door. "Yes, you do. And much more."

They made their way down the hallway, Rachel triangulating the location of the gunman based on wolf observation.

"Plan?" Rachel projected to Kamal.

"We break in and attack him."

That was straightforward. Her heart was pounding, fear dabbing her forehead and armpits with sweat. Tendrils of fire surged up her spinal column and flowed down to her hands. Rachel flexed her fingers, summoning the power.

Kamal motioned to the door. His wings were flat against his back, but he was still a large man. When this was all over, she had to learn more about the people she came from. She hoped there would be time.

"Now," Kamal said.

With a swift motion, Kamal kicked in the door and hurled himself through, his momentum carrying him inside. Rachel followed, quickly moving to the left.

The gunman, standing at the window with a rifle pointed down, whirled, clearly caught by surprise. The apartment was dimly lit, but Rachel found it easy to see, apparently another side benefit of her emerging Ifrit powers.

"Stay back!"

He was a slight man, perhaps five foot eight at best, but made bulky by the thick Kevlar he was wearing from head to toe. Only his head and hands were left uncovered. On the table in the room, otherwise bare of furnishing except for a single bed, were a myriad of weapons and war-making items, from handguns to grenades to the remnants of the bombs Phoenix had dispatched.

The man pointed his rifle at them, his hand completely steady on the trigger.

"It's over." Kamal lifted one wing to show the man he wasn't human.

"No, it's not."

She could hear the caravan drawing close to the hotel. They were out of time. "Stay back!"

Kamal moved, and the gunman fired toward Rachel. It was a shot designed to warn, not kill. Kamal froze.

"I said, stay back."

The gunman turned back toward the caravan. He aimed again, lowering the rifle.

Kamal moved, leaping toward the man. With a quick jerk, he pulled the blocker off the man's neck, sending it skittering across the floor. In the same motion, he knocked the rifle out of the gunman's hands. His momentum carried him out the open window. Glass shattered, and Kamal cried out as he fell. She hoped he would be able to steady himself in time not to crash into the humans. Rachel didn't know what that would look like—a shielded paranormal would nonetheless have bulk and momentum.

Then she was alone. With an angry gunman, armed to the teeth.

Rachel calculated the distance between herself and the tableful of guns. He still had the rifle.

"Aleric?"

He was engaged with Haures. Praying that Kamal would be back shortly, she looked at the gunman. Fire surged within her, heating her bloodstream.

"It's over." She gestured vaguely to the window. "The Chicago mayor is out of range."

"She is," the gunman agreed, and his voice had a strange, tinny quality. "I failed." He seemed unconcerned about the failure of his assignment. "You, however, are not out of range."

He cocked back the barrel. She heard Kamal pounding up the stairs again, heard Phoenix in the distance and even Griffin, engaged in his own battle, as clearly as her own thoughts. She wondered why Kamal didn't fly up instead of using the stairs.

"You. Will. Die."

On the last word, the gunman pulled the trigger once, even as Rachel dove to one side. The next bullet missed as well, sailing over her head as she continued to fall. The gunshots were loud, deafening.

No more fear, she thought. No more running.

Rachel rose. A look of surprise crossed the gunman's face. Flames licked across her body, and she let them come, allowing him to see. His eyes widened in terror but he raised the gun again. She only had seconds. Concentrating, Rachel dug for the power she had felt in Kamal when he melted the lock. Finding it, she directed the power at the gunman, and to her great satisfaction the gun melted, the barrel twisting toward the floor like taffy. The gunman gave a cry of dismay and cast the gun aside as if it burned him.

She had done it.

Even as she moved to throw fire at the gunman, an Ifrit plunged through the shattered window. At first she thought it was Kamal, but that couldn't be. She still felt him coming nearer.

The assassin took in the unfamiliar being and shot her a stare. "I win. House always wins." He grabbed a knife from the table, shoved it in his jeans belt and ran toward the door.

The being in front of her wasn't her grandfather. Kamal was near and getting closer, but his mind signature spoke of pain searing along his left wing. He had folded it along his side. She would have to trust him to stop the assassin.

Rachel faced the unfamiliar Ifrit. With a sickening thud in her belly, Rachel knew who it had to be. *"Get the man,"* Rachel said to Kamal.

She had a mental image of Kamal cornering the assassin on the stairwell, advancing toward him. The man looked left and right, a desperate expression on his face as her grandfather flapped his good wing, one hooked top scoring the man's shoulder. His eyes widened and he feinted as it to duck past Kamal, but Kamal flipped that same wing into the man's face, and he staggered.

"I am Farouk," the other Ifrit said to Rachel.

"I know," she said. At the same time she said it, Kamal roared and charged toward the door. Distantly she heard Phoenix as well, high up in the clouds.

Hampered by his injured wing, Kamal was not in time to dodge the man's direct attack when he yelled and came at her grandfather. He lunged at Kamal and jabbed at him with the knife. Pain seared down their mental connection as his weapon pierced Kamal's wing.

The Ifrit standing before her was as big as Kamal, with wings that spread across the window openings, blocking out the sun. There was no mercy in his eyes. This was the being who had killed her parents.

Rachel examined her options. The table full of weapons beckoned tantalizingly beyond the Ifrit. She feinted, trying to dive under his legs and grab something, anything. The Ifrit—Farouk—grabbed her arms, cuffing them behind her. Rachel kicked and clawed, but she was no match for the stronger being. He took the blocker from the floor and secured it around her neck.

The world went silent as the blocker shut out all mental communication. She could no longer hear any voices, and when she tried to transmit to Phoenix, she was met with a blank slate. A few weeks ago she would have welcomed it, but now it accentuated the plight she was in more effectively than anything that could have been said. Outside, she heard Kamal scuffling with the other man.

"You are coming with me."

Rachel looked up into the Ifrit's face. He gripped her with an iron grasp and without hesitation plunged through the shattered window and into the air. He dipped slightly and then turned and banked upward, Rachel in his arms.

Wind caught her as they shot straight up. Helplessness flooded her. He was the person who had killed her parents. He was the person who would have killed her if he'd seen her. Thanks to her grandfather, he hadn't known of her escape that day. She prayed that her grandfather was following now. She had felt his pain and knew that his wing was damaged. That had to be why he had run up the stairs instead of flying. If he could not fly she was already dead.

"Why?" she asked. "How did you find us?"

His grip tightened. "Your awakening shriek was loud across the mental plane and your mental signature apparent. As for the rest... Haures needed my help. The vampires offered more. They were quite eager to share your location. As for the why... You know why."

The spire of the Transamerica Pyramid drew closer. The many panes winked and caught the sun, reflecting Farouk and Rachel's approach. Far below, tourists and businesspeople bustled around. They weren't aware of anything, and for the first time, Rachel hated the knowledge that humans couldn't see paranormals. She automatically tried to reach out, only to be presented with the blank slate of the blocker.

Damn it.

The building grew nearer, and Farouk slowed and banked until they were hovering above one of the side areas. The spire was above them and the bulk of the building was below. Up closer, the finely crushed quartz that gave the building its light color winked and gleamed in the broad sunlight.

He dumped his bundle on the sloped concrete. Rachel slid slightly, her arms caught behind her. The ground far below tilted for a moment until she steadied.

The renegade Ifrit contemplated her from his superior height, a mixture of anger and disgust on his face. "You were supposed to be my daughter. You were supposed to be the combination of two powerful Ifrit clans, two bloodlines surging through you. Instead—" he looked at her with disgust, "—you are a weak half-human. You do not deserve to live."

She didn't know if anyone could hear Farouk, didn't know if someone out there felt the blankness where her mind had been. It hadn't taken her long to rely heavily on the mind talk, and now she didn't know what to do without it. Where were Phoenix and Kamal? The wolves?

Looking for her, of course. She was important to them. Despite her dire situation, a warmth went through Rachel. She had love. Here, at the end, at least she had that.

She struggled against the bonds. Could any humans see her, now that she wasn't in Farouk's grip? Or would her halfling blood shield her from human eyes? She wasn't sure which would be better. Rachel shot a look at the windows of the spire but could see nothing except the reflection of the city mirrored back to her. "I'm not sorry for what I am. My parents loved me. My grandfather loves me.

Phoenix might love me. It's more than you have."

Farouk's face twisted. "She was not free to love someone else. She was always intended for me."

Rachel shrugged, although with her arms behind her the action had little meaning. "Free will, pal."

"We don't hold to such ridiculous notions. Her parents were too easy on her. She was mine."

Hoping her terror didn't show, Rachel tried to keep her face calm. She would not give Farouk the satisfaction of seeing how scared she was. Her one regret was that she hadn't told Phoenix how she felt. She wished she'd said the words. She wished she had heard him say them back, if he did love her. She thought he did. She hoped he did.

"I am going to finish the job I began years ago, and then the clan will see I was right all along." With the sharp point of one of his wings, Farouk sliced through the rope bond. "You will look like a suicide, although they will speculate about how you got up here. It is fitting you should die from a fall. Your Elemental is too far away to save you. Your grandfather cannot stop it this time. He is too far away. He is hurt. So much the better." His look at Rachel could only be described as pure hate. "Goodbye, half-breed. You will not pollute our bloodlines."

Reaching over, he snatched the blocker from around her neck. Immediately, the chatter of minds began. Through them she heard the scream of Phoenix's call, searching desperately for her. She reached out and touched his thoughts. He was still in the air. He was too distant, and they both knew it.

Her grandfather was closer, but his inability to find them had cost him precious minutes. He was just far enough away to make this a tragedy instead of a last-minute rescue. Kamal had hauled the man to the broken street side window and shoved him out. Then as the man struggled, Kamal slashed at his throat and simply let go. Without watching the man fall, her grandfather took to the air through the window. People began pointing first at the man bleeding out and then up to the shattered window. They did not see the form already desperately flying toward her, favoring one side of his body as he caught the air.

Farouk shoved her, and Rachel's newly freed arms tingled. She flailed as she tried to catch a grip. She slipped and then slid over the edge. The building receded away from her. Farouk stood there for a moment then, with a powerful beat of his wings, took to the air.

"It is done," she heard.

The street rushed toward her, so fast, too fast. She threw her hands up, arcing fire along and through her body, but the wind kept snuffing it out. The stories of the Transamerica Pyramid soared past her as the ground got closer.

Impact. She landed, and her bones snapped. Phoenix was with her mentally, his mind howling, but still trying to soothe her. She knew her body was crushed. She couldn't raise her head. It was strange, this absolute lack of pain. Perhaps it wouldn't be so bad to die.

Blood seeped out from multiple breaks. The lacerations of her internal organs would have killed anyone, but she'd also broken her spine and crushed her lungs. Then the pain seared through her, even as her lifeblood poured out.

"Habibti!"

It was an anguished cry. Rachel saw her grandfather through dimming eyes as he landed awkwardly, staggering before regaining his feet and rushing toward her. At least she wouldn't be alone at the end.

"Tell Aleric I love him," she said, her voice growing weaker.

Kamal made a small sound, tears shining in his eyes. "Hang on, habibti. Phoenix is coming."

"He won't be in time." Her voice was resigned. She was aware that her life was ebbing out.

"I know."

"Rachel, please. I love you. Don't leave me." The anguished plea was far away as Phoenix's mind receded with the rest of the world. Rachel made one final effort to respond.

"I love you too, Aleric. I wish...for so much..."

Film covering her eyes, consciousness leaching from her, Rachel died.

Chapter Fourteen

Phoenix had miscalculated his enemies. The Challenge might have been about the Chicago mayor, but in the end it was really about Rachel.

"You were so easily fooled," Haures said from behind him. "Your Challenge cluttered your mind, and you didn't see the truth. You won your Challenge, but you lost everything. If we had succeeded, the assassination of the mayor might have triggered World War III, or it might not have. It's hard to know. Rachel is still dead. You failed. Fire will not call to fire."

It was all visible through Kamal's eyes. It was evident her life was fading. Massive wounds, too huge to survive, bloomed on her body, and far too much blood pooled under her.

"It's too late, Phoenix," Haures said with a gloat. "It's over."

"I love you," he called to her again but this time heard no echoing reply.

Kamal picked up her broken, battered body and rocked her. Then she was gone, the mind link snapped. Her arms going limp, Rachel stopped breathing.

Phoenix turned to his nemesis and hurled himself at her, cold fury surging through his veins. Haures flew a short distance away, out of his reach, gave him a mocking smile and vanished.

Phoenix's shout echoed through the clouds, washing through the minds of the other Elementals. The others, especially Griff, touched his mind with concern and alarm. Strangely, there was nothing from Sphynx. He flicked Griff and Ondine away, casting them out of his mind and slamming his shields down.

Gone. She was gone. Their time had been much too brief, and now she was lost to him forever. He had just met the woman he could build a life with, his fire half.

Phoenix turned and plunged toward the ground, his wings flat behind him as he plummeted. He relied on his automatic senses to get him there, as his mind was completely occupied with the pain of losing Rachel.

She was gone.

The next time he was called to the pyre, he would not rise. He would will it to be his last time. To hell with being an Elemental if he couldn't have her. He should have told her how he felt sooner. Now it was too late. It would forever be too late.

The tang of the city pervaded his nostrils as he got closer to the Transamerica Pyramid. Dimly he saw that the mayor's car was parked at the hotel, its flags flapping in the wind, surrounded by security. The heads of the cities must already be inside, attending their lunch. He had won his Challenge. In the past he would have been relieved and gratified that he had done his part to help humanity. Now, it didn't matter.

He landed by the tower, ignoring the tourists and businesspeople who gathered around the tableau. With a quick flick of his mind, Phoenix clouded all of them. As if in a walking dream, the people shuffled away.

Farouk's wings were bearing him out of the city even now. Through the minds of the wolves, he saw they were lurking around the body of the assassin. Police had been summoned, judging from the armed cops converging on the apartment building and the still body nearby. One assassin had paid, but the other had not. He would change that, with Kamal's help.

Kamal was there, holding Rachel's body, but he yielded to Phoenix as soon as the Elemental arrived. "I'm sorry, Phoenix."

"You were supposed to protect her," he said, his hands balling into fists. He wanted to strike something, but Kamal was the wrong target. It didn't matter. Nothing did.

"I was," Kamal agreed. "I failed. I underestimated Farouk. I will regret this for the rest of my life."

Part of him wanted to scorch Kamal to ash, but the man would not burn.

"You will make him pay?" Phoenix asked and Kamal nodded.

"If it is the last thing I do."

Phoenix pressed his forehead to her lifeless one. She was still warm, and it seemed as if all he would have to do was shake her and she would wake up. He even did that, shook her gently, and felt no response. There was nothing in his mind, no familiar echo of her mental signature.

Silvery tears ran down his face, catching at his nose before dropping off onto her clammy face. She'd never had a chance, not with the assassin and his weapons. Not with Haures targeting her. Not with Farouk gunning for her. The tears came faster and he began keening, moaning out a timeless cry of suffering and loss that echoed off the tall buildings around them.

He held her for what seemed an eternity, his tears falling until there were no tears left in him. Even then he held her, knowing once he let her go, he would be saying goodbye to her forever.

Finally, however, there was nothing to do. Gently he placed her on the ground and rose. He gestured to Rachel. "What is the Ifrit tradition?"

Kamal's eyes were moist, and when he spoke, his voice was rough. "We burn our dead." He paused. "But Phoenix…"

Phoenix waved a hand, stopping his words. "Will you…take care of her?" Grief flowed through him.

He wished she'd had time to use her Ifrit powers to their fullest. He wished she had lived to see another sunrise. Another sunset. He wished she could have lived to see the birth of their child, or maybe children, boys and girls, strong and wise like their mother. He wished for so many things, and none of them would come true.

Phoenix turned his head to the sky. Shaking his fists, he shouted his rage. "It's not fair! It's *not* right! This cannot end this way. You, whoever you are, make this right!"

Kamal remained motionless. "Phoenix, listen to me. The wolves, they have said, there is a possibility—"

"Damn you! Damn all of you! This should not be. Take me instead." Sobs caught his voice and he fell to the ground again. Picking up Rachel, he embraced her, uncaring of the blood on his shirt. The shirt was tattered and stained from his hasty flight with the bombs. It didn't matter. Nothing mattered. His tears fell on her still face. He'd rarely seen her face at rest, except when she was sleeping. It was always in movement, always alive and sunny, like her.

Phoenix wiped the remaining tears off his face and, with a still-wet hand, gently caressed her cheek.

She was dead. He had failed.

* * * * *

She was somewhere, nothing around her in any direction, in a kind of gray that seemed to stretch on forever. Rachel tried to reach out, first with her arms and then with her mind, but there was no response.

The events that she guessed had led her to this place surfaced slowly, like honey sluggishly rolling from a jar.

Was she dead? She was dead. She had to be dead. She remembered her life draining out of her, but it was dim and distant. She recollected fear, and then the emotion leaving her. She recalled her grandfather holding her hand, and nothing more.

She examined her body but there was no sign of wounds. Without emotion she saw she was naked. It didn't matter, here in this netherworld. In the distance there was a flicker of red and orange that could have been fire. Idly, Rachel tried to summon it but was unsurprised when her fingers failed to light.

She should have been upset, but there was no emotion inside her. If this was death, she was okay with it. Even that was abstract, like something she should be concerned about but wasn't.

There was a noise pinging against her consciousness, but she ignored it. Perhaps this nothing world would be where she simply drifted, not existing but existing. Perhaps she was just held here by a residue, and she would fade away in time.

The noise grew louder and her body twitched, reacting involuntarily to the persistent sound. There was a brief flash of color, a bright yellow, before the world faded to gray again.

She liked the gray. She would stay there.

* * * *

As if to punctuate the futility of any hopes he had regarding Rachel, his wings vanished. He staggered, tumbling over her, the awkward position he'd been in throwing him off-balance.

Gently he laid her back down on the ground and rose. The tears were still wet on his cheeks. They had dripped down onto her face and body, dampening her skin.

Mentally he reviewed the active volcanoes in North America. Hawaii had the closest one, but that volcano had too many tourists to be a safe place to end his days. Alaska would take longer, but it would be easier. Whatever happened with the other Elementals and their Challenges, they would have to face the next one with a new Phoenix. It was time for his part in this battle to be over.

"Don't do this, Aleric." It was Griff's voice, and it had an air of desperation but also of acceptance, as if he knew Phoenix's mind was made up.

"Sorry, friend. May your new Phoenix be powerful."

He shut Griff out and focused on his plans. By his estimation it would take a day of solid flight to get to Alaska. Once there, he would immediately plunge into Mount Cleveland, seeking out the fiery heart of the volcano. He didn't know if he could will himself not to rise, but he thought the power or powers behind this endless battle would heed his cry.

If not, he would find another way to die.

He shifted his gaze back to Kamal. "Take care of her. Perhaps we shall meet again in whatever afterlife there is."

It would be sooner rather than later.

Kamal put a hand on Phoenix's arm, but Phoenix jerked away. "Phoenix, you need to know something," he began, but Phoenix turned away.

"*Phoenix, stop.*" Sphynx's mental voice, the masculine voice of Masud only, boomed into his consciousness.

"*I have no choice. I cannot go on.*"

"*You must go with Kamal and Rachel immediately.*"

"*There is nothing to 'go' to.*"

Then he had no choice but to accept an image Sphynx forced into his mind. It had to be of the future, because she was still lying in front of him. It showed Rachel, her broken body bundled in a blanket, being borne to the wolf park.

Betrayal soared through him at the image. He had thought they would burn her. If there was an afterlife, he hoped he would meet Rachel in it.

"*You must go with Kamal. Now. Rachel needs you. This is what must happen. You will understand shortly. Now.*"

"*Rachel is dead.*"

"*Go.*"

Phoenix was confused, irritated and angry, but a thousand years of obeying Sphynx as their leader made him obey. He turned to Kamal. "Apparently we have to go to the wolf park."

As if summoned, there was a burst through the tourists, and Fenley and his son Artur were there, yipping and growling although they were in human form. They motioned to Rachel.

"We have to take her. Now," Fenley said, his tone urgent.

He didn't know why Sphynx was so adamant, but the oldest Elemental did not do things without a reason. He didn't know why the wolves were there, or why they had to go to the park, but it didn't matter. He would resume his quest to die after he found out why Sphynx was insistent—and why Kamal and the wolves were taking Rachel to the ground instead of the pyre, where she belonged.

He would do this one last task the elder Elemental demanded, and then go to his death.

* * * * *

The gray was flashing with yellow and green, like lightning streaking across the nonexistent horizon. Rachel should have been curious, but she didn't have any desire to go and find out why the gray was broken. It didn't matter. Nothing did.

Would she be allowed to rest? She was tired. She had never been part of anything until the last few weeks, but she could be part of the death that eventually overcame everyone.

Something tugged at her, as if a far-off thread were pulling her to the distance. She ignored it, willing it to go away. Annoyance flooded her, the first emotion she had felt since she found herself in the gray.

Then she focused. Red eyes danced in front of her. Those she knew. Rachel saw the insubstantial people Phoenix had called shadow people, wavering on the edge of her vision.

"Come. Join us."

Unlike the first time she had seen them, there was nothing between her and the wavering figures. Rachel took a step toward them. It would be easy. She could go with them now and walk into something else. All her troubles would be over. All her fears at an end.

Or maybe they weren't. Rachel stopped moving her feet, realizing she was beginning to follow them.

"No," she cried mentally and the figures took a step back. Her entire body shook, and the air waved as bright fire burst from her, aiming toward the shadow people. It seemed to arc from her in a way it never had before, and it struck in the flickering crowd. She heard a shriek and they vanished.

If she had said yes, she would have been lost to the world forever, doomed to become something else. Perhaps she would have become a shadow person, or perhaps she would have simply been lost forever. She would not, could not join the shadow people. But what now? She heard a short pop. Then there was a streak of yellow like she had seen before the appearance of the shadow people. She waited for several beats, but they did not reappear.

There was another noise. A staccato beating with a certain rhythm to it, like a drumbeat.

After a minute, she realized it was her heartbeat.

Her heartbeat? She shouldn't have one. Not in the dark, not in the gray. Not in this limbo, this potential afterlife. Whether she was with the shadow people or not, she was still caught in this other place. She shouldn't have been able to use her fire, but she had.

There was a path in the gray, like emergency lights on a plane aisle, leading into the distance. She couldn't see anything else.

Rachel didn't want to go. She wanted to stay right there. She could not have survived the fall. She did not want to be a ghost or some sort of shade haunting the world, and worse, haunting Phoenix. That was less of a life than the gray.

"Come, Rachel. Before it is too late."

Fear flooded her, nearly paralyzing her. Still, she stepped forward, first one step, and then another, until she was moving through the gray at a fast pace, the path acting as a guide.

"Come." The voice came from everywhere and nowhere at the same time. She didn't know the voice, but it was also familiar.

With reluctance, not wanting to move from the gray nothingness, Rachel nonetheless obeyed.

* * * * *

Phoenix didn't want to see Rachel's dead body. He didn't want to be reminded that the only woman he had ever truly loved would never be his to hold again. He wanted to remember her as he had seen her for the last time, vibrant and alive with her fire power, a woman who he thought would always stand by his side.

He wasn't sure why he had obeyed the command, but almost without being aware, he found himself at the park. The werewolves bore Rachel between them,

Kamal close behind. Phoenix observed the tableau like a spectator. Numbness laced his body and froze his spirit. He stumbled over a tree root and shrugged. Small injuries didn't matter. Nothing did.

He would have to fly commercial to Alaska. So what? He had the money, and it didn't matter how it was spent. Nothing mattered.

"Phoenix, quickly." He didn't know the voice.

Movement to the left caught his eye, a four-legged body pointing to the trees. The wolf howled and with his muzzle gestured to the forest clearing in the middle of the stand of pines. The wolf trotted toward it, pointing with its muzzle and yipping three times. With slow movements, dragging his feet with every step, Phoenix went to the clearing.

The wolves had formed a semicircle around Rachel's still form on the ground. Kamal was hovering when Phoenix came to rest beside him. Kamal studied Phoenix, his features unreadable.

Brienne, still in human form, stepped forward. There was an elongated crunching noise as Artur changed from wolf to human, but nobody moved. The young werewolf retrieved a satchel and handed it to Brienne.

Phoenix felt drained, empty of all emotions. Rachel's broken body was motionless, the wounds gaping and as ugly as he remembered. Blood, caked and crusted, was dried on her clothes in a hideous reminder of her mortality. She appeared deflated, her body malformed, bones sticking out at impossible angles. He'd seen crushed and dismembered people many times before, but they had never been his one true love.

"Why did you call us here?" Phoenix forced himself to look at her lifeless body. It would eliminate any lingering doubt about perishing in the volcano.

The grass around her began to wave. The wolves straightened her out, and Phoenix winced at the grinding of bone. He was surprised they bothered to concentrate on putting her body back together, but perhaps it was a wolf tradition.

He had lost everything that mattered, even though he had won his Challenge. The evidence lay in front of him.

"Phoenix, we are not so easy to kill. A part of Rachel lingers," Kamal said as if schooling a child. "I tried to tell you earlier."

Brienne examined her. Her gaze went first to Fenley, then Kamal and finally Phoenix. "You are assuming Rachel is dead. Do you have any more tears in you?"

His brow furrowed. "Why?"

"Tears of a Phoenix," Brienne said. "They have the power to restore life."

"Myth," Phoenix said. "I've cried before and it's never restored anything." His body shook as he struggled to contain hope.

"Try," Fenley commanded.

Try reverberated in his head, dancing around his skull.

Phoenix shrugged. It would be futile, but he would do anything if it meant even a smidgen of hope of restoring Rachel to life. Digging deep, he pulled the desolation out of his mind. Stepping forward, he forced himself to kneel in front of Rachel. As the tears fell, he let them roll off his chin and onto her still, pale face.

There was a faint shimmer in his mind as if someone was trying to probe him.

Brienne spared him a quick glance. "She is caught between staying and going. Her injuries were grave, but she is Ifrit. She tries to remain even now." She removed several items from her bag.

The shimmer in his mind grew stronger as Rachel's body heated. "I don't understand," he cried in desperation. She wasn't cold yet, but soon she would be. Cold, colder, coldest. Forever cold. Dead and gone. His only love, cruelly snatched from him. "She's broken beyond repair. Not even a paranormal could survive that fall."

"Support her head," Fenley said. Kamal muscled forward and took Rachel's neck, carefully inserting his hands under the spinal column. Phoenix cradled her head gently. The squishiness of her broken skull made him wince.

There was a long silence while it seemed as if nothing were moving, not even the leaves on the trees. His tears slowed, but the evidence of them lingered through the wetness on her face. He had thought the myth of Phoenix tears disproven, but perhaps he was wrong. His heart soared at the possibility.

"It is happening." The voice echoed as if from a distance.

There was a far-off presence, almost too faint to be detected. Then it grew stronger, a little stronger, and finally…

A shriek roared into Phoenix's mind, coming in on waves of pain.

"A…Al…Ale…Aleric?" The mental voice was feeble and quivery but unmistakably Rachel's.

"Love?" he called and heard an answer, as if far in the distance. It was dim and faint, but it was there. A flutter of movement, a tic, twitched in her leg. Phoenix grabbed for her hand. He squeezed and could have sworn there was a return squeeze, almost too soft to detect.

"No time for niceties." While Fenley's tone was harsh, there was a thread of relief through it.

"Blood. We're going to need blood. You." Brienne pointed to one of the nearby wolves. "Three pints. O-positive. And an IV."

"Take mine," Phoenix said, already rolling up his sleeve. "Take it all. Rachel, Rachel, it's not possible."

"I think your tears are enough out of you for today," Brienne said sharply. "I don't know what your blood would do to her."

Somewhere in the back of his mind, he heard a plaintive mental cry.

"I hurt."

"Start the IV. Keep her body straight. She is Ifrit. If she heals too quickly, we may have to reset any bones that don't knit properly. We may have more wounds to contend with," Brienne said.

Brienne started the IV, feeding blood into Rachel's arm, although her chest wounds were still large and gaping. It seemed as if the blood would just pump right out of her body again. Heat shimmered around them, her body rising in temperature.

"I'm here, love. Don't fight it."

Wounds began healing, closing like a shutter on a camera. Bruises faded and cuts mended. She seemed to lengthen, blackening the grass in an outline around her. Closer and closer the wounds came together, and finally sealed. First they appeared as an angry red pucker before they smoothed out, leaving no visible signs of trauma.

Several smaller cuts on her arms and body knit back together, and Rachel's eyes fluttered.

"Tell her to keep still. I think it's almost done." Brienne's relief sang through her words.

Heat poured off Rachel's body. With a series of crunches that made Phoenix flinch, Rachel's bones healed, one by one. Her hand sought his.

"I don't think she's going to burn up," Kamal said, but he seemed hesitant. "This is so far back in legend, I don't know what truth is and what was added to over the years."

"Stay still, my love. Just a little while longer."

Phoenix wasn't sure if it was his imagination or not, but it seemed to him the air was cooler than it had been a second ago. Then he noticed the heat shimmer lessening and the florid color of her face fading to normal.

Rachel tried to rise to a seated position, but Brienne held her down.

"Not yet," the woman warned. "Your body is still quite fluid. You need to be completely still for a little while longer. First, let me check you and make sure you healed properly."

She ran her hands over Rachel's face, making small adjustments to the bones and skin. Phoenix winced as she realigned a cheekbone that had started to knit a little crookedly, but smiled when the familiar contours of Rachel's beloved face returned. Brienne moved down Rachel's body, adjusting here and there as she went, and then beckoned for the wolves to turn Rachel over.

"Gently. Very gently," Brienne warned and motioned to Phoenix to release Rachel's hand. "You'll have her soon enough. She's my patient right now."

Nodding, Phoenix released Rachel's hand despite her mental plea not to.

"I want you perfect, love. It's only for a little while."

Brienne checked Rachel's neck and spine, making adjustments and alignments as she went. After what seemed like forever, it was over. Her spine was straight and mended, the bones solid. The wolves rolled Rachel back to her original supine position.

The Ifrit approached, a smile of profound relief on his face. Phoenix smiled back, the movement uncertain. He had kept himself apart from all others for so long, he didn't know what the right behavior was.

It was time to find out. With his love by his side.

Rachel's eyes opened. She observed the gathered crowd blankly.

"I don't understand. I died. I fell…the Transamerica Pyramid…nobody can survive that." She looked at her chest, at the blood on her clothes, and then at her healed body. "There was nothing, just gray. It was quiet there. Peaceful. I felt… nothing." She flushed. "I wanted to stay."

"You didn't survive," Kamal said gently, still kneeling next to Phoenix. "I was with you when you died. But you are Ifrit. We are hardy. You went to the gray?"

Rachel swallowed, making the barest motion of assent with her head. Brienne picked up a bag of recently arrived blood and inserted a tube into the IV.

"I don't understand." Rachel said.

"You need more blood. You lost most of yours." Her growling tone didn't give Rachel any room to argue. "Your man brought you back. There is a legend that the tears of a Phoenix can give life. But only if the Phoenix's heart is at stake. Wolf lore doesn't go back to the last time it happened." He glanced at Kamal.

Kamal's face jerked in a rueful smile. "We have never believed such a legend. I am happy that in this, the Ifrits were wrong."

Rachel tried to rise to a seated position again. Firmly but inexorably, Phoenix held her down with a hand on her shoulder.

"Don't rush it," he said and found to his dismay that his voice was barely above a whisper. "Is she still in danger?" His question was directed to Brienne, although he didn't move.

Brienne felt Rachel's chest, apparently checking her heartbeat. She examined Rachel's skin for any wounds and then, with a satisfied smile, shook her head, stepping back. "She is healed."

"You brought me back," Rachel said in wonder. She looked over at Brienne. "Thank you. I… Thank you."

Brienne said nothing. After a moment she crossed one foot in front of the other and bent her knees in a curtsy.

Rachel blinked but raised a hand in acknowledgment.

Phoenix bowed to Brienne from his seated position and then turned his attention back to Rachel.

"I love you," Rachel said, her voice breaking.

"I love you." He said it simply, his heart swelling in his chest.

Nobody moved except Brienne, who, with a nod, backed away from Phoenix and Rachel, joining Fenley a few feet away.

Phoenix slipped a hand under Rachel's body and helped her rise to her feet.

Unsteadily, Rachel gripped his waist, seeming to feel her legs under her again.

"Thank you," she managed, her voice still shaky. "All of you."

"Habibti," was all Kamal said.

* * * * *

Rachel kicked aside her tattered and bloody clothes with distaste. With a gesture, Fenley had sweats brought forth, and Artur handed them to Phoenix. He blocked the rest of the onlookers and helped Rachel into them. She would need a shower. Her body still felt unfamiliar and her mind strange. The events, all of them: the assassin, Farouk, the tower and finally the gray whirled in her mind until she thought she would collapse under the weight of it all. She died. She had died.

"You came back to me."

Rachel leaned against Phoenix, and his arms went around her.

Remains of tears were still evident on Phoenix's cheeks when he pressed his face to hers. The tears tingled and then seeped into her skin. Rachel felt like she had absorbed something into her body that would last a long time.

Something was different, and it was marvelous. Flexing her arms, Rachel concentrated, and in a moment power surged through her body. She had no aches or pains. It reminded her of when she had been a child and thought she was unbreakable.

"I was going to a volcano. I didn't want to continue," he said. "Not without you."

"Oh," she said simply.

Phoenix slid his arms down until his hands linked with Rachel's. "I am going to tell the other Elementals they will have to find another Phoenix in the future. When you die, I go, if I have to will myself onto the pyre."

"Aleric!" she exclaimed, turning her head to look at him. "No. You are an Elemental. You have a job to do. You can't give up immortality for me."

"I am not immortal, just long-lived. I can and I do give it up." His eyes glittered, leaving her no doubt he meant what he said.

She shook her head. "No. I will stand by your side. You will not stop being what you are. It's important. Please, Aleric. I love you too much to allow that."

There was never a question of refusing her. "If you're sure, my love. I want to be with you. I'll sacrifice whatever I have to."

Brienne gave them a small, private smile. "Your sacrifice may not be necessary."

Phoenix cocked his head, his confusion plain on his face. "What do you mean?"

"There is another part of that legend. The story tells that when Phoenix tears bring a person back to life, their life essence merges with the Phoenix. That person will live as long as Phoenix does. It's never been proven." She shrugged. "Time will tell."

"Be careful who you cry on," Fenley said.

Phoenix faced the group of wolves. "I owe you and your pack more than I can ever repay," he said to Fenley, his voice firm. "Anything you need, just ask."

Fenley shrugged, but he had a satisfied look on his face. "In these dark times it is good to have the Elementals to call on. I will remember your promise." He gestured to Rachel, who came forward, reluctantly releasing her hold on Phoenix. To her surprise Fenley lifted her into his arms and held her gently. There was moisture in his eyes. "Take care of Phoenix, lovely lady. I don't think your part in this saga has ended."

"Nor yours," Phoenix said.

"What comes next?" Rachel asked of Phoenix. "What about Farouk?"

Kamal's expression was grim. "I will find him. He is mine." The look on his face said that Farouk would not survive the encounter.

Phoenix studied Kamal for a long moment. "He will die."

"Yes."

"You can't stay here," Fenley said. "You should hide out for a little while until she's stronger."

"I would show Rachel some of the world," Phoenix said. "We won my Challenge, but this is far from over. There are still three other Challenges to win. We don't know their outcomes yet. I would do this in case…"

In case they needed to fight a final Challenge. In case that final Challenge ended the world. *If one fails, they all fail.* It should have terrified her, but as long as she had her fire Elemental, it would work out. They would face it together. Neither one of them were alone anymore. She wanted to spend her life with him and never be separated.

"You won," Fenley said again. "You did your part. You deserve a brief rest. There is more to come if the final Challenge comes. Pray your counterparts win their battles." Fenley cleared his throat. "We don't believe in human marriage, but there is a werewolf tradition of handfasting to show our commitment to each other. I perform the ceremony."

The implications took a minute for Rachel to absorb. Phoenix, on the other hand, looked startled, and then his eyes widened.

"Char and…" Phoenix broke off as if belatedly realizing how his oath might sound. "Time may be against us, Rachel. Let's make it legal. What do you say? Will you mate with me?"

She thought she should pretend indignation, but nothing but relief flowed through her. "What if time weren't against us?"

"I'm a warrior, an Elemental. I don't have much skill with feminine things. Even then I'd want to plan something grander. But right now I just want to be with you. Join your life with mine, my beloved. Let me love you for as many or as few years as we have left together."

There was only one answer, and as she wrapped her arms around him, it shone around them like clear, brilliant white light flecked, as always, with fire.

"Yes."

With the other wolves and her grandfather as witnesses, Rachel and Phoenix turned to face the werewolf to join their hearts and hands as one. Whatever time there was left to them, they would be together.

About the Author

Claire has written on and off for most of her life, starting with fan fiction when she was very young. She writes across a wide range of genres, and does not consider any of it off limits or out of reach. If a story calls to her, she will write it. She currently lives in Los Angeles and spends her free time writing novels and short stories, as well as doing animal rescue and enjoying the sunshine. Claire's website is www.clairedavon.com.

Interested in being on Claire's mailing list? Signing up is easy! Just go to: http://clairedavon.com/mailing-list/ and you will have access to news, as well as giveaways and special bonus content only available to her subscribers!

If you loved this book, then you're sure to love the second book in the series as well! Keep reading for an excerpt of Griffin's story.

AIR ATTACK
Elementals' Challenge, Book 2

When love drops from the clouds, the sky is the limit…

This is a bad idea.

The basket jumped and swayed in the wind, hauled upward by the unseen Demonos. Clea kept a tight grip on the thick rope, focusing on the Elemental next to her. Griff had his head tilted up, as if savoring the wind.

With his eyes closed she was able to study his classically handsome face. He seemed no more than twenty-five years old. It was only by looking in his eyes that you realized there was no way he could be so young. His blond locks and light skin, coupled with his features, suggested he had Scandinavian or Northern European ancestors, but the Italian he sprinkled through his speech pointed to Italy. Perhaps Northern Italy, like Milan or Venice. Or he was an ancestor himself. Did Elementals have children? She didn't know enough about Griff or the Elementals and resolved to scour the Internet as soon as she had Wi-Fi and some free time.

The basket continued ascending. She still couldn't see the person who manipulated it on the other end. It was an odd device, archaic and hand-woven, like something pulled from the past.

Clea knew as little about the Demonos as she did about the Elementals. The elders didn't want to remember the war. The pantheon had been wounded, their city destroyed, and that was all she had needed to know. It usually didn't matter to paranormals if the Elementals won or lost. If the Elementals won, then humanity was safe. If they lost, the consequences were only supposed to hurt humankind, but her pantheon had discovered that demigods could be counted among the casualties. She had no idea what Amai-te-rangi was, or what his powers were. She would find out. Her people would not pay the price of another Elemental failure.

Griffin's wing feathers fluttered on a gust of wind. As they continued up they passed clouds moving in the sky. She wondered how thick the troposphere was in Iceland. In the distance, still far above them, were a few planes flying in the stratosphere, taking advantage of its more stable air.

The clouds thinned until they were wisps of white against an azure sky. She shivered, her body reminding her how cold it was. The air was thinner than anything she'd ever experienced even in her brief mountain-climbing excursions. Breathing was harder at this height but not impossible. Goosebumps rose on her arms.

Griffin frowned, picked up the throw she'd retrieved from the couch, and put it over her. His warm hands against her chilled skin shot a bolt of sensation through her body, making her knees wobble. The basket began to slow.

"Looks like we'll stay in the troposphere. Sometimes Amai goes to the tropopause, just below the stratosphere. He likes it there." Griff's hands lingered on her shoulders.

"Are you all right?"

The mentally delivered question made her start in surprise. It indicated a concern for her welfare she wouldn't have thought the man would ask.

"Yes, thank you. Cold, and a little out of breath, but I'll be fine."

"We're almost there."

They came to a stop. The planes still flew above them, but they were closer now. The mountains and volcanoes of Iceland were small below them, the buildings mere dots. It was exhilarating as well as scary to be so high. They were high enough that they could see the curve of the Earth on the horizon.

The ropes grew taut and then began to float down. At first the form above them was indistinct. As it got closer she saw a giant man with dark chocolate skin. He was wearing only a loincloth, and his body was thick with muscle. The Demonos appeared as if someone torn from the pages of a history book, when the races didn't intermingle. He reminded her of what early sailors might have found when they landed on the islands of Oceania.

Amai-te-rangi jumped into the basket, which rocked at the movement. The ropes vanished into him. By the time he hit the bottom of the weave there was nothing visible supporting them, only basket, barely big enough for three, hanging in the troposphere.

The basket swayed in the higher winds of this layer of the atmosphere. Far below them the ground seemed infinitely far away. The sky seemed to go on forever above and around them.

"Griffin," Amai-te-rangi said. There was a metallic quality to his voice, like small iron shavings had been shoved down his throat and vocal box. Up close his chest was aggressively muscled and covered in tribal tattoos. She couldn't identify the circles and whorls but they had to relate to his heritage.

Clea studied Amai's face, committing it to memory. This was her enemy. This was the man, the Demonos, who had killed her brother. This was the man she would stop.

"Amai." Griffin nodded. It was a formal nod between equals. "Long time." He flipped a hand at the basket. "Still flying coach. Did you get new tattoos as well?"

Amai loomed like a giant tree dwarfing the tall Elemental. His eyes, black against his dark skin, gave nothing away. He did not answer Griffin, instead fixing him with that dark gaze. The silence stretched out for several moments.

"What's with the basket?" Clea said, and then clamped her lips together. She snapped her teeth with a clack, hoping the sound didn't carry.

Amai's slow sweep scanned her, the pace telling Clea the insult was intentional. There was an ancient intelligence in him, speaking of lands long forgotten, of times that existed only in legend.

Then Amai-te-rangi raised a shoulder. "*Kia orana*. We become what humans expect, over time. The legend the mortals created for me told of my landing in a basket to snatch up unwary humans to eat them. The basket stayed when I became the air Demonos. Do you like it?" He rocked the basket, tilting Clea downwards. She stumbled and slid. Griff's wings half unfurled, hampered by the conveyance.

He also started to slide, but reached out and gripped the side, stopping his fall. One wing, free of the basket, fully spread out. The feather tips caught the wind.

Clea tilted as the basket dipped, slipping down. It continued to slant, like a drunk person losing the battle with gravity. Her body slammed against the wood panels, and the hemp ropes creaked. Taking a deep breath, she reached inside, preparing her air powers.

"This is unworthy of you." The edge in Griff's voice was unmistakable. Demonos and Elemental stared at each other, their gazes locked. Before Clea could summon her talent, wind started, a small current out of nowhere, focused in a tight spiral. She felt a shove from below, and the basket once again became level.

Griffin and Amai had not broken their eye contact. Regaining her balance, Clea reached for imaginary dust motes, flicking them off.

"Challenge is here." Amai broke the staring contest and turning his attention to Clea. His eyes were deep and dark, and she couldn't pick out a color. There was something wrong with his face, and it took Clea a minute before she realized he had no hair on it. No eyelashes, no eyebrows, no fine hairs anywhere. "*Kairau*, leave," he said with a snarling tone. "This does not concern you."

Griffin's face didn't move, but mottled color bloomed on his cheeks. "Come here," Griffin said, without mentioning her name. He held out his hand to her. She shook her head, pressing her lips together.

"*We need to show unity,*" he said mentally. "*He called you a harlot.*"

"*I know.*" Clea's cheeks grew hot. She moved from the side of the basket she was on to the opposite corner where Griff still stood. He was surefooted and secure in his balance, his wings outspread.

When she reached him he opened a wing instead of his hand, and draped it over her. His feathers were warm and smooth. She could feel the tendons against her skin, strong and pulsing.

Amai-te-rangi raised an eyebrow. "A new pet, Elemental?"

In the distance a plane soared by, higher than the basket, leaving a small contrail in its wake. She peeked into the minds of the humans and verified that they saw nothing of the scene below them. It always seemed impossible that humans had no clue what went on around them, but the basket, and the people in it, were invisible to human eyes.

"I'm nobody's pet," she spat, grinding her teeth, resisting the urge to lunge at him. This…this *creature* had killed her beloved brother permanently. He had destroyed Patrik. The demigod could not recover from the grievous wounds Amai had inflicted on him. Patrik was gone in true, permanent death.

Griffin didn't answer. The silence lengthened, words falling flat and thudding on the basket floor.

"Go play elsewhere, *wahine*." Amai's voice was harsh. "You can't help him win this fight."

"Pantheons paid last time." The words were like acid in her throat. "It's hardly your turn on the chessboard."

Her voice shook, and Clea once again cursed her impulsiveness. Griffin hadn't said her name for a reason. Could Amai tell she was a goddess? If he hadn't known, he did now.

"*He aha hoki,*" Amai said. Clea automatically translated that to "*I disagree.*"

* * * * *

Never before had one Challenge come so quickly after the last. Griff had been looking forward to a century of idleness in Iceland. It was away from the day-to-day press of humans, giving him a measure of peace. If he wanted company, he could fly to civilization, by wing or by metal. Or company came to him when he was so inclined.

Now, instead of indolence and succubi, he had Amai to face. The basket was silly, but lethal. Griff had heard tales of the last Elemental who had dismissed Amai-te-rangi, then new to his Demonos role, as a threat. Griffin had assumed the mantle of the air Elemental after that mistake.

Griffin spared a glance for the goddess. He hadn't dealt with Clea's mother

Dodola Perperuna, a member of the ancient Slavic pantheon, since their failure in the previous Challenge. He owed her, and he would honor that debt. He would have thought Dodola would use the promise of an Elemental on something more substantial. There was more here than met the eye, but he had not yet picked it out. No matter. He would, before this was through.

The wind he had summoned continued to hold the basket steady. He could feel the tug on the corners as Amai tried to tip it sideways. He had already turned back to Griff, ignoring Clea. Amai didn't sense the power in her, but Griffin felt it like the eye in the middle of a hurricane. There was more to this minor goddess than was first apparent.

Her back was straight, wind blowing through the red hair that must have come from her father. Perun had blond hair, and Griffin didn't think the leader of the Slavic pantheon had sired this goddess. The blanket he'd settled around her shoulders lifted with the cross currents of his unseen struggle with Amai. Why the hell had Dodola sent her? Why had she come?

"There are reasons."

Griffin cursed at hearing Dodola's mental voice. He raised his shields until his thoughts were secure behind them. He had gotten lazy. Gorging on his own company had made him sloppy. He was going to have to get battle ready, and fast.

Amai's narrowed eyes moved from Griffin to Clea. Now he was sure Amai had gotten more tattoos in the intervening seventy years. They had a fresh look to them, as if he had them done recently, but Griff didn't know the symbols.

"Never a pet, Demonos." She moved out from the shelter of Griff's wings and to Amai. Not only was her voice steady, but so was her body. She walked across the rocking basket without hesitation. Clearly she had some air strength in her.

Amai snickered. "Griffin and I have a long history, *wahine*. He doesn't get involved with women. You are wasting your time, goddess. Gods have no part in this battle. Go back to your manna on Olympus."

"Wrong pantheon." Clea was face to face with the much taller and broader Amai. Griff probed and felt fear leaking past her shields, but it didn't show on her face. He stayed motionless, his wings up, poised for action. Stray currents touched his long braid, lifting the strands.

"Prepare, Elemental," Amai said. "Challenge is here." He turned his back on both of them. In retrospect, Griffin should have known what was coming.

"I tire of games," Amai-te-rangi said.

The basket flipped over, tipping out its contents. Then Amai and the basket soared up, too quickly to follow.

The small mountainado seemed to come from nowhere. The vortex hung vertical, created from sheer winds that hadn't existed a moment ago in this remote alpine pass. The strong gusts would have been damaging if there had been anything other than rocks and scrub trees of the high altitude of the mountain. What little snow there was mixed with the other detritus in a fierce spiral. The wind swelled around the flotsam and jetsam, tightening the coil. The mountainado blew on a downward slope and seemed about to head down, then it winked out and died.

Somewhere in a dark place there was a groan of frustration and anger.

"Try again," a deep voice said. "That pitiful display of power is not nearly enough to convince me you have a role in this battle."

* * * * *

"Father?"

Neit, the war god of the Tuatha Dé Danann, paused in the act of splitting a log and turned to the voice. The pile of wood was twice as high as it had been a short time ago.

"Aye, Cormac." He hefted the axe. Although the tool was heavy, little sweat showed on Neit's face or body. He struggled to contain the irritation still bubbling under the surface. Ever since he'd learned Dodola had sent Clea to the damned Elemental he had been in a temper. How could she direct Clea to another? Especially in this time of Challenge?

Cormac hesitated, and then stepped into the circle where wood lay around them. "Something in the air isn't right, so it isn't. Is it the Fomorians? Have our ancient enemies returned to these lands to fight?"

Neit shook his head, splitting another log. "There may be a day when we battle the Fomorians again, but it is not this day." He was not sure who his anger was directed at, but at this rate the Irish hills would soon be sparking with thunder and lightning.

Cormac nodded as if Neit's words confirmed something he already knew. "It's Challenge, it is, then," he said.

"Challenge does not concern ye." Even as Neit said it he wondered if it was true. Clea was with the air Elemental. Strange forces were at work, stirring ancients.

"It may yet, aye." Cormac picked up a log and swung it onto a pile. Dirt clung to the bottom of the log, showing grass roots and a few small bugs. "I am in the way of discovering it…" He trailed off. "I am not yet in the way of pinning this feeling down."

Badb, one of Neit's three wives, entered the clearing in her crow form. She landed, transforming into a woman who appeared to be in her forties, of average height and clad in a simple black dress the same color as the bird. Neit could not tell from the distance what Badb's temperament currently was, but if she had been angry she likely would have transformed into her crone. He breathed a covert sigh of relief. She may be his wife, but even Neit knew better than to anger the Morrigan, one of the most powerful gods in their pantheon. A triad goddess, the Morrigan, or the three Morrigna as his wives were sometimes called, were often associated with fate and influenced the outcome of war. One thing Neit knew for sure: his wives, all three of them, were great warriors in their own right, their worth in the pantheon great. Neit took a look at Badb and knew she had heard about Clea as well. The news had to be the reason for Cormac's visit. Although his son had never met Clea, they were fraternal twins, siblings in the way of gods alike and unalike.

"That's the way of it, then? Not Fomorians, Challenge?" Badb said, her voice harsh, as if some of the crow had lingered. Her laugh echoed of bird, more like a caw than anything human.

"Yea," Neit said.

He eyed the child, big and broad like him, and red-haired, but otherwise their similarity ended. It had been Cormac's choice to look a little rough, like the Celtic warriors of old.

Neit pushed a hand through his fire-red hair.

"What is it you're wanting of me, lad?" He handed Cormac the axe. As Badb watched, the men took turns chopping the wood.

"I don't know," Cormac confessed. "I'm feeling a pull. I do not understand but there is a difference to this Challenge, so there is."

Neit nodded. Although the color had not changed, the sky was darkening with a malevolence he could sense but not yet see. Could one of the true ancients be stirring? Their primary mother goddess Danu had not been sensed in centuries.

"I am after feeling it too." Neit glanced at Badb, who bobbed her head in a peculiar birdlike way. She did not yet know that Dodola had sent his daughter to the Elemental, but she soon would. He would need the wisdom of the Morrigan before long.

"It's watching we need to do." Cormac's sullen expression told Neit that his answer did not satisfy the boy. "Don't give out about acting." He would have to pay closer attention to Cormac. Neit wondered if he was feeling his sister.

Soon Neit would be demanding answers from Dodola. His long-ago lover could not put his daughter in danger without answering to him.

* * * * *

As if in slow motion, the wood disappeared and sky emerged. The buildings and landscape were far away, rivers too distant to be seen as anything more than small ribbons snaking through the earth. Even Hallgrimskirkja, the Lutheran church that was currently the tallest building in Reykjavik, was nothing but a dot below them. Clea's body stretched when gravity began to claim her.

Then she was falling much too quickly, the air plunging around her defenseless body. Her skin was pulling back from her face in a parody of the g-forces she had seen in shows where they simulated rocket travel.

She yelped once as she picked up speed. Clea took a deep breath, summoning her wind talents. The power gathered, a buzz starting at her fingertips and spreading to her palm.

"Coming."

Before she could act, there was a whooshing sound, but she couldn't tell if it was the weather or Griffin. Currents swelled up from below, pushing against her, and Clea marveled at the precision it took to form the wind underneath. Then Griffin's hands circled her waist, slowing the downward rush. It was similar to what he had done when he'd plucked her off the path to his mountainside home, but this time thousands of feet in the sky.

Clea's breath rushed out in a sigh of relief at the feel of him. Even in the chill of the troposphere he was warm, smelling of dew and musk.

"Thank you."

His strong yellow wings flapped, each pull slowing their combined fall further.

She was sure it was only a few seconds, at longest a minute, before the horizon stopped rushing around her body and the wind slowed. To her relief they now hovered in the air.

Patrik. She was doing this for him. She would have no interest in this Challenge if not for her brother. Otherwise, she would be far away from this battle. Madagascar, perhaps. There was a nice remote resort there where she could have explored the scenery. If not for Patrik, but there was the memory of her foolish brother who had tried to help Challenge and paid the ultimate price. She would fight this Amai, the Demonos with the ridiculous basket. She owed Patrik that.

"Come, let's get back to my place."

Currents of wind blew around and under them. Clea reached out to test the air. There was no need to supplement his gust with her own; he had more than enough. She cursed herself, wishing she had used her time to do more research before she had fled to the Elemental. She needed to know what Griffin's strengths, and more importantly, what his weaknesses were. Only then would she know what to focus on and how she could help. She couldn't lose any more family.

Inch by inch her fear began to leave her as Griff's strong wings beat in the currents. As they grew nearer Griff again made the same hand motion he had before, and the sliding door pulled back.

"Neat trick."

A rumble of laughter echoed in him.

He deposited her on the floor, landing her gently on her feet. Clea's hands and face lost their chill in the warmth of his remote home. To her dismay, her heart was pounding and when cold left her, beads of fear sweat bloomed on her body. Griffin poured her another glass of wine from the same bottle as before, saying nothing. His wings once again folded against his back.

"That was interesting." Small ripples danced across the red wine as Clea curved her free hand around the stem. In another moment she would be shaking. Too much had happened too fast. "Why keep the basket?"

"He doesn't need it to maneuver in air, but he likes to let the unwary believe what they will. Don't underestimate Amai," he said, steel in his tone. "The basket may look *stupido*, but he is ruthless and dangerous. He didn't kill my predecessor by being a fool."

Hoping her voice was level, Clea met Griff's gaze. "I have learned not to misjudge anyone. Danger comes in many packages. Still, you've got to admit it's ridiculous."

He flashed something that might have been a smile, but it was gone before she could be sure. "That's the point. It's a natural tendency not to take the ridiculous seriously, and he has caught many people by surprise that way. He was made into his current form by the primitive people of Mangaia, and he chooses to keep the trappings of his creation."

Griff didn't move, but he was in her mind, beating at her shields.

"Let's talk, Clea. Who is Patrik?"

She opened her mouth to speak but before she had any words, there was a crack of thunder. It was followed by another one, and another, until their surroundings seemed alive with electricity. Clea's hair floated out and Griffin's feathers stood up. There was a fleeting impression of a hooked nose on his face, like a beak. For a moment he looked like the half lion/half eagle that was his other form, before it was then gone.

Wind kicked up and swirled around the house, whipping the small trees at the bottom until their branches bent close to the ground. It picked up snow, sending it coursing through the air, and bits of debris whirled in the currents. Griffin still hadn't moved, cocking his head to one side.

"Amai's parting shot. He can be a child," he said. "I'll be right back."

Griff's power grew, almost a tangible force in him as he took in a deep breath. When he exhaled the wind stuttered and then stopped swirling. It began churning in the opposite direction, rising away from the house. Lightning streaked down, but before it could crash to earth, Griffin caught it mentally and sent the electricity back up the path it had followed, lifting his hands as if to direct the path. In the distance Clea heard a quick yelp before the storm was gone as fast as it had manifested.

The buzz in her subsided. There was no need for it yet. It may be best to keep her powers hidden until she had need of them. Amai was not the only one people often underestimated.

"Where were we? *Sì*, Patrik." Griffin dusted off his shirt, removing a few bits of litter. He smoothed the cloth down, eyeing Clea with an air of expectant waiting.

"I'd rather talk about my mother. Were you guys a thing? Did you sleep with her?" *The best defense…*

Griffin raised an eyebrow. "With Dodola? Of course. Your pantheon predates Christianity and doesn't have any so-called modern sensibilities." She could have sworn regret laced his features. "If you think Dodola sent you to me because we are related, that is not so. None of the pantheon can claim me as their father. Elementals rarely have children."

Clea shook her head. "Not that. I know who my father is. I've never met him but I know who he is, and he's not you."

"Ah." Griffin's single word held a wealth of meaning.

Clea swallowed, watching him as he crossed the room towards her. There was menace in his stride, the air of a stalking predator. He moved like the lion half of his Elemental namesake, quick and deadly.

"What are you doing?" she asked as he grew larger.

He was there, big and male, in front of her. The tips of his wings poked out over his shoulders. His blond hair and braid were tossed from the storm. He moved like a jungle cat, every inch of him screaming coiled masculine power.

"What am I doing?" His voice was low, and his blue eyes blazed. "Clea Perperuna, I am going to kiss you."

Clea was no stranger to lovers. Sex was casual in most pantheons, born of time and beauty, as well as immortality. She was not as stunning as most goddesses, but she'd had her share of men.

"I'm not a Perperuna," she murmured. "Even if Perun were my father, we take our names from the matrilineal side. When I need a last name, I use Dodolaka."

"I see," he said, his head drawing closer. She watched him descend until her eyes crossed and his face filled her vision. "I am corrected."

His lips were firm but gentle, gliding across hers and then pressing into them. She tasted the wine he'd sipped. He smelled of wind, and of the clean air after a hard rain. His hands rested on her shoulders, stroking the skin in a back-and-forth motion. He didn't ask and he didn't demand, he just kissed her mouth, over and over, until Clea sighed and opened hers. Then he deepened the kiss, moving to close his arms around the small of her back and pull her against his hard body.

She heard a rumble before she surrendered to the warmth of another person.

His tongue swooped into her open mouth to claim it. Clea returned the kiss, playing her tongue over his as a moan built in her throat. It had been too long since she had taken a lover. Twenty years was no more than a heartbeat to an immortal, but her body missed the touch of a man.

She pushed her hands under the massive wings, the feathers tickling her, and curved her fingers around his neck. All the while his tongue was thrusting into her mouth, seeking and finding her, doing battle before retreating only to come forward again. His breath was coming harder now, his impressive chest rising and falling, and his body stirred to life against hers. Moisture began to seep along her secret places. His length pressed against her belly. Just like the rest of his body, he was strong, hard and long where he needed to be.

It may have been decades, but she wasn't about to let the playboy of the Elementals have her that easily. He went through women like water, slipping from one to another with the ease of the liquid, flowing to the next without any remorse or concern. It would be easy to fall into bed with him, but it was too big a risk. There were depths to him that made the idea too dangerous.

She backed away from his warmth, meeting his crystal blue eyes.

"You live up to your reputation," she said, and was surprised when his face darkened.

Griffin stepped back, separating from her with a rapidity that made her blink. Clea missed him the moment he was gone from her and found herself wishing she hadn't spoken. The sensation dancing along her nerve endings told her that her body wanted something her mind wasn't ready for, and it wanted it from this Elemental. Whatever his reason for kissing her, she doubted it was for simple pleasure.

"Good to know," Griffin said. "You didn't tell me about Patrik. No matter. You will, in time. I will make sure of that."